HILDA

A
TYPICAL FAMILY
CHRISTMAS

LIZ DAVIES

Published by Lilac Tree Books

CHAPTER 1

'My mother is coming to us for Christmas,' Kate announced, then stepped back and waited for the fallout. A stunned silence followed, but it didn't last long.

'Why does *she* have to come?' Her youngest, Sam, was the first to object. 'It's bad enough having to put up with the other one.'

'*She* is your grandmother, and so is "the other one".' Kate did quotation marks with her fingers and glared at her son.

'Nana Peters does nothing but criticise,' Kate's middle child jumped into the conversation with a moany voice of her own. 'Turn the TV down. Do we have to watch that? Stop playing with your phone. Can't you sit still?' Portia's impression of her paternal grandmother was remarkably accurate. 'It's bad enough with her, but with Nanny Collins as well...' She trailed off with a dramatic roll of her eyes. 'I don't think I can stand two of them at the same time.'

'Look,' Kate said. 'I don't like it any more than you do, but she's coming and that's final.'

'What about Nana Peters? Does she still have to come, or is it a one in, one out kinda thing?' Sam asked, flicking Cheerios halfway across the kitchen at the sink. His aim was pretty good. 'Do we get a choice? If so, I vote for Nanny Collins; she's not as bad as Nana Peters.'

'They're both coming,' Kate said.

'But why?' Portia had gone from moany to whiney in a nano-second. Then her daughter's eyes widened and a look of horror crossed her goth-painted features. 'She's not staying the night, is she?'

Kate sighed, took off her rubber gloves, and

threw them in the washing up bowl. She resisted the urge to howl as they filled up with water. Damn it. Now she'd have to dry them out before she could wear them again. She hated not using rubber gloves.

'Yes, she is. They both are.' She failed to add that it wasn't just for the one night either. It would probably be at least two. If not more…

Pandemonium ensued. Even Ellis, who'd finally floated downstairs, her nose in her phone and buds jammed in her ears, looked up from Instagramming or Tindering, or whatever she was doing, and glared at her mother.

Kate turned her back on her furious children and fished the gloves out of the greasy, grungy water. She should have tackled last night's washing up last night, but she'd been too tired.

'Mum, Mum, Mum, Mum,' Sam shouted.

Portia shrieked something unintelligible and Ellis banged her hands on the kitchen table. Knowing the noise would only escalate, Kate took a deep breath and turned to face her aghast offspring.

The reason for the panic was clear – they lived in a five-bedroomed house when six bedrooms were needed if both nans were coming to stay. Someone was going to have to bunk up with someone else.

And none of the three someones in question liked the idea.

'I'm a boy,' Sam pointed out. 'I can't share my bed with a girl.'

'I'm not asking you to,' Kate said mildly. She didn't intend to ask anyone to share a bed – that's what blow-up mattresses were for, and the family had one of those in the garage, somewhere. But she did intend for two of her offspring to share a room, and the most logical candidates were the two girls.

Sam shut up and leaned so far back in his chair that the two front legs lifted off the floor. Kate had an unmotherly urge to give it a little push.

Her son had a smug smile on his face, and Kate could tell that her daughters were itching to remove it. They probably would do so later when she wasn't looking. To be fair to them, and Kate was the first to admit it, Sam often deserved it. He could be a right little so and so. Kate blamed his father.

Kate blamed his father for a lot more than Sam's attitude.

'What does Dad say about Nanny Collins coming for Christmas?' Ellis was the most adept of the three children at playing one parent off against the other. She was the eldest, ergo she'd had the most practice.

'Your father is fine about it,' Kate replied, taking a days-old loaf of bread out of the cupboard and hunting for something, *anything*, to make sandwiches with. Actually, she hadn't mentioned anything to Brett yet. She'd only found out herself last night during her twice-weekly call to her mother, and when she'd gotten off the phone she'd been so surprised that she'd needed a bit of time to process the information. The two nans disliked each other intensely and did everything they could to avoid being in the same place at the same time, so both of them coming to stay for Christmas was unheard of.

'Corned beef?' she asked her children hopefully, holding up a tin.

'I bet he isn't fine,' Portia said, not taking anything her mother said on face value, as usual. 'And no thanks, I'll risk school dinners. At least the baguettes there don't have mould on them.'

Kate looked at Ellis, who grimaced. 'One of the boys can do a McDonald's run,' her eldest daughter said.

'You know I don't like you eating that rubbish all the time,' Kate started to object, but Ellis quelled her with a look.

She thought about meeting her daughter head on, but with little more than semi-stale bread, corned beef (assuming she could find a way to open the tin because the little key thing which should be attached to the side of it was missing), or a rock-hard lump of Cheddar, she didn't have a culinary leg to stand on. Besides, at seventeen, Ellis was beyond her control when it came to what she ate in college at lunchtime.

She put the tin of meat back in the cupboard

and said to Sam, 'I'll give you money for lunch too, shall I?'

He hissed out a 'Yes!', and his eyes lit up with glee. No doubt he'd be disappearing out of the school gates and heading for the chip shop at the end of the road as soon as the lunch bell rang. At least the packed-lunch debacle had taken her children's minds off the impending grandmotherly visits, she thought thankfully.

Wrong.

'I'm not sharing a bed with *her,*' Ellis announced, jabbing a finger at her sister. 'She snores.'

'I do not! Anyway, you're on your phone all night kissy-talking with your boyfriend,' Portia retorted.

'What boyfriend?' Kate asked Portia with a frown, momentarily distracted from the issue of bed-sharing by this news. 'I didn't know you had a boyfriend,' she said to Ellis.

'That's because it's none of your business.' Ellis retorted.

'Look here, young lady, you're not eighteen

yet, you know.' The thought of her daughter being pawed by some hormone-driven boy filled her with horror.

'I wish I *was* eighteen, because then you wouldn't be able to tell me what to do.' Ellis flounced over to the table and threw herself onto a chair. The chair made an ominous creaking sound. After suffering three children living in it, so did a lot of other things in the house, including her.

'It doesn't work that way, Ellis,' she said, crossing her arms. 'While you're under my roof you'll do as you're told.' Oh God, she thought as she listened in dismay to the words coming out of her mouth; she sounded just like her mother.

'Ellis,' she said, in a more conciliatory tone, 'I know it's a difficult stage for you, being halfway between a child and an adult—'

Ellis cut her off. 'When will you get it into your head that I'm not a child? I can make my own decisions. I'm in charge of my life, not you or Dad.'

Talk of the devil...

Brett darted into the kitchen, his tie slightly askew and a dollop of shaving cream on his ear. 'Don't speak to your mother like that. Show some respect,' he said.

Kate did a double-take. It was very unusual for him to be around at this time in the morning (he normally scarpered off to work before the kids rolled out of bed). It was also unusual for her husband to manage more than a surly grunt. In fact, he very often didn't manage more than a surly grunt in the evenings, either.

She avoided eye-contact with him, hoping he'd grab whatever he came into the kitchen for and make a dash for it. She would break the news about the impending visit later, when he was in work and otherwise preoccupied. Then she could legitimately say she'd told him all about it and that he'd said, "OK, fine, whatever", like he usually did. One day she just might ring him up and tell him she wanted a divorce, just to see his reaction. He'd probably say "OK, fine, whatever" to that, too.

'You didn't hear what *she* said, did you?'

Portia jumped in, her hands on her hips, the black-painted nails reminding Kate of when her daughter used to come in from the garden covered in dirt because she'd been digging for worms. She missed those days.

'I heard enough to know—' Brett continued to argue, and Kate had to admire his tenacity at this time in the morning.

'Nanny Collins is coming for Christmas,' Ellis interjected, just as he was building up a full head of wrathful parental steam, which was a rare change for him.

'Nana Peters always comes to us for Christmas, you know that.' By this time Brett's expression was more perplexed than annoyed. Obviously, Ellis's words hadn't sunk in yet, and Kate braced herself. What was about to come next wasn't going to be pretty.

'Nanny Collins is coming this year, too,' their eldest stated, her tone expressing her hope that her father would do something about it.

'Eh?' Brett blinked. His mouth opened and closed like a netted trout, and his irritation with the children's attitude deflated like a leaky balloon. He even did a bit of a balloon squeak as the air seeped out of his lungs.

'Tell her, Dad,' Sam piped up, even though he was going to be the least affected out of all of the kids. 'Tell Mum it can't be both of them. One granny is bad enough. Two…?' He shuddered.

'Your father will do nothing of the sort,' Kate said, sounding pompous to her own ears. 'He's totally supportive. Aren't you, Brett?' Kate forced out the last sentence between gritted teeth, and glared at her husband, daring him to deny it.

'Er, um, well,' he began, then seemed to suddenly remember what had brought him into the kitchen in the first place, and made a lunge for the fridge door, yanking it open, and grabbing a yoghurt. He was usually out of the house by now and well on his way to work. But today, of all days, he had to walk in just when she was trying to get all three children fed, watered, and off to school or college, whilst slipping a piece of bad news in, hoping the day in between would give her offspring the time and distance they needed to process the information and come to terms with it.

Not a chance.

Not when their father was running late for once, and they could turn to him for back-up.

'Daaaad?' Portia whined. She really did take after her grandmother, Kate thought, and it wasn't a compliment.

Kate knew Brett wasn't geared up for a confrontation at this time in the morning, but it looked like he was going to get one anyway, and she watched him mentally put his manager head on and prepare for battle. He turned to Kate, using the tie-straightening gesture she knew so well.

'Is this true? Is your mother coming to us for Christmas?' he demanded.

'Yes.'

'I'm not sure I'm totally on board with that,' her husband said.

'Well, get on board,' Kate growled back, her patience rapidly evaporating. 'I've had to put up with your mother every year since time began; it won't hurt for you to put up with mine for a change.'

'But that means we'll have the both of them,' Brett said.

'I can see why you got that promotion last year,' she said. 'Was it for your mathematical ability or your powers of observation?'

'There's no need to be sarcastic.' Her husband sounded hurt. 'I just meant—'

'I know what you meant. You're going to have to suck it up, all of you.' She glared at her family. Her family glared back, although Brett's expression was more akin to desperation than defiance. He knew he didn't have a leg to stand on when it came to motherly visits.

'Right, you lot, get going or you'll be late for school.' She made shooing motions with her hands and tried to ignore the continuing rumbles of discontent. They'd get used to it – they'd have to. The nanas were both coming to stay for Christmas, and that was that.

CHAPTER 2

Kate sagged against the kitchen worktop and heaved a gigantic sigh. That went well – not. She hadn't expected it to. The children tolerated their grandmothers, but preferably singly. The thought of having to tolerate them both at the same time freaked them out.

She didn't blame them, because she felt the same. His mother, Nana Peters ("call me Helen, please, children, Nana makes me feel so *old*") had been coming to them for Christmas, and for any other holiday she could wrangle, since Kate and Brett had got married. Their very first

Christmas together hadn't been the cosy, cuddly Christmas she'd envisioned. Instead, it had been a be-on-your-best-behaviour-and-ignore-the-pointed-comments Christmas. No matter what Kate had done, it hadn't been good enough, and it had set the tone of her relationship with her mother-in-law ever since. There was always something that could be commented on. Twenty-one years later, the situation hadn't changed.

And, to add to the delights of the forthcoming festive season, Kate's mother was also descending on them this year.

She loved her mother dearly, of course she did, but being in her company for more than a couple of hours drove her to distraction – she was just so miserable. All the time. There was no let up. Where Helen was subtly critical and adept at uttering pointed barbs, Beverley moaned. Constantly. The weather was a favourite topic; it was either too hot, too cold, too wet, too windy, too icy, too…anything. And at this time of year, the festive season got a battering. Beverley

Collins hated Christmas and made sure anyone within earshot knew about it, sucking all the joy out of it for everyone else, until they were as miserable as she was.

It got on everyone's nerves, including hers.

Kate, herself, never particularly looked forward to Christmas because of Helen (she'd usually found it to be a case of grit her teeth and plough through it) but this year was shaping up to be particularly stressful.

It had been easier when the kids were younger. She used to suggest a walk between present-opening and lunch to get them out of the house and burn off some of the overwhelming excitement and give them all a break from being cooped up like so many squabbling chickens. Helen had always remained behind, but Kate had long ago decided that getting away from her mother-in-law for an hour or so, was worth having to come back to her kitchen to find Helen had been "helping" while she was out. So what if her mother-in-law had re-peeled all the potatoes because Kate had left the odd minuscule bit of skin on one? Or had made up a batch of batter for home-made Yorkshire puddings because they "taste so much nicer than shop-bought ones, don't you think?" Getting away from her for an hour or so had been worth it.

She might still have some luck with suggesting a walk with Sam, but not with the other two. Last year they'd refused to leave the house, too busy on their phones to want to have the bother of having to look where they were placing their feet, or to put on gloves which meant they couldn't waggle their thumbs at the speed of light over their respective screens. Perhaps she ought to buy the girls a pair of thumbless gloves each for their stockings, but she didn't think they'd see the funny side.

With a glance around the messy kitchen, Kate pushed herself away from the counter, feeling the stickiness of spilt orange juice under one hand and crumbs stuck to the other, and sloped off upstairs to get ready for work.

Brett laughingly referred to it as her "little

shop job", but Kate didn't find it at all funny. She took her job very seriously indeed. So what, if it was part-time? So what, if she wasn't paid as much as Brett? So what, if there was little or no prospect for advancement? She loved her work and not just because it gave her a little financial independence. It also gave her companionship, a structure to her day, and a reason to ignore the housework. That it also fitted in extremely well around the children was an added bonus.

Whenever Brett hinted that perhaps it was about time she got a "proper job" (he meant one that would mean she was out of the house from seven in the morning until six at night, the way his did) she felt like taking him up on his suggestion, if only so he'd appreciate how much she truly did around the house. It was OK for him – he didn't have to wash and iron three lots of school uniform. He didn't have to supervise breakfasts, ensure there was an assortment of stuff for lunches (although she'd fallen down dismally on that particular chore this morning), or feed three hungry mouths, none of whom wanted to eat the same thing at the same time. He didn't have to ferry the kids to drama and band practice (Ellis), piano and horse-riding (Portia), or football, cricket, and swimming (Sam). And that was without the constant demands to be driven here, there, and everywhere to meet friends in town, or to go to someone's house for a sleepover/ barbeque/trying-clothes-on-session/playing on the Xbox/party, or whatever social event her children simply couldn't survive without attending.

And don't get her started on the homework nagging, the piano-practice nagging, the nagging to put clothes/shoes/bags/equipment away, or the daily (sometimes thrice-daily when it came to Portia) dramas about lost phones, iPads, keys, favourite tops, the only pair of trainers to be seen in (Sam), or the thousand-and-one other things that her children seemed able to lose and then expect her to drop anything and everything to help them look for.

In reality they didn't do much looking – they

just stood around helplessly while Kate felt down the back of the sofa (not recommended without wearing protective gear) or under beds (ditto), while asking where her children had last seen the item in question, and receiving a sarcastic "I don't know, do I?" in return.

She shouldn't omit the cleaning, shopping, lawn mowing, car servicing (she didn't do the servicing herself – she paid a garage to do it – but it was up to her to do the booking in, the dropping off, and the picking up), the visits to dentists, doctors, hairdressers (barber's in Sam's case), the attendance at various school concerts and parents' evenings, and—

She picked up two wet towels from the floor of the en-suite and wondered where she'd gone wrong.

Not been firm enough, maybe? Not laid out her expectations in words of one syllable? Not made her displeasure clear?

She wasn't just referring to the children, either. This time, her ire was aimed at her husband, who'd left the wet towels on the floor (why he needed to use two of them when he showered, she had no idea), toothpaste spit on the basin, the toilet seat lid up, and he hadn't noticed the empty loo-roll holder. And this was just the bathroom. The bedroom fared no better – unmade bed, scatter cushions scattered, wardrobe and drawer doors left open, yesterday's boxer shorts, socks, and shirt on the floor, a half-drunk glass of water on the bedside table (Brett's side), and shoes left right where she'd trip over them. If she didn't know better, she'd have thought they'd been burgled.

The kids' rooms would be equally as bad, she knew. Maybe it was her fault her family were slobs. She should have trained them better, like recalcitrant puppies. But it had been so much easier and quicker, and far less stressful to do things herself. There were enough arguments in this house as it was, without hourly tantrums over who'd left the milk out, or whose turn it was to vacuum the stairs. She'd made a rod for her own back, and she suspected it was far, far too late to do anything about it now.

CHAPTER 3

Brett wasn't having a good day. He normally liked to be out of the house before the morning mayhem began, but he'd been running late this morning and had therefore been in the firing line between his wife and children, and between the kids themselves. Why did they have to be so stroppy and argumentative all the time?

Before they were born, he used to imagine fun-filled picnics with his future family; evening meals where everyone sat around the table sharing news about their day; lazy Sunday afternoons building forts in the garden out of chairs and draped sheets.

The reality had been somewhat of a shock.

It hadn't been so bad when Ellis arrived, but the cracks began to show when Portia got to about three-years-old. By the time Sam appeared on the scene, the two girls had declared all-out war on each other, and now that all the children had reached their teens (more or less – at eleven, going on twelve, Sam was nearly there), they appeared to hate the very sight of each other.

Family time together was either non-existent, or it was spent wearing a hard hat and bullet-proof vest. There seemed to be no in between.

And now with Christmas bearing down on them at a rate of knots, he not only had his mother to contend with, but Kate's was threatening to show up, too. He just hoped that mangy pooch of hers would be put in kennels for the duration. The dog was a menace. Beverley treated it like a baby, and the damned thing ruled the roost. It had even growled and snapped at him the last time she'd come for one of her infrequent visits, and all because he'd tried to shoo it off the sofa. Dogs belonged on the floor, not on the furniture, in his opinion. He'd been picking canine hairs off his trousers for weeks afterwards, despite his mother-in-law's insistence that poodles didn't shed or moult.

He glanced out of the partition window and into the open-plan office beyond to see his staff with their heads down, beavering away on the new project. He should be doing the same, but all he could think about was his mother's inevitable reaction when he plucked up the courage to tell her that Beverley would also be joining them for Christmas.

The two women had never got on, and he had no idea why – so the best thing to do, in his opinion, was to keep them apart, and it had worked quite well so far. His mum stayed with them every Christmas, even though she only lived a few miles away, because he hated to think of her waking up to a quiet and empty house on Christmas morning, and because she insisted on visiting. Her friend, Rosemary, spent the festive season with her son and his family, so Helen didn't see why she couldn't spend it with her son. Brett made a point of fussing over his mother and making sure she had a good time, so that she could report back to Rosemary that she'd been treated like a queen and hadn't had to lift a finger.

The arrival of Kate's mother this year would change the whole dynamics.

He'd better warn his mother that Beverley intended to join them. It would give her time to get used to the idea; besides, she'd probably enjoy complaining about it to her cronies beforehand.

He checked the time, wanting to make sure it wasn't so early that she still might be in bed, but not so late that she'd gone out for one of her manicures, or hair appointments, or for coffee and cake with Rosemary and the rest of the elderly ladies in her friendship group.

Ten-thirty. Perfect, he should be able to catch her on her landline, when she was more likely to be on her own. She did have a mobile but he didn't want to risk calling her when she had an audience to play up to.

'Mum? It's Brett,' he announced.

'I know who you are,' she said. 'I gave birth to you.'

'Right, yes, OK..' Why did she always manage to put him on the back foot? She had this uncanny knack of making him feel twelve-years-old again. How did she *do* that?

'What do you want, Brett? I'm just about to leave for choir practice.'

Oh yes, he'd forgotten she'd recently developed an interest in singing. From what he could recall though, he hadn't considered his mum to have a particularly tuneful voice, but if it made her happy...

'I just wanted to let you know that Beverley will be joining us for Christmas this year,' he said, then waited for the explosion.

'Beverley, who?'

'Kate's mother.'

'Oh. *Her.*' The "her" was said with a sneer.

'What on earth for? It's a long way to travel for a bit of dry turkey and a spot of overdone Christmas pudding.'

Brett wondered if it was worth his while to take his mother to task for her disparaging remarks regarding Kate's cooking, but he decided against it. He'd not change her mind, and besides, he had bigger fish to fry this morning.

'Her sister is going out to Australia to visit her daughter, so Beverley would be all on her own over Christmas, if she doesn't come to us. We wouldn't want that, would we?' he said.

The silence on the other end told him that Helen didn't give two hoots whether Beverley was on her own or not, as long as she wasn't anywhere near Helen.

'Mum? Are you still there?'

She gave a deep sigh. 'I suppose I can put up with her for one day. I'll have to, won't I?'

Oh, hell. His mother thought Beverley was only coming to them for Christmas lunch itself. Although why she'd assume such a thing when

Beverley lived a four-hour drive away, was anyone's guess.

'Er, Mum, she's staying for a couple of days, not just for lunch.'

'She's *what?*'

Brett could almost hear his mother bristling on the other end of the phone. He could picture her drawing herself up to her full height and pursing her lips. Her indignation might have made him laugh, if it wasn't so heartfelt.

'When is she arriving?'

'Christmas Eve, I think.' That's when she always went to her sister's, so he felt it safe to assume that's when she'd turn up on his doorstep.

'I do hope you don't expect me to share a bedroom,' his mother said. 'I like to have my room to myself.'

Brett didn't bother pointing out that "her room" was, in fact, the spare room, and it was also the one Beverley stayed in on the rare occasions she came to visit. She didn't like travelling much, did his mother-in-law, expecting Kate and the rest of the family to visit her instead, even though she had a car and was perfectly capable of driving.

'I'm sure Kate will sort something out,' Brett murmured, although what the sleeping arrangements would be exactly, he had no idea. He'd leave that for his wife to deal with. If this morning's squabbling was anything to go by, she'd have a fight on her hands.

'Brett?' Brett looked up to see his boss's head poking around the door. 'All set for the meeting?'

What meeting? 'Oh, uh, yeah. I'll be right there.'

He waited until Clara, aka The Abyss, had left – he referred to her in his head that way because when he looked at her, Brett imagined he was staring into an abyss; the woman had no soul; she was a workaholic who couldn't understand that people had lives outside of the damned company – then said, 'Look, Mum, I've got to go, I'm in work. We'll speak later, yeah?'

'We most certainly will. I'm not at all happy about the situation, Brett, but if Beverley does have to be there, I'll simply have to make the best of it, won't I?'

As will we all, Brett thought. Then his mother said something that made his blood run cold and his heart sink to his boots.

'I've got an idea,' she said. 'Instead of coming to yours on Christmas Eve like I normally do, I'll arrive on Wednesday and get myself settled in. I expect Kate will welcome having another pair of hands, now that her mother is coming, too.'

I bet she won't, Brett thought.

Oh, lord, his wife was going to go ballistic when he told her.

Merry bloody Christmas, everyone.

CHAPTER 4

Doris had a cup of tea waiting for Kate when she walked in the door of the charity shop where she worked.

'I'll just take my coat off,' Kate said, as she did every morning, and went out the back to hang up her coat, scarf, and hat, and put her bag under the chair.

One of the volunteers was already there, sorting through some plastic bags of donations, and he sent her a small, hesitant smile. He was probably in his late seventies (Kate had never asked) and lived alone. He was shy, kept himself to himself, preferring to root through other people's cast-offs rather than interacting with the customers, but turned up unfailingly three times a week, Mondays, Wednesdays, and Thursdays. What he did on the other two days, Kate had no idea. She'd asked him once, but he'd just coughed, and carried on steam-cleaning a pair of trousers.

He was one of a handful of volunteers. Doris was the shop manager and Kate was the only other paid employee, because she stood in for Doris on her boss's days off or when she had a holiday.

Kate walked back into the shop, casting an experienced eye around as she headed for the counter and her mug of tea. After she'd drunk it and had a quick chat with Doris, she intended to change the window display this morning. Keeping it fresh was what brought the customers in and, despite it being a charity, the shop had to make money.

The Christmas decorations could do with a bit of tweaking, too. The tree next to the window leant drunkenly to one side, and the angel on the top had fallen off.

Still, the shop did look festive, and carols were playing quietly in the background, loud enough to be heard, but not too loud so as to annoy their (mostly) elderly customers. Someone, probably Doris, had plugged in a Christmassy air freshener, and the scent of berries and cinnamon filled the air.

'What's up?' Doris asked her, handing her a mug of hot, sweet, steaming tea.

'Mothers.' She said it in an apologetic tone, knowing Doris had lost hers a while back, but also knowing the older woman would understand.

'Which one – yours or his?' Doris knew all about Kate's fraught and delicate relationship with both women.

'Both. Mine has decided she's coming to us for Christmas.'

'She invited herself?'

Kate nodded, sipping her drink and wishing she had a packet of biscuits to go with it. With all the chaos of this morning, she'd forgotten to have breakfast. She'd nip out to the baker's shop across the road later and get some mince pies to share, along with some fresh bread to replace the mouldy loaf she'd absentmindedly put back in the bread bin.

Doris said, 'She's never come to you for Christmas before, has she?'

'No, and that's her argument. That and the fact that we always have Brett's mother to stay. I can hardly say no to having mine.'

'She *is* your mother,' Doris pointed out, gently. 'No offence, but why would you want to say no?'

'You haven't met my mother.' Kate's reply was accompanied by a grimace. 'His mother constantly nit-picks, but I can ignore that, most of the time – I've had lots of practice. But my mother is just so joyless. She's constantly miserable, and her biggest gripe around this time of year is that she hates Christmas. She doesn't see the point in it, can't wait for it to be over, and tells everyone in earshot over and over again.

She just brings the whole atmosphere down.'

'Has she always been like that?'

Kate put her mug down and stared into space, thinking. 'When I was growing up, I think she quite liked Christmas. I can't remember her being miserable about it.'

'What changed?'

'I'm not sure. I can't say it was because she and my father split up at Christmas, or anyone died around then. Dad left in March and my gran, Mum's mother, died in early summer. Not the same year, thankfully!' Kate gave a nervous laugh. 'Grandad passed away in September, so I've no idea why Christmas is such a horrible time for her.'

'What about when the children were small?' Doris wanted to know. 'I can understand how some people can lose the magic of Christmas or become disillusioned by the materialistic side of things – it happens to a lot of people as they grow older and their kids have lives of their own. But usually, the arrival of grandchildren brings Christmas back to life for most people.'

'Not for my mum. It just made her grizzle and whinge even more, usually about the number of presents they've been given.'

'What does she normally do at Christmas?'

'She spends it with her sister, my aunt. They take it in turns to stay in each other's house, but this year my cousin, Aunt May's daughter, moved to Australia, so Aunt May is spending Christmas and the New Year down under. I would have invited Mum to come to us for Christmas, of course, I would have – I wouldn't want her to spend it on her own – but before I had the chance, she told me she was coming to stay with us and that I was to buy a bottle of gin. A large one. I'm not sure if it's meant for her or for me.'

Doris chuckled. 'Drink it anyway. The drunken haze might help to take the edge off.'

'In that case, I think I'll start now. Brett isn't exactly over the moon at the thought of having both our mothers under the same roof. The last time that happened was at our wedding, and I don't think he's looking forward to repeating the experience. The kids are squabbling already –

mainly about who's going to sleep where. The most logical thing would be for both grannies to share the spare room because it's got a double bed in it, then no one is put out. But I can't see that working out. They can't stand the sight of each other. So...' Kate heaved a sigh – that was all she seemed to be doing lately – and said, 'one of the children will have to share and it's not going to be Sam, because he's a boy and, in his words, he can't share his bed or his room with a girl. Ellis and Portia didn't like that idea either, although they hate their brother for being allowed to stay in his room on his own.'

Doris was trying not to laugh, and Kate nudged her with an elbow.

'It's not funny,' she said. 'It's like trying to prevent World War Three from breaking out in our house. So much for brotherly, or sisterly, love. The three of them can't stand the sight of each other. Whenever I hear a young mum saying she wants to have another baby because she'd like a brother or a sister for her first child, I feel like inviting her round to my house at breakfast time.

It'll soon put her off having another baby just so the first can have a sibling, I can tell you.'

Kate snorted, continuing with, 'Not only are the sleeping arrangements a bone of contention, but Ellis decided to become a vegetarian last night, Portia says she doesn't believe in Christmas anymore and says the whole thing is pointless – although when I suggested we take her presents back to the shop for a refund, she had an absolute hissy fit and accused me of trying to ruin her life – and his mother informed me last week that she has both a gluten and a dairy intolerance. Oh, and my mother is bringing her smelly, incontinent dog with her.'

Doris was chewing at her lip and trying to control her laughter. 'A typical family Christmas, then?'

'I wish! Once, just for once, I'd like it to be the way it is on the telly. You see these adverts where everyone is happy and smiling, sitting around a table groaning with food. No one is necking back the vodka, no one is wishing the little bang in the crackers was a ruddy great big one, no one is wondering why they didn't think of putting sleeping tablets in the gravy before dishing up the Christmas lunch. And no one is wishing they'd booked into a bed and breakfast in the middle of nowhere, just to get away from it all. And that was last year, with just the one nan. This year is shaping up to be even worse.'

'It's only for a couple of days,' Doris said. 'I'm sure you'll cope.'

Kate, on the other hand, was almost certainly positive she wouldn't.

CHAPTER 5

'You're what?' It was Friday evening and Kate was wrestling with the laundry. She stopped trying to fold a king-sized sheet while holding the phone wedged under her chin, and dropped the item she had been about to iron back into the laundry basket.

'Arriving on Monday,' her mother said.

'You're supposed to be coming on Christmas Eve.' That would have given Kate nearly a whole week to mentally and physically prepare for the onslaught; the house was a tip and there wasn't a decoration in sight.

'I never said when. You just assumed,' her mother stated.

'You always go to Aunt May's on Christmas Eve.' When Kate had spoken to her mother yesterday evening and Beverley had informed her of her plans, she'd made no mention of arriving *before* Christmas.

'May only lives four miles down the road. You live four hours away. Why you felt the need to move to the Midlands is beyond me. Your Brett had a perfectly good job in London.'

Kate sank slowly down onto the nearest chair and resisted the urge to hang up on her mother. No matter how many times Kate had explained that Brett had been offered a promotion, with a better salary and everything that went with it, Beverley had chosen not to hear. Not to mention the fact that London hadn't suited her husband. He'd never settled there, and had taken the very first opportunity to return to the area he grew up in. Besides, they now lived in a lovely big house in a lovely little village; rather than in a tiny house, which was all they would have been able to afford if they'd stayed in London. They had fresh air, open fields, and the River Severn on their doorstep. OK, the river wasn't quite on their doorstep, but it was only a few miles away.

Her mother said, 'If you think I'm travelling halfway across the country on Christmas Eve, you've got another think coming. I'm far too old for that.'

Kate rolled her eyes. At seventy-one, her mother was hardly a frail old lady.

'I'm coming on Monday,' Beverley repeated. 'It's cheaper on Mondays.'

'What is?'

'Train fare.'

'Aren't you driving up?'

'All that way? No chance! You know I don't like it on the motorway. As it is, I've got to change trains twice, and I'm not getting any younger, you know.'

Kate shook her head in exasperation.

'You can come later in the week, Mum,' Kate suggested, desperately. 'I'll pay for your ticket, if it's the money that's worrying you.' Please say yes…please…please…

'No, I've made my mind up. I'll see you on Monday. And I hope you're not expecting me to share a room with Brett's mother.'

'Er, no, I—'

'Good. You can fetch me from the station. The train gets in at four o'clock. Don't be late. I don't want to be hanging around on a draughty platform. The cold will play havoc with my arthritis.'

Kate stared at her phone for a long time after her mother ended the call. Then she placed it gently on the table, stood up and walked to the door leading out to the garden, opened it, stuck her head outside, and screamed.

A flock of crows which had settled down for the evening in the tall fir trees beyond the garden, were startled by the noise, and flapped into the air in a flurry of squawks and jet-black wings.

Murder, she thought haphazardly. It wasn't a flock, it was a *murder* of crows.

How apt, because that was exactly what she

felt like committing.

'Did you say something?' Brett asked, strolling into the kitchen, his eyes on his mobile, his index finger jabbing at the screen.

'Not really. I was screaming. My mother just told me she's arriving on Monday.'

'That's nice,' Brett said absently, and Kate realised he wasn't listening to her. 'I told my mum that your mother would be joining us for Christmas this year,' he added.

'Oh? How did it go?'

'I don't think she was too pleased.'

'If she doesn't like it, she'll have to lump it. Or not come herself. I know which I'd prefer.' Kate muttered the last bit under her breath.

'She doesn't want to have to share a room. You know she's such a light sleeper.'

Kate knew all right. Helen had told her. Many times. Usually accompanied by some acerbic comment about the children being too noisy. What did she expect Kate to do, Sellotape their mouths shut? Tie them to their beds so they didn't run up and down the stairs (apparently, they stomped up and down them, and not walked like normal people). Send them away for the duration?

'She's worried your mother's snoring will keep her awake,' her husband added.

'My mother doesn't snore.' She paused. 'Does she?'

'I've no idea,' Brett said.

'And even if she did, how would *your* mother know?'

He shrugged. 'Anyway, she says she can't possibly share a bed, even a double one, with your mother, because of her allergies.'

Kate's eyes widened. 'Your mother is allergic to my mother?' Kate knew she sounded as incredulous as she felt.

'Don't be silly. She's allergic to dogs, and even though the damned poodle will be in kennels, its hair gets everywhere. Beverley will have some on her clothes, in her bag – everywhere,' he repeated.

'Mum didn't say anything about putting Pepe in kennels for Christmas,' Kate said. 'She'd never do that.'

'Oh? I assumed—'

'You assumed wrong. I fully expect Mum to bring Pepe with her; she always does, so why should this visit be any different?'

Brett scowled. 'Because my mother is allergic to dogs.'

'Since when? She's never mentioned it before,' Kate pointed out. If Helen was allergic, then Kate would have been told all about it. Many times.

Pepe was coming for Christmas, too, and that was that. He always slept in a little basket at the foot of Beverley's bed and Kate couldn't see any change in the situation this time. Although she didn't like him sleeping upstairs (he was prone to the odd accident), Kate couldn't be bothered with the drama which was certain to unfold if she tried to insist that Pepe's place was in the kitchen.

This time it was Brett who rolled his eyes. Kate suspected there would be a great deal of eye rolling going on before the Christmas holiday was over.

Brett repeated. 'Either way, it wouldn't be wise putting both mums in the same room. One of them wouldn't survive the night.'

'Because they'd try to kill each other?' Kate uttered a semi-hysterical giggle, then closed her mouth quickly, worried that she was already starting to lose it and the nans hadn't even arrived yet.

Brett gave her an odd look. 'No, because although the bed is a double, it's too small for both of them. One of them would end up falling out, and at their age it could mean a broken hip. And we both know what that could lead to.'

'The fallee would have to move in with us, and I'd end up murdering her?'

Another odd look from her husband. 'What I meant was, a broken hip can lead to pneumonia.'

'Oh, right.' Could it? Was there a direct correlation between hips and lungs? Kate thought not. But what did she know? Brett claimed to have far more medical knowledge than she did because he was in the pharmaceutical business; although Kate wasn't aware that the act of working in the office of a company which manufactured and distributed drugs made him any kind of medical expert.

'Can you close the door?' Brett asked, finally looking up from his phone. 'You're letting all the heat out.'

'Sorry.' She'd been leaning against the door jamb, hoping her husband would wander back out of the kitchen so she could have another scream, but with him giving no indication he was about to leave, she closed the door and leant against that instead.

"Letting all the heat out" indeed. That was the least of their worries. Sometimes Brett sounded old and grumpy. Forty-eight wasn't old, though, not these days. Neither was forty-six, but this evening Kate felt every one of those years piling up on top of her and weighing her down. She wondered if her husband ever thought the same way about her – that she was getting old. Was she, God forbid, starting to sound, look, and behave like her own mother? She bloody hoped not, but now and again she could hear traces of Beverley Collins in her voice when she shouted at the children or nagged them to do this, that, or the other.

Then something brought her out of her musing and into the present.

'—which is why she's coming a couple of days early,' Brett was saying.

'Pardon?'

'*I said,*' Brett began, with exaggerated patience. 'That's why she's arriving a couple of days early.'

'Who is?' Kate felt a flutter of panic in her chest.

'My mother. I swear you don't listen to a word I say.'

Brett had stolen her line. He was the one who never listened, who always swore blind she'd never told him something when she so definitely had.

'Your mother is arriving early,' she repeated woodenly, the flutter becoming a full-blown flurry of ink-black wings.

'That's what I just said. It's all right, isn't it? She's coming on Wednesday to spend a day or so with us on her own, before your mum gets here. She's used to having us all to herself, so having Beverley here is going to be a bit of a wrench. I thought we'd have a leg of lamb for supper. She'd like that.'

I bet she would, Kate thought. And who was going to have to rush home from work and cook it? Not Brett, that's for sure. And she'd just proved a point; she'd clearly told him only a few moments ago that her own mother was arriving on Monday, and it had gone straight over his head.

Oh God, she'd have to break it to the kids, and she'd have to force one of the girls out of her room for the best part of next week, and not just for the couple of nights that they'd been anticipating.

'Where's Ellis?' Kate asked.

'Out.'

'Out where?'

Brett gave her a helpless look. 'How should I know? She's seventeen.'

'Portia?'

'Out.'

Kate should know where her children were. She was their mother, after all. But they'd arrived home from school earlier than her because she'd had to drop off Brett's dry cleaning and do the food shopping for the coming week on the way home. When she'd got in, it was to find Sam waiting impatiently for a lift to his friend's house in the next village (although he hadn't asked her beforehand – he just expected to be taxied there and back), and therefore she hadn't managed to catch up with either of her daughters yet.

'Taylor's party?' she guessed. It wasn't the first Christmas party her middle child had been invited to, and Kate suspected it wasn't the last. The kids had only broken up from school today and there was a whole week to go before the big day finally arrived, and most of it was filled with parties.

'Yeah. You missed the sequinned top drama,'

Brett said, sounding aggrieved that his wife had the misfortune of being out and leaving him to deal with it.

Pity, she would have loved to have been home for that. *Not.*

'We'd better get a Christmas tree, and fetch the decorations from the garage tomorrow,' Kate said, her brain beginning to rev like a car with a newly-passed-their-test teenage driver at the wheel. She could feel the cogs spinning furiously as she thought about all the things which needed doing. She'd originally (stupidly) assumed she'd have a whole week to prepare for the impending visits.

Now it was only two days before the first of them arrived, that was all. The weekend, which was already full of stuff that needed to be done, had suddenly become a great deal fuller. Today was Friday. Christmas Eve was next Saturday. That was a whole week away, a week in which she'd planned on doing all the things she'd now have to cram into two days.

A thought struck her. Two thoughts, actually.

One of them was the worry that if Brett's mother realised her nemesis was turning up earlier than expected, she would also try to bring her arrival date forward. And the second was, Brett would be in work all next week, and so would she.

That meant the children would be on their own in the house with one or both of their grandmothers.

It also meant that the grandmothers would be on their own with each other.

OMG!! Could this Christmas get any worse?

CHAPTER 6

'Where are you going?' Kate demanded, seeing Brett shrug on his coat and pick up his car keys.

'I promised I'd join the guys for a quick game of golf.'

'In this weather?'

It was lunchtime on what was almost the shortest day of the year; the day was sullen and overcast, it was dank and cold out, and there were barely three decent hours of daylight left. She should know, she'd just done the supermarket run and she was bloody freezing, Besides, she had so much to do, she could use her husband's help, starting with carrying all the shopping in from the car.

'I promise I'll wrap up,' Brett said, dropping a quick kiss on the top of her head and patting her on the shoulder.

'But, there's the tree to fetch, I haven't finished cleaning yet, there's a pile of ironing to do—'

'That's why I thought you'd be better off with me out of the way.'

'What about the kids?' By that premise, then surely she'd be better off with the children out of the way, too? 'Couldn't you take them when you go to get the tree? I'm sure they'd love to go with you.'

Kate was fairly certain they wouldn't, but the three of them under her feet wasn't conducive to blitzing the house successfully.

From past experience, she knew that as soon as she'd cleaned the mess away from one room, it would reappear again in the form of half-drunk glasses of juice, abandoned homework, thoughtlessly kicked off shoes, and the thousands of other items that her family seemed incapable of returning to their rightful places. If they were all out of the house at the same time, at least she'd have a fighting chance of tidying up, and she didn't want to put any of the decorations up before she'd given the house a good clean.

'Aww, I would, but I promised the lads I'd play a round. The club isn't open over Christmas and this'll be my last game of the year. You can pick the tree up tomorrow. The garden centre is open on Sundays.'

Kate sighed, exasperated. She'd dearly love to slope off for a game of golf (OK, maybe not golf, or any other game for that matter, but having a couple of hours to herself sounded good), but she had far too much to do. Brett, she knew, couldn't understand her need to clean before his mother's visit.

She was pretty sure he didn't notice the mess or the crumbs dotting the kitchen floor, or the smears all over the shower cubicle, and if he did, he wouldn't be unduly bothered – probably because he knew the cleaning fairy would pay the Peters' house a visit and the cleaning would magically get done.

But neither had he been on the receiving end of his mother's barbed, subtly pointed comments and criticisms regarding Kate's housekeeping and parenting skills. If Kate could head the woman off at the pass, she would; having a clean, tidy house would give Helen one less thing to mention.

Of course, Helen would still find things which weren't up to her exacting standards – her visit wouldn't be complete unless she did – but the less ammunition Kate gave her to fire, the better.

Fine, Kate thought as Brett walked out of the door; *leave me to do all of it, why don't you.* At least her own mother (although she could be a pain in the backside) didn't constantly and snidely criticise her, even if she did complain a lot, as the children rightly noted.

Kate decided to start with stuffing the school uniforms into the washing machine so it could carry on doing its thing while she hauled bag after bag of groceries out of the boot and into the kitchen.

'Ellis? Portia? Sam? Would anyone care to give me a hand?' she called up the stairs.

Even as the words left her mouth, Kate realised she'd asked a daft question; of course her children wouldn't care to give her a hand. They'd pretend they hadn't heard her, and by the time she'd tramped upstairs, told them what she wanted, waited for them to finish applying fake tan/ this game/ listening to this track/ sending a text/ watching the latest episode of The Kardashians/ painting toenails/ speaking to X, Y or Z, she might as well have just got on with it and carried the shopping in herself. She could have done that, put it away, made herself a cup of tea, drank it, *and* had the washing machine go through half its cycle before any of the children made a move to help her.

'I'll just do it myself then, shall I?' she muttered, stomping out to the car and coming back with several bags in each hand. 'Just like I do everything else around here. One day, I'm going to go on strike and see how everyone likes it.'

But not now, not today – she simply had too much to do…

CHAPTER 7

Golf was a game not at its best when it was played on a dismal and murky Saturday lunchtime in late December, but Brett desperately needed some time-out. If he stayed at home, Kate would get him doing stuff and the kids would hassle him, and he simply couldn't face it. Besides, the whole polite competitive camaraderie of playing a round of golf was therapeutic, and if he only got an hour in, at least he could relax at the "nineteenth" hole with an orange juice and some non-committal chat about the boxing, or something similar. He would have preferred something stronger than juice, but he didn't think Kate would appreciate him asking her to pick him up after he'd had a few beers and then having to bring him back tomorrow to fetch his car.

His wife was quite tetchy these days and having both their mothers coming to stay with them for Christmas had sent her into overdrive. She should learn to chill out a bit. So what if the skirting boards were dusty, or the fridge needed cleaning? No one would notice, and if they did, neither mother would care. They were here to spend the festive season with the family, not to pass judgement on Kate's housekeeping skills.

Brett pulled into the carpark, cut the engine, and took his phone out of his pocket with the intention of switching it off – he didn't want to receive any work calls right now – then saw he had a missed call from his mother. He might as well phone her back, otherwise she'd only keep calling, and he'd bet his left arm that she'd manage to phone exactly when he was in the middle of taking a crucial shot.

'You rang?' he said to her, as he walked into the clubhouse.

'I just wanted to let you know that I've bought Portia the most gorgeous blouse for Christmas. It's in a pretty shade of lavender. Do you think she'll like it?'

An image of his youngest daughter dressed from top to toe in her usual black, with heavy black makeup around her eyes (when she was allowed to wear any) popped into his head. It would be nice to see her in some brighter colours for a change.

'I'm sure she will,' he said.

'I've got Ellis a cookery book, and Sam a model car.'

'Wonderful!' Brett said with forced jollity. Ellis didn't know a hob from a microwave and Sam hadn't played with cars since he was eight, but it was the thought that counted.

'I'll give them money, of course,' his mother added, 'but I want them to have something to open on Christmas morning.'

At least she'd given him the heads-up so he

could ensure his offspring were wearing suitably grateful expressions on their faces when the time came to open their presents. He didn't want any kind of atmosphere, although there would probably be enough of that between his mother and Beverley anyway. He simply couldn't understand why the two women didn't get on.

'Listen, Mum, I've got to go, I've another call coming in,' he said, his heart sinking to his golf shoes when he saw it was The Abyss.

'Morning,' he said to his manager. 'Or is it afternoon now?'

'I don't know and I don't care, not when we've got Craig Wesley chewing my ear off about The Southern Chemist contract. He wants a report on where we are with it, and he wants it yesterday. I'm in the office right now, but I can't make head nor tail out of the contract, so I need you in as soon as possible. If we don't get this sorted before Christmas none of us need bother coming in after the New Year.'

Brett sighed. What a bloody mess; he'd told The Abyss that the contract wasn't anywhere near ready to be signed because of some fundamental delivery issues, but she didn't seem to care and neither did Craig Wesley, Head of Operations.

It didn't matter if he went into the office or not, in terms of getting a signature from anyone in The Southern Chemist, because no one would be available until Monday. But if he didn't go in, he'd be accused of not showing enough dedication and commitment to the company. It didn't matter that he was in the office by seven-thirty every morning and didn't leave until six in the evening. No one cared a fig about his commitment then...

The way things were going, he might as well move his sodding bed into his office and be sodding done with it.

Shoulders slumped and his feet dragging, Brett walked slowly back to his car.

There must be more to life than this, surely? he thought. *There must be.*

CHAPTER 8

'I don't care, I'm not having her sleeping in my bed.' Portia folded her arms across her chest and stuck out her chin.

It was Sunday evening, Kate had work in the morning, she'd not managed to get half the things done that she'd wanted to do, and now Portia was up in arms again about the ensuing sleeping arrangements.

'It's not for long,' Kate pleaded.

'It's for a week,' Portia shrieked. 'A whole week! Why do they have to stay here for so long? Haven't they got homes of their own?'

'Don't be so silly. And try to have a bit more empathy.'

'Like you have, you mean?'

'Now you're being cheeky.'

'I'm simply telling the truth. I'm not having a wrinkly sleep in my bed. It's gross.'

What a charming expression, calling older people wrinklies, Kate thought, sarcastically. 'Your grandmother isn't gross. Brett, back me up, here.'

'Eh?' Brett glanced up from the TV. Countryfile was on. Kate hadn't realised her husband was so into what was essentially a programme for farmers. He'd never shown much interest in anything agricultural before. Funny that...

'Never mind,' she said. 'Portia, you'll do as you're told. You're moving into Ellis's room for a few days, and that's that.'

'You can't make me.' Portia's chin protruded even further.

Kate disliked the defiant, sulky look her middle child often wore. It was getting to the point where Kate had forgotten what her daughter looked like without her face contorted in teenage angst or plastered in a layer of makeup. Only the other night, she'd found herself slipping into Portia's room while she slept, to remind herself just what an attractive girl her daughter was. Her face smoothed by sleep and free of black kohl around her eyes, Portia had looked less like a sullen teenager and more like the child Kate wished she still was.

'Watch me,' she growled. 'I can take your phone off you for starters.'

The horrified look on Portia's face nearly made Kate laugh.

'Tell her, Dad! She can't do that! It's not fair!'

When Brett merely grunted, his attention firmly on the TV screen, Portia gave an almighty shriek, whirled on her toes, and flounced out of the living room. Kate flinched as Portia slammed the door hard enough to crack the plaster on the walls.

She rubbed her face with her hands. Why did kids have to create so much drama? Why couldn't they simply accept things for what they were and just get on with it? It wasn't as if this was a permanent arrangement.

For once in her life, she would like a happy, peaceful Christmas. No arguments, no squabbles, no shouting, no complaints. And no being piggy-in-the-middle, trying (usually unsuccessfully) to play referee, to smooth motherly oil on the troubled waters of her children's lives, to keep the peace between the generations and try to ensure everyone had a good time. Or, at the very least, didn't kill each other.

Kate didn't hear the door open and when Ellis appeared, ghostly and silent, ethereal in a floaty dress and several chiffon scarves, saying, 'I don't blame Portia – it isn't fair,' Kate let out a small shriek.

'I wish you'd stop creeping up on people,' Kate grizzled.

'I don't creep. I walk normally. It's not my fault you're going deaf.'

'I am not going deaf,' she objected.

'Nanny Collins is. It's supposed to run in families.'

Kate gritted her teeth. She wasn't interested in winning an argument over whether she was going deaf or not. She wanted to get the sleeping arrangements sorted out before her mother arrived tomorrow afternoon. There was no way she was having this kind of drama when the first of the grandmothers turned up. Of course, it was logical that Beverley slept in the spare room, considering she would be staying the longest. But Kate wanted to sort out which bedroom Helen would be sleeping in before her mother witnessed the children's strenuous arguing.

'I don't see what the rush is,' Brett said, from the depths of the sofa. Damn it, she'd forgotten to take the cushions off and vacuum down the sides. No doubt his mother would accidentally on purpose lose something, which would necessitate her sticking her hands down the side of the sofa and grimacing at the serious number of crumbs, hair bobbles, and sweet wrappers which were probably down there.

'My mother won't be here until Wednesday. That's three whole days away. Plenty of time to shift one of the girls and fumigate her room,' Brett said.

'The sooner we get the sleeping arrangement sorted, the longer everyone has to get used to the idea. I *told* you, *my* mother is arriving *tomorrow*.'

Ellis's ears pricked up. 'She's what? *Why?* Nana Peters doesn't usually arrive until Christmas Eve. Why isn't Nanny Collins coming on Christmas Eve, too?'

Kate couldn't face telling Ellis that Nana Peters was also arriving early. 'I'm picking your nanny up from the station at four,' she said, firmly.

'Effing hell,' Ellis muttered. 'Can this Christmas get any worse?'

'Probably,' Kate muttered in reply.

Ellis looked so indignant, Kate wanted to slap her.

Brett didn't look much happier. In fact, instead of giving her the support she so desperately needed, his whole demeanour was one of long-suffering exasperation. How dare he be this put-out, when she'd had to put up with his mother every year; but the one time her own mother wanted to spend Christmas with them, he was making it sound as if Jack the Ripper was descending on them for a spot of tinsel and turkey.

'Why is she coming so early?' Ellis whined.

'Something to do with the trains,' Kate said vaguely, not wanting to get into the whys and wherefores. It wouldn't make any difference, anyway. 'She's arriving tomorrow, so you'll just have to suck it up,' Kate added. 'As will your sister.'

'I'm not sharing my room with Portia for a whole week. She's so bloody annoying.'

She's not the only one, Kate thought. 'You'll do as you're told, and so will Portia.'

'It's not fair. You've got a giant super king-sized bed. I've only got a small double.'

'First world problems,' she said. 'There are people in the world who'd think they'd gone to heaven if they had your bed.' Oh, shit, she couldn't believe she'd said that out loud.

Ellis gave her a scathing look, which Kate felt was quite deserved. 'If you're that bothered, why don't you give up your room? Nanny Collins could sleep in there and Nanna Peters can have the spare room, like she usually does.'

'And where would your father and I sleep?'

'In the living room. You're always saying you don't know why you bought that tent in the first place, because you never use it.'

Kate barked out an incredulous laugh. 'You want your parents to sleep in a tent in the middle of the living room? It'll ruin the carpet.'

More scathing looks. Ellis was very good at them. 'I meant that you could sleep on the blow-up mattress.'

Kate had already thought of the blow-up bed, and was about to broach the subject, hoping it would stop the girls squabbling about having to cuddle down under the same duvet. They'd bought the tent several years ago with the intention of enjoying family holidays where they could get away from it all and be at one with nature. But there'd been so much complaining and grizzling about not being able to plug in hairdryers and other essential beauty appliances (the girls), mobile phones (all of them, including Brett), and the Xbox (from Sam, who'd smuggled it into his rucksack), that she hadn't bothered suggesting it again.

Kate said. 'Brett, go and fetch the airbed from the garage and blow it up. We can put it on the floor in Ellis's room, and Portia can sleep on it.'

'Oh, for fuc—'

'*Excuse me?*' Kate interjected, before her daughter said something Kate would have to take her to task on.

'Nothing. I hate this family, I hate Christmas. I wish I was eighteen already and could move out!'

Another flounce, another slam, different daughter.

Kate breathed out slowly, counting to ten, and wishing Ellis was eighteen, too.

What was she *thinking*? Of course, she didn't

want her oldest child to move out. The idea was ludicrous.

But it would solve the sleeping arrangements issue, wouldn't it, a treacherous little voice whispered in her mind.

Oh, shut up, she told it.

CHAPTER 9

Brett stalked out of the kitchen, muttering under his breath. It was dark, cold, and raining outside, and he had no intention of scrabbling around in the garage looking for the air bed. He'd do it tomorrow after he came home from work. It wasn't urgent; Beverley would have the spare room and his mother would have either Ellis's or Portia's room. Besides, his mother wouldn't be here for a couple of days yet. There was plenty of time to sort everything out. He'd dig out the decorations then, as well. Not that they had a tree to hang any of them from, but it was a start.

He wondered vaguely what Kate had been doing all weekend, considering she hadn't been to the garden centre to buy a tree yet. There was a time when the Buying of the Tree was a much-looked-forward-to family event and done with a great deal of seriousness, but that had all changed over the years. Last year, if he remembered correctly, Kate had taken a grizzling, complaining Sam with her to help choose one. It saddened him that the kids were growing up so fast and no longer wanted to do the things they'd always enjoyed doing together. These days, his daughters were more interested in hanging out with their friends, rather than spending any time with the "olds", as he'd overheard Portia refer to him and Kate. Huh! *Old* indeed. He wasn't even fifty yet; he had a good long way to go before he considered himself old.

He didn't want to call his mother, but he thought he'd better warn her. If she turned up on Wednesday to find Beverley already here, he'd never hear the last of it, and neither would anyone else. He thought it best to tell her now and give her some time to get used to the idea.

'Hi, Mum, just to let you know, Beverley will be here before you,' Brett said as soon as his mother answered. 'She mentioned to Kate that she's arriving tomorrow.'

'Tomorrow?' Helen shrieked, and Brett winced, holding the phone away from his ear for a moment.

'Er…yes?'

'Why?' His mother's voice was sharp. 'She didn't tell you the reason why she's descending on you so early?'

'I'm not sure. Something about trains?' Kate had probably told him, but if she had he'd not been listening.

'I see,' Helen said. Her voice was frostier than a snowman at the Arctic. 'Did she say what time?'

'Kate's in work until five, so unless one of the children are at home and can let her in, I expect it'll be the evening.'

'I see,' his mother said, again.

'Sorry, Mum. I know you were looking

forward to spending a couple of days with us on your own, but it can't be helped. We'll still have a nice Christmas, yeah?'

'With the woman who keeps saying "I hate Christmas"? Hardly likely, is it? I mean, I'm not all that keen on Christmas myself – you don't seem to enjoy it as much when you get older, I've found – but at least I don't keep mentioning it all the time. We all know it's a waste of money and too commercialised, but we just grit our teeth and get through it.'

With that, she hung up, leaving Brett staring at his mobile with a bemused expression. Bloody hell, his mother made Christmas sound as bad as having a root canal. He hadn't realised she felt like that about it. But now she'd come to mention it, he didn't feel as excited as he used to. All Christmas meant to him this year was having some time off work. Because the offices would thankfully be closed, there was no way The Abyss could bully him into going in, like she'd done yesterday. It didn't help his festive spirit that Kate had practically cold-shouldered him for most of the weekend after he's gone out to play golf. He could have come clean and told her he'd had to go into work but he didn't see why he should have to explain himself. If he wanted to wind down on the golf course at the end of the working week, then he shouldn't be made to feel guilty about it. It wasn't as if he didn't pull his weight – he worked damned long hours to keep his wife and children in the style they'd become accustomed to. OK, he mightn't do much around the house, but in the summer he was responsible for the garden, and he mowed, trimmed, and weeded everything to within an inch of its life. All Kate had to do was plump up the cushions on their patio chairs, pour herself a glass of something long and cold, then sit back in the sun and enjoy the fruits of his labour.

To be honest, he thought she had the better end of the stick in their relationship. She was never stuck in work at seven-thirty in the evening. She was always home well before then, pottering around in the kitchen or doing a bit of ironing while listening to Radio 4. Hardly taxing, was it?

Brett found he wasn't looking forward to Christmas at all this year. What with his mother joining forces with the "I hate Christmas Crowd", Portia already in that particular club although Brett was at a loss to see what a teenager could find to dislike about Christmas, and Kate stressing herself out over being the perfect wife, mother, daughter, cook, hostess, and so on. Sam would probably be wedged in his room with his headphones on, Ellis would waft in and out whenever she felt like it, and he didn't even want to mention all the squabbles which usually took place and didn't need to be exacerbated by enforced jollity and awful TV. He almost wished he could run away for a couple of days and wait for it all to be over and for everything to return to normal.

With a mutter and a frown, Brett threw himself on the sofa and buried his nose in the paper. Maybe all the cheating, lying, assaults and thefts in the news would cheer him up.

Huh!

CHAPTER 10

Monday didn't start off particularly well, what with Kate having been awake half the night (this seemed to be becoming an issue – apparently it was the perimenopause), then, as a result, sleeping through the alarm. Which had Brett moaning that he was late for work because she hadn't woken him up.

Since when had it become her responsibility to wake him up? He was a grown man, with an alarm on his phone, and opposable thumbs. Surely he was capable of ensuring he was awake in plenty of time to get ready for work without having to rely on her?

Clearly not.

She thrust a pack of hastily made and not-particularly-edible-looking sandwiches into his hand, and practically pushed him out of the door into the darkness of a late December morning.

It was supposed to be the longest night soon, Kate thought, as she began to get ready for work, although she had a sneaking suspicion that the following few days were going to feel twice as long as they actually were. Three times, as long, maybe.

She watched her husband unlock his car and get into it, wondering what had happened to the days when he'd give her a kiss before he left. He always used to, without fail. Until one day, he'd stopped doing it. She hadn't noticed at first, and couldn't honestly point to a day and say, "there, that was it – that was the day my husband stopped kissing me goodbye in the morning"; the kisses had simply trailed off. Maybe she'd been too busy sorting the children out, had been too preoccupied with the routine of chivvying her offspring into getting out of the door with food in their tummies, clothes on the their backs, and all the necessary bits and pieces to get them through their day, to notice that she hadn't been kissed on a particular day. Then one day must have become two, and two had developed into three, until there came a point where Kate couldn't remember the last time he'd kissed her goodbye.

He was still the man she'd married. A little paunchier around the middle, but she could hardly talk. Three children and no time to oneself, didn't encourage a pin-up body. Some days she was grateful to have brushed her hair. His was receding a little, but not so as you'd notice, and he'd collected a few lines around his eyes. Not classically handsome (no chiselled jaw or six-pack), Brett was quietly pleasant to look at. His face wouldn't be the first man a woman would look at if she walked into a bar, but when she did see him, her eyes would be drawn to him again and again. At least, that's what it had been like for Kate, some twenty-odd years ago.

She wondered if it would be the same now, were she to meet him for the first time.

Damn, look at the time. She'd better get a move on, and not stand in the doorstep staring at the space where Brett's car had sat a few moments ago. She couldn't remember if she'd waved him off or not. She suspected she hadn't.

Going back inside, she closed the door gently, not wanting to wake her slumbering offspring. The reason was purely selfish and had nothing to do with letting them have their beauty sleep. Although she hated leaving the kids alone every day during the holidays, she couldn't face their combined whining, so a blissful non-school morning without it would be wonderful.

There was a time, and not all that long ago either, when she used to force them to get out of bed, made them eat breakfast, gathered everything they could possibly need or want for the day, and bundled them off to the childminders, despite Ellis's vehement protests that she was old enough to take care of herself.

Then there came a period of allowing them

to stay in the house, with supervision. Kate might only be in work for six hours, but children could get up to a considerable amount of mischief in that time, despite her employing a baby-sitter in the form of one of the young mums in the village who needed a bit of extra money. Kate often slipped home during her lunch break to make sure they hadn't set fire to the house or had hung one of their number by their ankles from the bannister, because one day she'd caught the girls just about to string Sam up, and had rescued him in the nick of time. The mum had preferred spending time on Snapchat to watching the children, and Kate had very nearly given up work altogether at that point, to stay at home to look after them.

Rather unfairly, now that Ellis was seventeen and Kate worked slightly longer hours, Kate relied on her to keep the other two in check. She was only a few minutes' drive away, and Mrs Pemberton, the middle-aged lady who lived next door along with seven cats and a husband no one ever saw and who Kate wasn't entirely sure existed, popped in now and again to check on them.

Today Ellis was going into town to do some Christmas shopping, Portia was going riding and would be at the stables all day, and Sam was going ice-skating. One of his friend's mothers was taking three of them plus her own to Telford ice-rink. All Kate hoped was that no one broke anything.

She stuck her head around each child's bedroom door before she left and hoped that with the three of them out all day, the house might remain relatively clean and tidy. She wouldn't get a chance to dash home before she picked her mother up from Worcester station, which entailed a drive into the centre of the city at the start of rush hour and back out again. She was having to leave work early as it was.

She thought she'd done well to get into work on time, and she was in the middle of congratulating herself when she tripped over a pair of legs jutting out of the shop doorway and fell flat on her face.

'You alright, love?' a gruff male voice asked.

Kate raised her head to see a pair of stained trousers with a soiled blanket tucked around them.

'Ron. Hi.'

''Ello. Got any change?'

As a matter of fact, she didn't, but she did have a hot cup of tea, and some cheese and chutney sandwiches she could give him. He looked like he could do with a new pair of trousers, too, and a fresh blanket.

She pushed herself to her knees and slowly got to her feet. Thankfully, it hadn't rained last night, but her jeans were damp and there was dirt daubed down the length of them.

'You really shouldn't be lying there,' she said to him

'Sorry. Did you hurt yourself?'

'I'm fine. I'm not saying you can't use this doorway, because you can. Doris doesn't mind. What I'm saying is, you should have gone to the shelter. It's too cold for you to be outside this time of year.'

Ron gave her a blank look. Kate had lost count of the number of times she'd suggested him going to the shelter, but as far as she knew he'd never done so.

Hang on, why was he sprawled out in the shop doorway at this time in the morning, anyway? The charity shop should have opened half an hour ago.

'Where's Doris?' Kate asked, aiming the question at no one in particular.

'Don't know.'

Feeling a little uneasy, Kate fished her keys out of her bag and unlocked the door. 'Wait there for a moment,' she said to Ron, and she stepped inside hurrying to the rear to flick the lights on.

No sign of Doris.

Kate got her phone out.

Ah, Doris had sent her a message; she was sorry, but she thought she was coming down with the flu, and could Kate man the fort?

Kate groaned. Not today, please not today. Bang went her hope of getting away early. She'd have to call her mother and tell her she'd have to take a taxi. But first, there was Ron to see to. Not only did she feel immensely sorry for him, but he was no good for business. People didn't like having to step around a homeless person to buy a pack of charity Christmas cards, and although Kate herself didn't mind him being there, Head Office did.

She invited him in to choose a pair of trousers, while she put the kettle on to boil and dug out a clean blanket to give him. When he was done and she'd sent him on his way with a mug of tea and her lunch, she aired the shop out (bless him, he couldn't help it, but he did whiff a bit), then she spent the next hour or so putting fresh stock on the rails while serving customers.

Later, she texted Doris to say she hoped she felt better soon, phoned each of her children to make sure they were out of bed and doing whatever it was they were supposed to be doing today, and tried to call her mother. No answer. Kate wasn't surprised.

Despite Beverley and Helen being roughly the same age, Helen had a far greater grasp on technology than Beverley. Helen used Facebook, had an email address, and thought internet shopping was a new sport. Beverley turned her mobile off to save the battery and complained bitterly when no one called her as a result.

Which is exactly what her mother would do later, when Kate failed to show up at the station.

She'd turn her phone on then, quick enough.

Kate shuddered. She wasn't looking forward to that conversation.

CHAPTER 11

'Kate? Kate? Where are you? I've been waiting for ages, and Pepe, the little love, is shivering.'

'Mum?' Kate whispered into the phone because she had a shop full of customers and she didn't want them all to overhear her conversation.

'Who else would it be? Where are you? It's seven minutes past four.'

'I'm stuck in work. I did try to call but your phone wasn't switched on. Can you get a taxi?'

'No, I can't.'

'Why not?'

'I can't carry my cases that far.'

Cases? As in, plural? How many had the woman brought with her? 'I'm sure there are railway staff around who you can ask to help take them to the taxi rank.'

'I can't see anyone, except for a boy who looks like a cow.'

'Pardon?'

'Chewing the cud. Nasty habit. If I see him spit his gum out on the ground, I'm going to go over there and give him a piece of my mind.'

'Please don't.'

'Are you coming to fetch me?' The belligerent tone had become wheedling and rather pathetic. 'I don't like it here on my own. I don't feel safe.'

Oh, for God's sake! 'Mum, I'm in work. I can't leave for another half an hour.' At the earliest, and even then she'd be closing the shop before the designated time.

'That's right, put your job before your family,' her mother said, abruptly becoming quarrelsome. 'Like you always do.' Then she added, sharply, 'I'll wait here for you, but don't blame me if I come down with a cold. Or worse.' And with that, her mother hung up.

Kate quietly seethed while trying to call Ellis.

No joy.

Portia?

Nope.

She didn't bother phoning Sam. He wouldn't be home for ages yet, and anyway, he wouldn't have a clue how to turn the oven on, take the casserole she'd prepared earlier out of the fridge, and then put it into the aforementioned oven. It would be beyond him; yet he was perfectly capable of taking his TV apart and putting it back together again, with no ill effects except for the loss of Channel 5, which, in reality, was hardly any loss at all.

Supper would simply have to be late. There was nothing Kate could do about it.

As soon as she feasibly could, Kate locked the shop and hurried to her car, pulling her hood over her head against the misty drizzle. Mizzle was it called, or drist? She hoped her mother had found refuge in the waiting room and wasn't standing on the platform, getting drenched, just to make a point.

But when she got to the station, her mother was nowhere to be seen.

Worcester Foregate Street railway station had only two platforms. *Two*. So how could Kate not find her mother? She checked in the waiting room, but there was no sign of her.

She went back into the ticket area. Beverley wasn't there, either.

She hurried outside, just in case her mother had been hovering on the pavement and Kate had walked right past her without seeing her.

Still no sign.

Beginning to get anxious, Kate asked one of the staff, 'Have you seen a plumpish lady in her seventies, with lots of luggage, and a poodle?'

'No, sorry, love. Have you tried the waiting room?'

Kate smiled her thanks. Now she really *was* starting to worry. Maybe her mother had decided to get a taxi, after all? She tried her mother's mobile, but it wasn't switched on. Of course, not

– why would it be? Then she dialled the landline hopefully, only to realise that even if her mum *had* taken a taxi, she wouldn't have been able to get into the house because no one was home yet.

Kate tried Ellis and Portia again. Both calls went straight to voicemail. Then she tried Sam on the off chance, but he didn't pick up. Neither did Brett.

'Oh, shut up,' she muttered, to the annoyingly chirpy Wizzard as the song blasted out of the loudspeaker system. Kate, for one, was immensely glad it wasn't "Christmas every day". In fact, once a year was proving to be too frequent. If she heard one more carol or one more Christmas song about peace and goodwill, she thought she might scream.

There was nothing for it, but to go home and hope her mother was on the doorstep.

When Kate got there she saw that Beverley wasn't – but Helen *was*.

Or rather, her mother-in-law was sitting in her car outside the house, with the engine running, tapping her manicured nails impatiently on the steering wheel.

'About time,' Helen announced, when Kate pulled up behind her on the drive and got out of her car.

'Have you seen my mother?' Kate asked.

'Hello, to you, too.' Helen's voice dripped sarcasm. 'No, I haven't seen your mother, thank God,' she added, then peered at her. 'Should I have?'

'I was hoping she'd be here. I went to fetch her from the station, but she wasn't there.' Kate glanced around the close, as if she expected her mother to be hiding behind a bush, or something.

Hang on, why was Helen here? 'I thought you weren't arriving until Wednesday?'

Helen waved a hand in the air. 'Oh, you know...' she said. 'Are you going to let me in? I'm desperate for the little girl's room.'

'Um, yes, OK.' Kate unlocked the front door and pushed it open. 'Look, I'm going back to the station, to see if I can find her. You know where the kitchen is; make yourself at home.'

Helen glanced at the slim, gold watch on her

wrist. 'It's getting late. Where is everyone?'

'Brett's still in work, Sam is on his way back from Telford – he's been ice skating – Portia's been to the stables, but she should have been back by now, and I've no clue where Ellis is.'

'What time will you be back?'

'When I've found my mother,' was Kate's grim reply.

Helen stared past her and into the road. 'I don't think you need bother. If I'm not mistaken, that's Beverley in a taxi.' Helen's tinkling laugh set Kate's already frayed nerves on edge. 'I thought she'd turn up like a bad penny.'

Kate shot her mother-in-law a pleading look. Please, please don't let the whole week be like this…

Helen mistook it. 'I know, dear, I'm not too happy she's here for Christmas, either. Right, I'm off to powder my nose. Bring my case in, would you?'

Powder my nose – who said things like that anymore? And, *bring my case in* – did Kate look like a servant? Then she instantly felt contrite.

The woman was nearly twenty-five years older than Kate; of course Helen shouldn't be expected to carry her own luggage.

Plastering a welcoming smile on her face, Kate hurried towards the taxi, whose driver was making no attempt to help her mother with *her* luggage.

'I'll get it,' Kate said, hauling the first case out of the boot and eyeing the other two with dismay. Why her mother had to bring all this with her, Kate had no idea.

Her mother, after waiting in vain for the driver to get out and open the car door for her, eventually clambered out with much huffing and puffing, and a great deal of indignity, as her skirt rode up her legs.

It didn't help that she was trying to hold Pepe under one arm and her voluminous handbag in another. She was also clutching Pepe's blanket, another bag with an umbrella sticking out of it, and a small paper bag which looked ominously soggy.

'Here,' her mother said, thrusting the paper

bag at Kate.

Kate took it. It was dripping slightly, and she wondered what it contained.

'Pepe was sick,' Beverley announced. 'I tried my best to clean it up, but I ran out of tissues.'

Kate closed her eyes slowly and counted to five, before opening them again.

'He's probably caught a chill.' Her mother straightened her skirt as best she could without having any spare hands. 'If you hadn't abandoned us at the station, none of this would have happened. Pay the man, and mind you don't give him a tip. He doesn't deserve it.'

Kate watched her mother totter up the drive, and then turned back to the taxi, catching the driver's eye. The poor man deserved a medal, not a tip.

'Hang on, let me get the rest of the cases out, then I'll get my purse,' she said to him.

She put the nasty paper bag on the ground, hauled the other two cases out, and fetched her handbag from the car. Giving the taxi driver almost double the cost of the fare (there was a faint whiff of vomit emanating from the car's interior), she watched the poor man leave, wishing he'd taken her with him, dog-sick smell or no dog-sick smell.

Sighing, she turned to grasp the handle of the nearest case and stepped straight onto the paper bag.

The squelching noise was bad enough, but when the stench of half-eaten dog food and bile wafted up her nose, Kate almost gagged. Dear God, but the stuff was all over her shoe...

She took a step. The bag clung to her foot.

She tried to shake it off, but it hung on in there, forcing her to bend down and remove it with her fingers.

Trying not to breathe and thankful it was dark, so she couldn't see the mess too clearly, Kate gingerly placed the broken, soggy bag in the nearest flower bed. She'd deal with it later.

Walking on her heel, with her toes not touching the paving stones because she didn't want risk spreading the disgusting mess all over the drive, Kate hobbled towards the house, leaving the cases where they were. First of all, she needed a bucket of hot, soapy water and some disinfectant to wash the remains of Pepe's little present away, before she moved the luggage.

Her mother met her at the door, just as Kate was attempting to ease her shoe off.

'There's someone in my room,' Beverley announced. 'It's Helen.' From the tone of Beverley's voice, anyone would think Satan himself was staying the night.

'*Helen?*' Oh, God, Kate had forgotten Helen was here.

'I thought she doesn't usually turn up until Christmas Eve?' her mother said.

'She's here early. Just like you are.' Kate used the edge of the doorstep to lever her heel out of the shoe, then turned to go inside. She vowed to speak to Brett later; he could bloody well have warned her!

Her mother was blocking the way. 'Where am I supposed to sleep, that's what I want to know?'

'Look, Mum, go inside. Let me clean this

mess up and bring your cases in, then we'll sort something out.'

She wondered if she should take advantage of the fact that the girls were out, to install her mother in Portia's room and put the inflatable mattress in Ellis's. Faced with a fait accompli, neither of them would be able to do anything about it.

Or would they?

Kate had a horrid feeling they'd make a scene, and the last thing she wanted was to make her mother feel unwelcome. She might be miserable and moany, but she didn't deserve to feel as though she wasn't wanted.

Anyway, Brett still hadn't fetched the blasted mattress from the garage yet, and he hadn't brought the decorations in, either. Damn him. And they *still* didn't have a tree.

Kate tried to move her mother away from the door so she could get past, when she became aware of Pepe wriggling frantically in her mother's arms.

'He needs to go pee-pee,' Beverley said,

placing the poodle on the ground and scrabbling around to get a hold on the thin, red leather lead, which went with his thin, red leather, diamante-encrusted collar.

Unfortunately, it slipped through her fingers, and Pepe, probably sensing unexpected and very welcome freedom, took the opportunity to make a dash for it, darting between Kate's legs and down the drive.

'Stop him!' Beverley shrieked. 'Oh, my baby!'

Kate, on the edge of the stone step and with one shoe on and the other off, made a pathetic lunge for the trailing lead, and lost her balance.

She tottered precariously for a long, long second, wind-milling her arms, before losing the fight to remain upright, and falling face first onto the drive.

'Argh!' she grunted as she hit the ground with a thud.

'My baby, oh my baby. He's getting away.' Her mother shuffled toward her, then stepped over Kate's prone body and tottered down the drive after the poodle.

She wished *she* could sodding well get away, she thought, as she levered herself on to her knees and assessed the damage. Anywhere but here would do.

'Pepe, Pepe, darling, come to Mama,' Beverley called. 'Ooh, he's heading for the road. Stop him, Kate.'

She shook her head in disbelief. How the hell was she supposed to stop a determined poodle who was in full flight, when she was barely able to stand up?

Carefully, she got to her feet; nothing appeared broken (except her spirit, but that was an old injury), although her knees were sore where she'd landed on them, and her wrist ached from her attempt to prevent herself face-planting the concrete paving stones. It was a wonder she hadn't broken her collarbone or fractured a kneecap.

Taking a shaky breath to steady herself, she peered down the drive. Pepe was nowhere to be seen, but it wasn't surprising – spotting a small black dog in the darkness of a December evening was never going to be easy, despite the streetlights.

Her mother, however, was clearly visible, prodding at the bushes which divided Kate's drive from the one next door, and calling, 'Darling, come to Mummy.'

Kate sighed and groped around with her foot. Finding the shoe she'd just taken off, she slipped it back on again, and went to help her mother search for the dog.

'Pepe! Pepe!' she called, pausing in between as though she expected the dog to answer her.

Nothing.

Her mother's voice was becoming increasingly high pitched, which might be a good thing, Kate decided – if it went high enough, only Pepe would hear it, and everyone knew dogs responded to those high-frequency whistles that humans couldn't hear.

'What on earth are you doing out there?' Helen called.

Kate looked over her shoulder to see her mother-in-law standing in the window of the spare bedroom, or "her" room, as she liked to refer to it, silhouetted against the light.

'Looking for Pepe,' Kate replied loudly, following it with, 'Damned dog,' under her breath. As if she didn't have enough to do this evening. If she didn't get the casserole in the oven soon, they'd be eating it at midnight, and now she had her mother-in-law to contend with, too.

Oh, there was Pepe, in the Edmunds's garden, which was on the opposite side of the road and three doors down.

'Mum, I can see him. Pepe! Pepe! Here, boy.' Kate made kissy noises in the hope it would entice him to come within lead-grabbing distance.

Pepe ignored her. He continued to sniff and rootle in the rose bushes, before lifting his leg and giving the plants a quick watering.

Kate took the opportunity to hobble painfully across the road while he was stationary, and hoped his widdle would last long enough for one or the other of them to catch him. Her mother was hurrying along the pavement on the opposite side of the road, with the clear intention of trying to intercept her pet.

The poodle saw them coming long before either of them got close enough to attempt a rugby tackle, and certainly not close enough for a foot to stamp on his trailing lead.

Pepe was off, tail in the air, scampering into the middle of the road and dodging his would-be captors with ease.

Headlights, the growl of an engine, the squeal of brakes, followed by her mother's strangled scream, brought Kate skidding to a stop.

'Pepe! My darling! Oh God, they've killed him,' her mother shrieked, scurrying to the front of the vehicle to inspect the damage.

'Mum, don't look,' Kate called, but it was too late.

Beverley came to an abrupt halt, her eyes on the ground just in front of the car.

Kate knew her mother's horrified expression would stay with her forever.

'Mum,' she whispered, her heart going out to her.

'Nanny?'

'Portia?' Kate said, seeing a young girl emerge from the car.

'What's going on?' her daughter wanted to know.

'Get back in the car!' Kate yelled. 'Portia, for once in your life, do as you're told and get back in the car.' Portia didn't need to see poor Pepe's remains smeared across the road.

Her daughter ignored her, walking around the bonnet to join her maternal grandmother in their examination of Pepe's corpse.

Kate finally limped over to the car, steeling herself for the unpleasantness.

Pepe wasn't there.

'Is it all right?' a female voice asked, through the car's window. 'I didn't see it in time. It should have been on a lead.'

'We know,' Kate muttered, raising her voice to say, 'I think he might be underneath your car.'

'Oh. Yuck. I'll reverse a bit, shall I? You can't

leave him there.'

'Who's that?' Kate whispered to Portia out of the corner of her mouth.

'Alice's mum. She gave me a lift home because you didn't come to pick me up,' Portia hissed back. 'Is Nanny's dog under there?'

Kate nodded. 'Poor thing. You don't need to see this and neither does Nanny. Why don't you take her back to the house?'

'Nah, it's OK.'

'It's not going to be pretty,' Kate warned.

'I'll be fine. We dissected a frog in school last term. It was a bit gross, but I wasn't sick or anything.'

You mightn't be, Kate thought, *but I'll probably barf, and what about my mother*? Not only that, who was going to move it? Pepe couldn't be left in the middle of the road. Oh, God, would she be expected to do it? She bet she'd have to bury him, too.

The car slowly moved backwards.

Kate made a "keep-going" motion with her hand.

The car continued to reverse.

Nothing. No sign of Pepe.

Four feet, five, seven...ten.

No dog.

Kate's mother let out a little cry of relief and sagged against Portia.

Portia grimaced and pushed her away. 'Get a grip, Nanny. Pepe's not been squashed.'

'Where is he, then?' Beverley wanted to know.

Kate shrugged. The rest of the family should be home soon – they could help her mother find him. She was going indoors to get changed, to make sure Helen hadn't donned white gloves and wasn't running her cotton-clad fingers along the skirting boards to check for dust (not that her mother-in-law had ever done such a thing, but Kate wouldn't put it past her), and to shove that damned casserole in the blasted oven.

She stalked off as best she could, considering her knees still ached, and made her way back to her house.

Her mother's cases were where Kate had left

them, so she grabbed hold of the nearest and began dragging it up the drive, when something made her pause.

What was that...?

Oh, dear God. It was Pepe, and he was enthusiastically eating the contents of the paper bag which Kate had placed in the flower bed a few minutes earlier.

How Kate didn't throw up there and then was a miracle.

CHAPTER 12

Kate's husband was seriously cheesing her off. He'd arrived home only a few minutes ago, when she was up to her armpits in drama, and what had he done? Kissed his mother on the cheek, said an off-hand hello to hers, then sloped off into the living room, slumped into his favourite armchair, and hid behind the newspaper.

He hadn't even remembered to take his shoes off, and Kate was certain there were faint marks of whatever Pepe had eaten for breakfast and which were now liberally smeared on the drive, daubed all over the cream carpet. In her haste to reach the downstairs cloakroom and deal with her own nausea, she'd totally forgotten that she'd intended to fetch a bucket of hot water to swill the drive down.

His mother was sitting in the armchair, glasses perched on the end of her nose, head buried in a magazine.

Her mother was standing in the kitchen fretting about where she was going to sleep.

'I always have the spare room,' she said, for the fifteenth time. 'When I come to stay, you always put me in the spare room.'

'Yes, Mum, we do. But you're never here at Christmas, and Helen is. She always has the spare room when she comes to stay, too.' Kate didn't add that it seemed Helen had arrived early for the sole reason of claiming the spare room as her own – the wily old bat.

'So where am I going to sleep?' Beverley wailed. 'Oh, I knew I should have stayed at home and not bothered you. I could have bought one of those microwave meals from the supermarket for Christmas dinner. It would be just as nice.'

Thanks, Kate thought – her mother had just compared her cooking to a supermarket meal, and her carefully-planned turkey lunch hadn't come out of it too favourably. She peeled some potatoes and threw them in a water-filled saucepan, debated whether to chop some of the wilted parsley which was currently sitting in a pot on the windowsill, to use as a garnish, and decided against it. After all, she couldn't possibly compete with one of Asda's finest ready meals, and her mother-in-law wasn't too impressed with her cooking, either. She may as well have ordered a takeaway and be done with it. Crossly, she yanked the oven door open and checked the casserole.

'You're not bothering me, Mum,' Kate said, through gritted teeth. 'We love having you. Now stop worrying, we'll sort something out.'

'I don't want to be an inconvenience. If you think it's too much trouble, just say, and I'll go back home.'

'Don't be silly. You're here now, and we're going to have a lovely Christmas, aren't we,

Sam?' she added to her youngest child, who had just sauntered into the kitchen. 'Did you have a nice time? I expected you home before now. How are you so late? Say "hello" to your grandma.'

'I would if you'd let me get a word in,' Sam replied.

He looked tired, dark circles under his eyes and his skin was pale. Kate hoped he wasn't coming down with something, not with a brace of elderly ladies in the house, who'd be certain to catch whatever it was he might be coming down with.

'Hiya, Nanny.' He got the orange juice out of the fridge and poured himself a large glass.

'You'll rot your teeth if you drink all that,' Beverley observed, and Sam rolled his eyes. 'Come and give your old nan a kiss.'

The look of horror on Sam's face when his grandmother opened her arms and puckered her lips, made Kate smile. She quickly wiped the smirk off her face and replaced her grin with a "go on then, do as you're told" expression.

Her son allowed himself to be hugged,

although he did manage a well-executed turn of the head, so his nan's kiss fell somewhere around his ear rather than on his cheek. As soon as she let go, he stepped away smartly and retreated towards the door and freedom.

'Are you hungry?' Kate asked him. 'Tea won't be for ages yet, but I can make you a sandwich to tide you over?'

'Nah, I've eaten. Jack's mum took us to a Harvester on the way home.'

He tried for the door again.

'Did you have a nice time?' Kate persisted. Since he'd started in high school, he'd become recalcitrant and rather reluctant at sharing much. It wasn't so very long ago that he used to want to share every last detail of his day with her. Now she was lucky if she got an "all right".

'It was all right,' he said.

'Just all right?'

'Yeah, it was good.'

'Did you do much skating.'

Sam shrugged. 'S'pose.'

'Did you fall over?'

He shrugged again.

She let him go. Trying to hold a conversation with her son was worse than trying to hold one with Pepe.

'I can't believe how much he's grown,' her mother observed. 'Though, I suppose when you don't see your grandchildren much, they will have shot up.'

'You saw him in October, remember? We all came down to Brighton at half term?'

'That was ages ago.'

'Seven weeks.'

Beverley huffed. 'Where am I going to sleep, that what I want to know? Will I have Portia's room? I don't want Sam's – it smells of feet. Ellis's has the nicest outlook, though, with its view over the garden. Portia's is at the front and I don't like sleeping at the front, it's too noisy with all that traffic.'

Kate ground her teeth. Too noisy, indeed? They lived on a close of only twenty or so houses. It was not noisy! Her mother, on the other hand, lived three streets back from Brighton's busy and popular promenade.

Kate caught Ellis's eye as her daughter peered around the kitchen door, and she shook her head. Don't you dare start an argument right now, she tried to warn her.

Ellis floated in, a beatific smile on her face. 'Hi, Nanny,' she said, and moved into her grandmother's embrace without being prompted. She didn't even pull a face.

Kate narrowed her eyes. The girl was up to something.

'We've sorted the sleeping arrangements out,' Ellis said, still smiling. 'I've given my room a good clean, ready for Nanny.'

'Oh, that's nice of you,' Beverley beamed. Turning to Kate, she added, 'You could have told me I was having Ellis's room, or do you like to see me worry?'

'You're OK with that?' Kate asked her daughter.

Ellis nodded, still smiling.

Kate peered at her, trying to work out if the smile was genuine or not.

It *appeared* genuine enough.

Maybe Ellis was finally growing up. She *was* seventeen, after all. It was about time she took responsibility and stopped acting like a spoilt teenager.

Kate felt herself welling up, and she blinked away the tears. Her little baby was turning into a lovely young woman. She was so proud of her.

'Is Portia all right about it?' Kate asked, hoping some of Ellis's new-found maturity would rub off on her sister.

Ellis blinked. 'Yeah, of course, why wouldn't she be?'

Kate almost mentioned the arguments and tantrums over who was going to sleep where, but decided it was best not to say anything. There was no point in dredging it up again, especially when her daughters had come to terms with the situation and had sorted it out between them.

'I know it's putting you out, Ellis dear,' Beverley said, shooting a barbed glance at Kate, 'but you can come in whenever you want, to put your make-up on or get dressed.'

'Oh, that's OK.' Ellis waved a hand in the air. 'I'm taking what I need with me. Don't worry, Mum, I'll be back early on Christmas morning. I don't want to miss the present opening. Ooh,' she squealed, clapping her hands. 'This is going to be so much fun.' Then she twirled on her heel and darted to the door.

'Wait a minute, what do you mean "you'll be back early on Christmas morning"? Where are you going?' Kate demanded.

'To Riley's house.' Ellis said, over her shoulder.

'Come back here.' Kate waited for her daughter to sidle back into the kitchen. 'Who's Riley?'

'A friend from school.' Ellis refused to meet her eye.

'I've never heard you mention her before.' Kate's heart thumped and a shiver of worry slithered down her spine.

Ellis shrugged.

For God's sake, why did all her kids shrug? Was it something they were taught in school –

"Today we're going to learn about the Industrial Revolution, but first we'll do five minutes of shrugging".

'Who is she, and where does she live?' Kate demanded. 'I'm sure her mother won't be too happy to have a stranger descend on her for Christmas. Anyway, that doesn't matter, because you're not going.'

'Mum!' Ellis stamped her foot. 'You can't stop me, it's all arranged, he's—' She stopped, her eyes widening, and she bit her lip.

'He? *Riley is a boy?*' Kate's mouth dropped open. Her daughter was not only planning to be absent for Christmas, but she was planning on spending it with some spotty git with an excess of hormones and an urge to do something with them?

Over her dead body.

'Duh, yeah...' Ellis recovered quickly, folding her arms and scowling.

'Don't you "duh" me, young lady. How am I supposed to know who Riley is, considering you've never mentioned him before? And no, you're not going to stay with some boy for Christmas. Or ever.'

'I thought you'd be pleased—'

'Yeah, right. How on earth you thought you could get away with pulling a stunt like this, is beyond me.'

'Fine.' Ellis stamped her foot again. 'I'll stay here, but don't expect me to give up my room, and I'm not having Portia sleep in mine, either. If you're so keen on having the wrinklies to stay, then one of them can sleep in *your* bed!'

With that, Kate's lovely, mature, thoughtful daughter, whirled and stormed out through the door, slamming it so hard it rattled the mugs hanging from the mug tree on the counter.

Kate stood there, aghast and embarrassed. How dare Ellis behave so badly in front of her grandmother. And how dare she give the impression that neither of the old ladies was wanted.

A sob came from Beverley, and Kate turned to see tears sliding down her mother's face.

'She's a teenager,' Kate said, as if that

simple fact both explained and excused her eldest daughter's appalling behaviour. 'I'm sorry you had to see that. Of course, we're delighted to have you and Helen for Christmas. If it was up to me, you'd spend every Christmas with us.'

Kate crossed her fingers against the fib. It wasn't that she didn't love her mother, she did, but Beverley could be so joyless.

'Don't cry, Mum,' Kate said, cursing her children from here to next week. 'I'll sort something out.'

And she did, just not in the manner she'd been expecting.

CHAPTER 13

Brett was turning purple. It didn't suit him, Kate thought, not with his light brown colouring and grey-blue eyes. He stopped blowing, held the nozzle which protruded from the inflatable mattress firmly closed, and panted.

'Isn't there a thingy you can use to blow it up?' Kate said. 'You know, a foot-pump? I'm sure we've got one somewhere,' she added, as she wrestled with putting a fresh cover on the spare duvet.

'Its's in the garage,' Brett puffed.

'Why don't you go and get it?' She shook out

the now-covered duvet vigorously, making a loud thudding slappy sound.

'Shh, you'll wake Mum,' he hissed, flicking his gaze towards the ceiling.

The spare room was directly over the living room, but Kate guessed Helen wasn't asleep yet; she was probably lying there, quietly seething, and plotting her revenge.

'Well?' Kate said. 'Go and get it, or you'll still be blowing this thing up in the morning.'

'I can't believe you did this to me. Us,' he amended quickly. 'Besides, I can't get it.'

Kate wasn't sure where to start. She picked the last comment as the line of least resistance. 'Why not? I thought you said it's in the garage.'

'It is. The light in the fluorescent tube has gone.'

'So?'

'It's pitch black in there.'

'You managed to find the air bed.' Her reply was rather on the tart side. Kate had had enough of this day – she just wanted to get to sleep. She had a feeling she'd need as much rest as possible to cope with the next few days. Or plenty of gin. Maybe both...

'I knew where that was,' he explained. 'The foot-pump could be anywhere.'

'Take a torch?' she suggested, starting to lose patience. Did she have to think of everything?

She looked up from stuffing a pillow into its pillowcase to find her husband who, she reminded herself, held down a quite senior and very responsible job, with a sheepish expression on his face.

'The torch is in the—' he began to say.

Kate finished it for him '—the garage. Why is it in there?' The torch was supposed to live under the sink. That's where they always kept it.

'I left it in there the last time,' Brett admitted.

'Oh.' Kate thought for a second. 'So, the fluorescent tube didn't just die tonight, then?' She'd assumed he'd gone to switch the light on earlier, only for it to fail.

'Er, no.'

Great. He knew it had needed replacing but

hadn't bothered to do anything about it. Serves him right, she thought, that he was now forced to blow the air bed up by hand. Or should she say, by "mouth"?

Brett took an extremely deep breath and returned to the arduous task of inflating the mattress using only his lungs.

Kate left him to it and sat on the sofa. The TV was on low, but she found she couldn't focus. There was something she needed to get off her chest before she'd be able to sleep.

'What did you mean, "did this to *me*?",' she asked, after a moment. 'I did nothing to you. If you'd have given me the slightest bit of support, instead of letting me deal with this on my own, Ellis and Portia would be bunking up together right now, and we'd be sleeping in our bed.'

Brett looked up at her, his lips puckered around the little tube, his eyes bulging slightly.

'But you didn't say a word,' she continued. 'I'm fed up of playing bad cop.'

Brett stopped blowing. 'I'm pretty sure I don't play the good one.'

'That's because you opt-out of playing altogether. Avoidance isn't a valid parenting strategy.' Although, she had to admit, it had generally worked for him in the past.

'You should have put your foot down,' he said.

Kate glared at him. 'I did. Then when I appealed to you to back me up, you said you couldn't deal with it right now, because you were going to play a game of squash. That was Friday night, and there's not been a peep out of you since.'

'You haven't said anything since then, either, so I assumed it was sorted,' Brett said.

'No, it wasn't sorted. Ellis made my mother cry.'

'You need to speak to her in the morning.'

She slapped the arm of the sofa in frustration. 'I've got an idea, a radical one I admit, but why don't *you* speak to her?'

'I'll be in work.'

'So will I.'

'Are you saying you intend to go to work and

leave them here alone? The two mothers and the kids?' Brett looked horrified.

'You stay home, if you're so worried.'

'I can't. Do I have to remind you that I'm the main bread-winner?'

'Don't start,' she warned. 'You might have a high-powered job and earn three times the amount I do, but my job is important, too.'

'Four times.'

'Eh?'

'I earn four times more than you.'

Kate blinked slowly. 'I can't believe you've bothered to work that out.'

'It doesn't take a mathematical genius. Just look at your wage slip, then look at mine.'

'Fine. If you really want to do this now—' She took a deep breath. 'I've spent eighteen years raising your children. I didn't have the luxury of being able to work my way up the greasy promotion pole. *I,*' she poked herself in the chest, 'wasn't able to work at all until a few years ago, because I was too busy cooking, washing, ironing, cleaning, sorting out school uniforms, bandaging grazed knees, taking the children to the park, to swimming lessons, to piano, to school, to dental appointments, to the opticians, to the doctor, on playdates. I was the one who stayed up all night with them when they were ill. I was the one who sponged them down when they had a temperature. I was the one who cleaned up sick...' she trailed off, remembering Pepe's little accident.

Nothing had changed – she was still cleaning up sick. In fact, she was still doing all the jobs she'd just listed, but with the added burden of working, too.

'It's called division of labour,' her husband replied loftily. 'You did your part, and I did mine.'

'Really? I didn't realise that doing your part meant a total abdication from anything parental, including telling your spoilt brat of a daughter that she has to do as she's told, whether she likes it or not.'

'Which one?'

'Excuse me?'

'I asked, which daughter, because from

where I'm standing both of them appear to be spoilt.'

'And that's my fault, too, is it?' Kate cried.

'Shh, you'll wake my mother,' Brett said.

'Sod your bloody mother.'

There was a noise from the hall, and the pair of them paused.

Helen stuck her head around the door. 'Is everything all right? I thought I heard voices.'

Brett shot Kate a "now-see-what-you've-done" look. Kate resisted the urge to stick her tongue out at him.

'We're fine, Helen. Why don't you go back to bed?' Kate said. She could do without this right now.

Helen didn't move. 'Brett, darling, is there anything I can do to help? Take a turn at blowing that thing up?' Helen said.

Kate almost choked on a laugh as she tried to keep it in. *Helen, blowing up an air bed?* Ha, ha.

'I can manage, Mum, but thanks for asking,' Brett said, with a smile which Kate wanted to wipe off his face. He never looked at *her* in such a considerate and grateful way.

'I hate to think of you being ousted from your bed, especially since you have work in the morning,' Helen said, her voice oozing concern and sympathy. 'Wouldn't it have been better to have come to some other arrangement?' This last comment was aimed at Kate.

'We'll sort something else out for tomorrow night,' Kate said, gritting her teeth. If she kept on doing that, she'd have to see a dentist before too long.

'I do hope so; Brett needs his rest. And to think of Beverley with that big bed all to herself, while poor Brett has to sleep on the floor...' Helen gave a little twist of the mouth and a sigh to accompany it.

'I've got to sleep on the floor, too,' Kate pointed out.

'Ah, well, Beverley *is* your mother, and her visit *is* quite short notice. We all have to make sacrifices.'

Kate wasn't quite sure what sacrifices Helen

had made.

Another false sympathetic smile from her mother-in-law was accompanied by her saying, 'Besides, you don't have to go to work tomorrow. Brett does.'

'I do.'

'Do what, dear?' Helen asked.

'Have work tomorrow. You'll have to amuse yourselves, I'm afraid. I'll be back in time to see to the evening meal.'

Helen frowned. 'I see,' she said, frostily. 'I hope it won't be as late as tonight's was. I'm sure it was delicious, but I don't like eating at nine o'clock. I find it gives me heartburn.'

Kate had observed Helen merely picking at her food, wearing a slight moue of distaste as she did so.

She rolled her eyes. Between rolling and grinding, she wasn't going to have much of a face left by the time the mothers went home. 'I'll see what I can do,' Kate said, trying not to snarl.

Helen gave a tiny gasp, her hand went to her chest, and her eyes widened. 'I've just had an idea. How about if Beverley has my room?'

Helen's face was open and guileless, but Kate wasn't fooled. 'Are you offering to sleep down here, on the air bed?' she asked sweetly, knowing Helen would never make such an offer, not in a million years.

'Good lord, no!' Helen exclaimed. 'I was thinking that your bed is so big, that Brett and I could share, then everyone will have a good night's sleep.'

That suggestion was wrong on so many levels that Kate honestly didn't know where to start. First, her mother was probably asleep by now and wouldn't take kindly to being woken up to move rooms. Second, why should Brett get a better night's sleep than she was going to have? Third, ew. Just ew. The thought of Helen snuggling up to Brett made her stomach turn. Fourth, the only reason Helen was even suggesting this, was because Kate and Brett's huge attic room with its luxurious en suite was gorgeous, and Helen was insanely envious that Beverley was getting to sleep in it and she wasn't. Ha, you old hag, Kate wanted to shout – you thought you'd get one over on my mum by arriving early, did you? Wrong! Beverley had certainly come out on top in the war of the bedrooms.

'No, thanks, Mum,' Brett jumped in before Kate opened her mouth. To be fair to him, he looked as shocked at his mother's suggestion as Kate felt. 'We're fine as we are for tonight. Go back to bed, eh? I'll see you in the morning.'

'If you're sure…?'

'I'm sure.'

Kate and Brett watched as Helen retreated, closing the door behind her, then Kate sagged against the sofa. 'I can't believe she said that.'

Brett looked thoughtful.

'Don't you dare!' she warned, seeing his expression. 'It's wrong and downright odd to share a bed with your mother. I wouldn't dream of getting into bed with Sam and he's only eleven.'

'It'll only be for the one night,' he began.

Kate decided to try a different tack. 'If you

disturb my mother at this time of night, I'll never forgive you. She feels bad enough as it is, without making her feel worse.'

'She didn't look as though she felt bad – she looked like a cat who'd got the cream when you suggested she could have our room.'

Yes, Kate silently agreed with him; her mother had looked positively *gleeful*. That was the word. Or was smug a more accurate one? The self-satisfied look she'd given Helen, must have made Helen's blood boil.

It was pathetic, the way they acted. Beverley was well aware that Helen always came to them for Christmas. She was also well aware that Helen stayed in the spare room. Which was why Kate was certain her mother had arrived as early as she had – in order to bag the spare room for herself. It was also why Helen had brought her arrival date forward (twice!), to make sure she got the spare room, too.

Absolutely pathetic.

Therefore, it was quite ironic that Helen had got what she wished for, and still thought she'd been dealt a poor hand.

Kate's wish was that the pair of them would grow up.

She felt like there weren't three children under this roof tonight but six, including her husband. No, make that seven – Pepe the poodle was just as much trouble as the rest of them.

Her patience having finally deserted her, Kate scooted down on the sofa, pulled the duvet over her, and closed her eyes.

'What are you doing?' Brett asked.

'Going to sleep.'

'On the sofa? What about the air bed?'

Kate opened one eye and squinted at the semi-inflated mattress. 'You can have it.'

'It's not fully blown up yet.'

'Then I suggest you get on with it.'

'What am I going to put over me? You've got the duvet.' He sounded so plaintive she didn't know whether she wanted to hug him or slap him.

Slapping won. 'Tough,' she said. 'Use one of the sheets in the utility room. They're clean.'

'I haven't got any pyjamas.'

'Oh, for God's sake.' Kate threw the duvet off and scrambled to her feet. She'd reminded him earlier to gather what he needed prior to letting her mother into their room, but what had he grabbed apart from his work clothes for the morning and his toothbrush? A golfing magazine from the little rack next to the loo in the en suite; as if he was going to get any time to read it.

Dear lord, did she have to do everything?

Stomping into the utility room, Kate dug around in her ironing pile for a clean sheet, then dug around some more for his pyjamas. The top and bottom were mismatched (she guessed they must have been in there a while, like the odd-sock pile in the bottom) but they'd have to do.

Muttering crossly under her breath, Kate returned to the living room, to find Brett sprawled on the sofa, the duvet tucked firmly around him, snoring his head off.

Wonderful!

CHAPTER 14

The following morning, Brett thought it best to be mouse-like and not wake Kate. She was fast asleep, curled up in a ball on a couple of cushions which she'd taken off the armchairs and put on the floor. Tiny little snuffles came from her half-open mouth, and she was deep in the land of nod. At least *she* appeared to have had a decent night's sleep, unlike himself – he'd spent half the night tossing and turning, the sofa proving to be too short and too narrow for his long frame.

He resisted the urge to give his wife a nudge with his foot.

If he woke her now, he'd have to listen to her nagging and, frankly, he could do without having an ear-bashing before he'd even got into work. He'd get enough of that when he was at his desk; he didn't need it at home, too.

He was right – by nine-thirty he'd come to the conclusion that if anyone else thought that giving him a bollocking was a good idea this morning, he might just throw his toys out of his pram and bugger off home.

To be honest, the only thing preventing him from telling The Abyss that he didn't feel very well and leaving work for the day, was the knowledge that the kids were all off school and the two mothers were in residence. He'd not get a scrap of peace, and he could really do with some right now.

Seventy-three emails to clear, two meetings to attend, a presentation to prepare, and now his mother was texting him some rubbish about Beverley thinking she'd broken the toaster, when she hadn't, but was too daft to realise it wasn't plugged in, and asking what time would he be home because she intended to cook the evening meal.

Brett hoped to God that his mother had OK'd it with Kate first, because he knew his wife had planned the meals for the week and for all over Christmas as well. She always did. If you looked up "organised" in the dictionary, Kate's name would be under it. His wife wouldn't be too pleased with having her meal plan wrecked. That she could swap it around wouldn't occur to her; spontaneity wasn't a word he'd use if asked to describe Kate.

Have you checked this with Kate? He pressed send then returned to his inbox. If he could delete a few of the emails that didn't concern him, he'd be able to see the wood from the trees.

Ping. He glanced at his mobile.

I thought it would be a surprise. It would be that, all right, he thought. **We can eat at a more reasonable time,** she'd added. Then, **Did you sleep well?**

Not really

You shouldn't have given up your bed for Beverley.

Brett knew that, but he also had no idea what had happened last night. One minute he'd been sitting on the sofa minding his own business and trying to ignore all the squabbling, and the next Kate had informed him that her mother was having their room for the night and they were to sleep in the living room on the blow-up bed.

He should learn to be a bit firmer and say no, but he had enough on his plate at the moment without silly little domestic dramas. There was always a crisis of one sort or another in his house, and if he reacted to even a fraction of them, he'd have been a basket-case by now.

Thank God Christmas only lasted a couple of days – any longer and he'd be on the first flight out of the country he could get. Outer Mongolia sounded nice. Or maybe not "nice", but distant. He'd dearly like distant right now, especially if that meant putting several thousand miles between him and Clara The Abyss Jenkins, then that would be just fine with him.

Speaking of which, like a genie who could be conjured merely by thinking about it, his boss appeared in front of him.

'Have you spoken with anyone from The Dragonfly Corporation yet? I thought you were going to set up a meeting this side of Christmas but there's nothing in my diary. And the new warehouse is having picking problems. I'd go over there myself and sort it out, although it should be your job, but I'm going to be tied up with—'

Yep, tied up – that's exactly what he'd like to do to his boss. Tie her up somewhere, pop a gag in her mouth, and leave her there for a few days. Not too long – he wasn't a sadist – but just long enough to clear the backlog of work that was sent his way, without giving her the opportunity of throwing yet more at him.

He knew the company was struggling, he knew The Abyss was under pressure from above and that she was filtering it down to the staff she managed, but if any more stuff was piled on him, he had a feeling he'd be squashed flat by it. It wasn't just him either. Everyone in the company was feeling the pressure, and they were all close to cracking.

Clara flounced out of his office, shaking her head at his lukewarm response, and he knew she'd see it as a lack of commitment on his part, or accuse him of not taking the situation seriously, but for God's sake he was doing his best. They all were. Aside from working twenty-four hours a day, seven days a week (and the thought had occurred to him that maybe she'd like that), there was nothing more he could do. His department needed more staff, but with a hold on recruitment he wasn't going to get more anytime soon. This put added pressure on everyone else when someone was on holiday. The Abyss frowned on that too; he hadn't told Kate, not wanting to worry her, but last summer Clara had hinted most strongly that he shouldn't take the two weeks annual leave he'd booked (the family was off to Menorca) and that he was needed in the office instead. Of course, he hadn't complied, and she'd been on his case ever since.

It didn't help that the pressure she was putting on staff, was starting to lead to burn out, and one or two key people had already either resigned (not to be replaced, obviously) or had gone off sick with stress.

If she wasn't careful, Brett would be joining them.

His phone buzzed and he glanced at it. It was his mother. Again. He could do without this right now, but he knew from experience that if he didn't answer, her next step would be to phone him.

There aren't any Christmas decorations up, he read.

I know

Why not?

Kate hasn't bought the tree yet.

I see. Shall I buy one?

Do you mind?

He didn't want his mother to feel as though he was putting on her, but it would be an immense help. She didn't come to visit in order to clean the bathroom (he'd once come home from work to find her balancing on a stool and trying to tackle the cobwebs on the bathroom ceiling), or to cook (she often pitched in to give Kate a hand, and she was quite a good cook). She was here to enjoy some family time, and to have a rest.

Of course I don't. I can see Kate is busy. It's a shame that the rest of the family has to suffer. It doesn't look at all Christmassy she replied.

That would be great, thanks.

At least that was one less job Kate would nag him about.

The decorations are in a box in the garage he added.

He didn't want his mother to go and buy new ones when they already had a boxful. Some of them were rather old and shabby, he had to admit, but they'd do for this year.

There was another reason for him agreeing to let his mother loose on putting the decorations up – it would give her something to do and keep her occupied. If she was busy, she'd be less lightly to cause ructions with Kate's mum.

There we go, he thought, feeling satisfied with himself. Two birds with one stone. His mother would feel useful, and Kate had one less job to do. Result!

CHAPTER 15

It was with a sense of dread that Kate left the house that morning. Three stroppy teenagers (OK, two and a half), two grannies, and one disgusting dog weren't going to make for a very happy household. Brett had buggered off at the crack of dawn, leaving her to it. Kate, taking the coward's way out, had left shortly afterwards, having been awake for hours because the half-blown-up bed had stubbornly refused to stay half-blown-up and had gradually deflated throughout the course of the night, until she'd resorted to stealing the cushions off the armchairs and lying awkwardly on those instead.

Brett, on the other hand, seemed to have had a very good sleep indeed, thank you very much. She knew, because he'd snored throughout most of it. Typical though, she'd just about managed to drop off, and half an hour later Brett had got up for work, making enough noise to wake the dead. Stubbornly, Kate had pretended to be asleep, not wanting to have him chew her ear off at seven in the morning.

She, herself, had crept out of the house shortly afterwards, having taken the quickest, quietest shower in the world, and not bothering with breakfast or even a coffee. The sooner she was out of the house, the better. If she'd had to speak to either of the nans, she mightn't have been responsible for her actions. And as for her daughters…Grrr.

The cafe opposite the shop wasn't open yet, and Kate checked the time.

Crikey, she really *was* early.

'You're early,' Ron confirmed.

He was huddled in the shop doorway,

underneath several blankets and inside an artic grade sleeping bag. She knew it was good to -20 degrees Celsius, because she'd bought it for him. Having such a good sleeping bag didn't mean it was a good idea for Ron, or for anyone else for that matter, to spend the night outside, though. Far from it – the temperature was hovering at around freezing.

'Come inside,' she suggested. 'I'll put the heaters on and make us both a nice, hot drink.' Then, as soon as the café opposite opened, she'd buy them a bacon sandwich each.

'Why are you so early?' he asked, unravelling himself from his cocoon and clambering stiffly to his feet. 'Doris never arrives before half-past eight.'

While Kate set about making tea, she said, 'It's a long story.'

'I've got time to listen.'

He wasn't wrong there, Kate thought, so she offloaded, big time, letting it all out in a cathartic release of frustration.

At first, Ron listened with a sympathetic

expression on his face, but as the story unfolded and she got to the part where Brett stole her sofa and made her sleep on the floor, Kate could see that he was having difficulty holding back a grin.

'It's not funny,' she protested, a smile threatening to escape.

'Yes, it is,' Ron insisted. 'The two grans sound a right laugh.'

'You try living with them,' she retorted, then realised what she'd said. 'Sorry.'

He shrugged. 'It's OK. I like my life just the way it is.'

'What do you like about it?' she wanted to know, genuinely curious. The thought of having little or no responsibility was appealing, but the thought of living rough most definitely wasn't.

'No walls. No worries about finding enough money for the rent, or paying the bills. No one to answer to…' He trailed off.

'If someone offered you somewhere to live, would you take it?'

'Probably. Not many people want to be homeless.'

Kate suddenly felt very guilty. She had a spare room (or she would have after Christmas and the mothers had gone home) – the least she could do would be to offer it to Ron. God knows what her kids would make of it. Or Brett. She'd better talk it over with him first.

'Sometimes, I wish I could run away from it all,' she said, abruptly. 'Not permanently, never that, but just for a few days or a week or two, and let them get on with it.'

'Why don't you?'

Kate gave a self-conscious laugh. 'Oh, you know...'

'No, I don't.' He took a grubby hankie out of his pocket and carefully wiped his mouth, paying attention to his overly-long whiskers.

Kate wondered what he'd look like without them. She didn't think he was all that old – somewhere in his late forties, perhaps. It was difficult to tell under the straggly beard and the grime.

'I've never had a mother-in-law or kids, teenage or otherwise,' he continued. 'It must be... interesting.'

'That's one way of putting it. Look, I'm sorry to dump all this on you.' Ron didn't need to hear her moaning about her insubstantial problems, when he didn't even have a roof over his head. The differences in their situations seemed to put her ridiculous complaining into perspective.

'It's OK. That's what friends are for,' he replied, and Kate felt ridiculously pleased that he thought of her as a friend.

'What are you doing on Christmas Day?' she asked, impulsively. Surely neither Brett nor the children could object to having another person at the table?

He sent her a quizzical look. 'The same thing I do every day.'

'Why don't you come to us for lunch?'

His smile was rueful. 'I don't think that would be a good idea, do you?'

Kate bristled. Brett, the nanas, and the kids would just have to suck it up. If she wanted to invite someone to lunch, then she damn well would.

'I think it would be an excellent idea,' she retorted. 'You need a meal and we've got plenty of food.'

'I mean, I don't do houses or happy families. But thank you for the offer. Bring me some turkey sandwiches instead, the next time you're in work.'

He got up to leave, the warmth of the heater having loosened his joints and muscles, his movements more fluid.

What was his story, she wondered, for the umpteenth time. What series of events had led to him living on the streets?

He seemed a reasonably intelligent guy, had always been pleasant to her, and he didn't appear to have an alcohol or a drug problem. She wondered if she should ask. Would he think it nice of her to take an interest, or would he think she was just being nosey?

'I'm going to grab a bacon sandwich,' she said, seeing the café was now open. 'Let me get you one.'

Ron didn't object; he never turned down the

offer of food and waited patiently in the warm until she returned with a sandwich and a cappuccino.

'Where would you go?' he asked, around a mouthful of bread and bacon.

'Pardon?'

'If you were to run away, where would you go?'

'I dunno, I've never thought that deeply about it. The coast, maybe.'

'Which one?'

'The south? Cornwall? Devon?' she shrugged. The idea of getting in her car and simply disappearing was an inviting one; where she'd go, and what she'd do once she got there, was another thing entirely.

'Brixham's nice.'

'It is? Isn't is near Torquay?'

Ron nodded. 'It's not as far as Cornwall, easier to get to. Straight down the M5 to the end, then turn right. More or less.'

'Where else have you been?' she asked, curiously. This was the first time Ron had spoken about himself.

'All over England and Wales. Haven't made it up as far as Scotland yet. It's on my to-do list.'

Kate smiled. Who'd have thought Ron would have a to-do list?

'I'm going to try to get up there this summer,' he added.

Now she came to think about it, she didn't see Ron around hardly as much in the summer as she did in the winter. 'Do you always come back to the Worcester area?' she asked.

'It's my home,' he said. 'I was born not far from here. I like travelling, but this is where I belong. Right, thanks for the food; I'd better get off before you open up.'

Kate watched him go, wondering what he'd be doing for the rest of the day, and she hoped he'd find somewhere warm.

She was just about to unlock the door and let the first customers in (no Doris again today), when her phone rang.

It was her mother. 'I can't get your toaster to work. It's broken.'

'It was fine yesterday,' Kate said.

'It's not fine today,' Beverley snapped. 'What am I supposed to have for breakfast?'

'There's cereal in the cupboard, or you could make yourself an omelette—'

'I always have toast. Besides, I don't like your cooker. It's too complicated.'

'You only have to turn the knob.' Kate's nerves began to fray slightly; nothing significant, just a little unravelling around the edges. 'Never mind, why don't you ask one of the kids to have a look at it?'

Her mother snorted. 'They're not up yet. None of them. Only Brett's mother and I'd prefer not to speak to her.'

OK, Kate thought, that wasn't so surprising when it came to her children still being in bed, considering they were teenagers and had no school to get up for. 'One of them will be up soon,' she said. 'Give it half an hour.' She crossed her fingers. It was only just nine o'clock. Beverley would be lucky if she saw them before eleven.

'I suppose I'll have to go without,' her mother

said. 'Oh, and just to let you know, Pepe had a little accident.'

'What sort of accident?'

'He did a whoopsie in your bedroom. I've cleaned it up, but it's left a bit of a stain.'

Marvellous, sodding marvellous. Her bedroom carpet was cream; neither the smell nor the stain would be easy to get rid of.

'It wasn't his fault,' Beverley was saying. 'We ate so late last night, it gave me heartburn, so I was awake half the night, which meant I slept late this morning, and Pepe couldn't hold it.'

Kate heard the unspoken accusation that Pepe's little accident was Kate's fault.

'I'll spray some vinegar and bicarbonate of soda on it when I get home,' she said. 'That's supposed to be good for urine smells.'

'It wasn't urine,' her mother said. 'He did a Number Two.'

When she hung up, Kate resisted the urge to hold her head in her hands and howl.

It was only nine a.m. on day one. There were another six days to go before the mothers departed. Kate didn't know how she'd get through it without having a breakdown.

At this rate, she wasn't sure she'd make it to lunchtime.

CHAPTER 16

'Where is everyone?' Kate asked, throwing her coat over the bannister, dropping her bag next to it, and hearing a remarkable lack of noise. There was also a strong smell of roasting meat; lamb if she wasn't mistaken. She guessed it was the lamb she'd planned for Wednesday, the day she'd originally thought Helen would be arriving.

The living room contained her mother, who was knitting furiously, Pepe, who was curled up on the sofa and sleeping peacefully, and no one else.

'There you are,' Beverley said, looking up

from her needles. 'About time, too. I've been on my own all day, with no one to talk to. It's worse than being at home.'

Kate glanced over her shoulder at the clock in the hall; it said five thirty-three, her usual time for getting home. Then she looked back into the living room. Something wasn't quite right…

'Who put the tree up, and what's it doing *there*?' she asked.

'Hello, dear,' Helen said, sailing in from the kitchen wearing an apron, a full face of make-up, and a satisfied expression. 'Do you like it? I hope you don't mind, but I threw out those hideous decorations and bought a few new ones. There's a lovely little shop in the village that stocks the most delightful things.'

Kate didn't know where to start.

The most obvious place to begin was that the tree on which those new decorations were hanging, wasn't a proper tree; it was silver and artificial. Kate always had a real tree. It was one of the family's traditions that they went to the garden centre as a family and picked one out.

OK, they hadn't done it last year, because Ellis had been on some sort of eco-warrior high horse and had objected to the cutting down of trees purely for the entertainment of the masses. Portia had appeared to have lost interest in all things Christmas, except for telling Kate what presents she would like, the details of which changed on a daily basis, until Kate had no idea what to buy the child. Sam was the only one who'd gone with her, and together they'd chosen a lovely little tree, not too big so that it overpowered the room, yet full enough and tall enough to make a statement.

'Where did you get it?' Kate was staring at the huge monstrosity which took up most of the space in front of the bay window and then some. The top branch was slightly bent because the tree was a fraction too tall for the height of the ceiling, and the star sitting on it leant drunkenly to the left. Kate always placed the tree slightly to the side of the window, so it was visible from the road, but not totally blocking all the weak winter light. And she preferred an angel on the top – the one she and Brett had bought in a little Christmas market in Copenhagen the year they were married. It might be old, but it held memories, as did every other bauble she'd lovingly and meticulously collected.

'I took a little run out to the garden centre,' Helen informed her.

'Oh, lovely,' Kate said, weakly. Inside she was seething. How dare her mother-in-law decide to buy their tree without consulting her? How dare she throw out the family's decorations? Kate would like to throw her mother-in-law—

'You're welcome,' Helen said. 'I thought it would save you a job, as you're rushed off your feet. I put the lamb in the oven, too, and prepared the veg. Dinner should be ready in half an hour.' She paused and threw Beverley a supercilious look. 'You know how I like to keep busy; I can't just sit around all day. Unlike some people.'

'There's no point in keeping a dog and barking yourself,' Beverley muttered, peering over the top of her glasses.

'You didn't need to buy any decorations,' Kate said quietly, hanging on to her temper by a very fine thread indeed. 'There's a box full of them in the garage.'

'I know, dear. Tatty old things. I put the box next to the wheelie bin,' Helen said, 'ready to be collected by the bin men.'

'Right.' Kate, with another look at the hideous tree with its red and gold decorations, stalked outside to rescue the box of ornaments, and marched back with it. She popped it into the cupboard under the stairs for now. As soon as Helen had gone to bed, Kate intended to replace each and every nasty plastic bauble with those beautiful, unique decorations the family had lovingly collected over the years.

'Are the children around?' Kate asked, following her mother-in-law into the kitchen to find Helen squinting through the closed oven door.

'You need to give this door a wipe over,' Helen said. 'Some nice hot water, a squirt of washing-up liquid, and a good application of elbow grease should do the trick.'

Kate knew the oven needed cleaning, but it was the least of her worries. It frequently needed cleaning. So did everything else in the house. It must be nice to have all day, every day to yourself, she thought, with nothing to do but potter. No job to go to, no children to taxi around, no parents' evenings to attend, no—

'Where are the children?' she asked again. Whatever they were doing, they were being suspiciously quiet about it. When it came to kids, silence was never golden unless they were asleep, and sometimes not even then she'd learned, after a disastrous incident with the washing machine and a bag of flour.

'No idea. They come and go as they please. I think Sam's in his room,' Helen said. 'He's been in there all day.'

Kate held back a sigh. Trust the kids to disappear when the nanas were here, but she didn't blame them. She wished she could disappear, too. 'I'll get changed, then I'll take over from here. You sit down and put your feet up,' Kate suggested, meaning "please get out of my kitchen".

'Nonsense! I've started, so I'll finish.' Helen made shooing noises with her fingers.

Kate obediently shooed, her quiet seething becoming more of a bubbling simmer. She knew Helen meant well, but honestly! There was being thoughtful, and then there was being downright interfering. Her mother-in-law had always been the same – Kate had never felt good enough; no matter what she did, Helen managed to make her feel inadequate and sub-standard. The oven door remark was just the latest one in a whole line of similar comments, stretching right back to before Brett and Kate had got married.

It had started the first time Kate had met Helen. Some comment about Kate's hair, which had been long, dark and straight, and how Kate could inject more body and life into it if she'd had a good few inches chopped off the ends. Apparently, a decent cut would take care of all those split ends, too, according to Brett's mother. And Brett, bless his oblivious little cotton socks, had wondered why Kate had taken exception to the suggestion. 'She means well,' Kate remembered him saying.

Kate knew exactly what Helen meant, and the comments had persisted ever since, couched as "helpful" suggestions. Which was why there was absolutely no point in challenging her. The one and only time Kate had done so, had resulted in Kate looking like the bad egg and her mother-in-law snivelling daintily into her handkerchief and tearfully telling Brett that she had no idea Kate felt so antagonistic towards her, when she was only trying to help.

Of course, Brett took his mother's side. He always did.

'Are you OK, Sam?' Kate asked, popping her head around her son's door. He was sitting in the dark with only the light from his Xbox for illumination. God knows what game he was playing, but the green colour on the graphics made her son look like an extra out of The Walking Dead. His grunt of acknowledgement was also oddly similar to the noise the creatures made.

'What have you done with yourself today?' she persisted.

'Nothing.'

'What time did you get up?'

'Dunno. Late.' Sam didn't take his eyes off the screen.

She gave up and went to find one or the other of her daughters. Without any luck. Both rooms were empty, although she did notice the pathetically deflated air bed on the floor in Portia's room, with the foot pump in a prominent position next to it, and took an educated guess that Helen had put it there.

Her mother-in-law certainly had been busy, but if Helen thought that either Ellis or Portia would be happy with the arrangement, she was sadly mistaken. For one, Ellis would vehemently object to sleeping on the floor – in her eyes, being the eldest gave her certain privileges, and bunking down on a wilting airbed wasn't one of them. Neither would she want Portia in her room.

Kate smiled grimly. She knew exactly what Helen was playing at; she must have heard Beverley saying she preferred Ellis's room last night, and had therefore put the air bed in there which, if her plan was successful, would mean Beverley would have to sleep in Portia's room, instead.

The sneaky old bat.

Kate found she was quite looking forward to her daughters' return home. Under the current circumstances she had to grasp any chance of amusement with both hands, however small, and the sight of the inflatable mattress would certainly provide that.

Then common sense kicked in and she realised what a pair of brats both girls would appear to be, and she didn't want her mother to witness yet another "who's going to end up with nana sleeping in their room" episode. She couldn't even blame Helen – not really. Even if her mother-in-law hadn't turned up so early, Kate would still be facing the same situation, just in reverse; her own mother would have been firmly ensconced in the spare room and everyone else would have been fighting over where Nana Peters would lay her hairspray-encrusted head.

Blowing her cheeks out, Kate plodded across the landing to the stairs leading up to her and Brett's attic conversion, wondering if it was better to just leave things the way they were. Her mother could continue sleeping in their bed, and Kate and Brett could sleep downstairs in the living room. It wouldn't be so bad once he'd blown the air bed up, and it was only for a few nights. Everyone would be happy – except for her and Brett, but that was nothing unusual – and she was prepared to do anything to make the festive season pass a little smoother and ensure they all came out of the other side alive.

It was amazing how quickly a brownish stain right in the middle of a pristine cream carpet could change a person's mind, Kate thought, a few seconds later, as she surveyed her bedroom.

She tried to console herself with the fact that at least her mother had tried to clean it off, as she stripped off the bedding and hunted out some fresh linen in preparation for her and Brett moving back into their own room this evening.

After changing out of her work clothes, she bundled up the sheets and made her way downstairs, full of determination to tackle her girls. If either one of them said a peep about sharing, she'd stop their pocket-money for a month. She'd take their phones off them; she'd take their Christmas presents back to the shops; she'd—

'Arggh!'

Kate, unable to see where she was placing her feet because of the load of washing in her arms, stumbled over Pepe, and landed heavily on her knees in the hall. There she remained for a long, long second, in that state between injuring oneself and not yet feeling the pain but knowing it would be monstrous when it arrived.

Oh, dear God, here it comes, she thought, as a shock wave travelled up from her poor knees and into her hips. Bloody hell, but that sodding hurt; she was sure she must have broken something or dislocated her kneecaps.

It took a while to realise that the whimpering she heard wasn't coming from her, but from Pepe, who was sitting on his fluffy haunches and gazing at her with concern.

The dog was a damned menace.

With a lot of groaning and considerable effort, Kate struggled to her feet, rubbing her knees and wincing. It hurt so much, she almost felt sick with it.

Pepe watched from the side-lines, his head cocked to one side. She couldn't decide whether he was commiserating with her, or whether her predicament amused him.

'Go away,' she hissed at him.

Pepe whined a reply but didn't move.

Leaving the washing where it was and continuing to massage her damaged kneecaps, she staggered into the living room.

Her mother hadn't moved from her chair and was still knitting with a speed suggesting the end of the world was nigh if she didn't hurry up and finish the garment she was working on.

'It's for you,' Beverley said, holding up her

creation proudly, and momentarily taking the wind out of Kate's proverbial sails. 'Do you like the colour?'

'Yes, lovely.' Mustard yellow wasn't her favourite shade, but it was the thought that counted. 'What is it?'

'A pullover.'

'Great. Look, Mum, you're going to sleep in Portia's room tonight—'

'She's got to you, hasn't she?' her mother interrupted.

'Pardon?'

'That woman. *His* mother. I could tell she wasn't happy with me having her precious son's room. I know she put the air bed in Portia's room, because I saw her do it. Oh, she thought she was being sneaky, but she can't pull the wool over my eyes. I know what she's playing at. She'd give her right arm to have your lovely room.'

'Everything alright, Beverley?' Helen said from behind Kate, and Kate jumped, the movement sending fresh waves of pain through her knees.

'Tickety-boo,' her mother replied. 'I was just telling Kate that I had the best night's sleep ever last night. It's so peaceful at the top of the house, away from the racket the children make. Isn't it kind of Kate and Brett to let me have their room?'

'Mum, I—' Kate began.

'The pair of them will do anything to make my stay pleasant – I'm sure they do the same for you, don't they?' Her mother smiled sweetly then said to Kate, 'You're such a good daughter, and I do appreciate you putting yourself out for me.'

Kate, ignoring Helen's thunderous expression, turned slowly on her heel and walked back into the hall.

She was just in time to witness Pepe cocking his leg on the mound of sheets on the hall floor and giving them a liberal sprinkle.

CHAPTER 17

After the day he'd had, Brett was seriously considering jacking it all in. He'd get a job in a pub, or on a farm, or sweeping the streets. All those were perfectly good, respectable jobs. They all provided a valuable service, and they all had the minimum risk of receiving snotty emails from snotty clients. None of them would involve trying to persuade reluctant and suspicious companies to buy your company's product because you told them it was better than any other company's product, when in fact there wasn't an iota of difference between them. None of those jobs would involve trying to screw said companies out of as much money as possible, while said companies were trying to pay as little as possible.

He was sick of it. Sick of the pressure, sick of the never-endingness, and really, really fed up with the commercialism of it all. Brett, who'd once won employee of the year, hated being employed by the company he was with.

Also, he had The Abyss for a boss.

He couldn't wait for midday on Friday, when the whole place would shut down for the Christmas period and he could forget about bottom lines and targets for three and a half lovely days. It didn't matter that the two nans would both be there, bickering and trying to outdo each other.

It didn't matter that the kids would be squabbling and trying to get their own way at their siblings' expense. It didn't matter that he and Kate might very well be at each other's throats trying to keep the various factions happy, and only succeeding in cheesing everyone off.

Anything was better than having to go to work and—

'Why is that bloody dog pissing in my hallway?' Brett dropped his briefcase on the floor, thought about what he'd just seen the dog doing, and hastily picked it up again.

'Because it can?' His wife sounded slightly hysterical.

He knew how she felt.

'Please will you do something about it?' he asked and stalked past her, ignoring her glower.

'Brett, darling! I thought I heard someone come in.' His mother was in the kitchen presiding over a leg of lamb, the enticing aroma of roasted meat and rosemary filling the air.

It looked delicious. His mother had always been an excellent cook.

'Mmm, smells good,' he said, pulling one of the chairs away from the table and putting his briefcase on it. After the scene in the hall, he wasn't going to take any chances on having it watered by a poodle. He'd never get the smell out for a start.

Kate strode in, clutching a wriggling Pepe.

She ignored both Brett and his mother, opened the door to the garden and thrust the dog outside, shutting it firmly behind him. Then she strode back out of the kitchen.

Two seconds later, she was back with the urine-covered sheets. She stuffed them into the washing machine, threw a washing tablet in after them, slammed the door, and strode back out again.

Brett exchanged a meaningful glance with his mother. Kate was doing a lot of glowering and striding.

Why the hell did Beverley have to bring that dog with her? She knew what an inconvenience it was, and the animal's tendency to pee everywhere didn't exactly endear him to anyone. Pepe was partial to the odd growl and snap, too, the nasty little thing.

'Ignore Kate,' Brett said to his mother, conscious of her rather hurt and slightly incredulous expression. 'The dog just peed on the washing. Oh, hello, love,' he added as his eldest breezed into the kitchen. 'You're just in time for dinner.'

Ellis stared at the leg of lamb and shook her head. 'I'm going to Riley's house. We'll grab something later.'

'Who's Riley?'

Ellis's expression was pitying. 'Don't you and Mum ever talk? He's my boyfriend. I've only come back to have a quick shower and get changed.'

'You've got a boyfriend? Since when? Who is he? Does he go to the same college as you? How old is—'

'Speak to Mum, she'll fill you in. Hi, Nan.'

Brett watched his daughter wave airily in her grandmother's direction, open the fridge, grab a carton of juice and breeze back out of the kitchen.

He blinked.

Helen frowned. 'I take it from that, Ellis won't be joining us for dinner?'

'It doesn't sound like it.'

'What about Portia?'

'What about her?'

'Will she be eating with us?'

'I've no idea,' Brett said. 'Is she in?'

'She's not been in all day. When I say, "all day", I mean since this afternoon. She didn't get up until ten-past twelve, then she waltzed straight out. Goodness knows where she's gone. Maybe Kate can enlighten us.'

'Pepe, Pepe.' Beverley's high-pitched, silly voice, the one she used when talking to her dog and which irritated the hell out of Brett, could be heard calling from the living room.

'He's in the garden.' Brett shouted.

His mother-in-law barged into the kitchen, the door thudding open, and Brett winced. Between her and his kids, the door and the plaster around it wasn't half taking a battering.

'Outside?' Beverley shrieked. 'He'll catch his death. It's freezing out there.'

It's not much warmer in here, Brett thought, when Beverley glared at him and his mother as though they were the ones responsible for Pepe's banishment to the great outdoors.

Beverley quickly let the dog in, bending down to check he hadn't developed frostbite during the two minutes he'd been outside, cooing to him as if he was a little baby.

Brett grimaced, caught his mother's expression of distaste, and rolled his eyes. He had a feeling he'd be doing a lot of eye-rolling before Christmas was over.

Pepe, none the worse for his brief expedition into the garden, slipped past his mistress and positioned himself under the kitchen table, his nose twitching avidly and his gaze on the roasting tin sitting on the counter.

With a huff, Beverley returned to the living room, satisfied that her pooch was in no immediate danger.

'Mark my words,' Helen sniffed. 'She'll be back in that chair. She's hardly moved from it all day while I've run myself ragged trying to help *her* daughter out. Did you see the tree I bought, and the decorations? I threw out those scruffy old things and replaced them with some lovely new ones.' She sniffed again. 'I must say, Kate didn't seem all that appreciative.'

'I'm sure she is,' Brett hastened to reassure her. He was pretty sure his wife wasn't (from the mood she appeared to be in) but he couldn't face his mother's sulking; not after the day he'd had.

'Come and see.' Helen ushered him out of the kitchen and into the living room, sending him a meaningful look when her prediction of Beverley sitting in the armchair once more had come true. 'Isn't it lovely?' She nodded towards the tree.

Brett winced. God, he bet Kate hated it. They always had a real tree, but he supposed what with the mothers turning up early, his wife hadn't had a chance to buy one.

Brett felt a faint wave of nostalgia course through him – he used to like the tradition of visiting the garden centre and each of them picking out a new bauble. He stared at the generic gold and red shiny plastic decorations, and wondered what had happened to all those carefully chosen ones... didn't his mother say she'd thrown them out?

Shit, she *had* said that. He'd better go and

retrieve them before Kate found out. She'd go ballistic.

At least the lights were pretty, all twinkly and white. Kate always insisted on multi-coloured lights, to go with the multicoloured and totally mis-matched decorations.

His wife did have a point, he mused, staring at his mother's tree – this one was generic, corporate. It was similar to thousands of others in offices and shopping centres all around the country. It might be attractive but there was nothing individual about it. Never mind, he decided, it was up now, and there wasn't any point in causing a fuss. He just wanted to get Christmas over and done with without incident.

Crash!

It came from the kitchen.

'What the hell...?' Brett pushed past his mother, wondering if she'd left something in the oven and it had exploded, although the noise sounded more like something had fallen.

He shoved the door open, registering the resounding thump as it banged against the wall, and came to a halt.

Pepe was crouched over the leg of lamb, which was now lying on the floor, meat juices sprayed across the tiles, the roasting tin upended next to it. The dog wore a cat-got-the-cream expression and was worrying at the joint, tearing bits of meat off as fast as his sharp little teeth would let him.

Helen let out a shriek, right in Brett's ear.

Brett yelped, the dog growled a warning, and his mother collapsed back against the nearest counter, fanning herself with both hands, her face the most alarming shade of puce, her eyes wide and furious, like a pair of glass marbles.

'The lamb, the lamb,' she wailed.

Beverley stuck her head around Brett, let out a shriek, and dived towards the dog, who growled even louder.

'No, Pepe, no. Naughty dog! Brett, take it off him before he eats the lot,' his mother-in-law cried.

'He can bloody well have it,' Brett retorted. 'If you think I'm going to eat any of it when a dog has slobbered all over it, you've got another bloody think coming. We'll have something else for dinner.'

'I don't care what you have for dinner – if you don't take it off him, Pepe will be sick. He could be seriously ill,' Beverley added with a wail.

'Good,' Helen snarled from where she was still leaning against the wall, her pretend almost-faint having had no impact whatsoever.

'I'll do it, shall I?' Kate pushed past Brett, strode up to Pepe and wrestled the leg of lamb from him. There was one point, Brett noticed, where the dog refused to let go and was hanging on for grim death, while dangling two feet off the floor, but eventually his wife won, and she threw the joint in the bin.

Pepe, his meal unfairly stolen, slunk out of the kitchen with Beverley hot on his heels, probably to make sure the animal wasn't about to expire from leg of lamb poisoning.

Brett, thinking he should do something to help, took a step towards the roasting tin, and slipped on the spilt fat. His legs shot out from underneath him and he landed with a sickening thump on the very unforgiving marble tiles.

'Oomph!' The breath whooshed out of his lungs, and he lay there winded.

Kate, his formerly loving, tender wife (it had been a while, he was forced to admit) stepped around him to pick up the roasting tin, threw that in the general direction of the sink, grabbed a roll of paper towels, and proceeded to wipe up around him.

The last thing she did before striding out of the room once more, was to grab a handful of the takeaway menus which sat on the shelf above the kitchen table, and throw them at him.

As a flurry of glossy folded menus fluttered down onto his chest, all Brett could think was, Merry effin' Christmas.

CHAPTER 18

Sam was in his element. 'The dog ate our dinner,' he giggled for about the fourth time. 'You wait until I tell Jack. He'll be well jeal.'

Portia blew in through the front door just as Kate was unpacking the delivery, and she could hardly contain her delight when she saw what was for dinner. 'Pizza! Yay! And it's not even the weekend. You can come again, Nan.'

Kate wasn't sure which grandmother Portia was speaking too, and she didn't care as long as the child was playing nice. She knew it wouldn't last, though. Portia hadn't seen the blow-up bed in Ellis's room yet, and neither had Ellis, because she was still out.

Kate prayed it wasn't noticed until after they'd eaten. She honestly couldn't face a showdown right now.

'Right, everyone, help yourselves,' she said, opening the boxes and taking lids off dips.

Somehow it didn't seem right to eat pizza and everything that went with it at the dining room table; it was usually a sit on the floor and dive in kind of meal, with the various boxes and cartons spread out around them. But Kate didn't think Helen would contemplate sitting on a rug to eat her evening meal, and Kate wasn't sure her mother could get down that far, or if she could, whether she'd be able to get back up again without the assistance of some mechanical lifting equipment.

Kate normally loved pizza from Domino's but this particular meal had developed a subtle flavour of disappointment and disapproval, which affected her appetite.

Everyone else appeared to be enjoying the

selection of pizzas and sides – although enjoying was the wrong word to use when it came to Helen as her mother-in-law picked and poked at everything on her plate with a long-suffering expression on her face. Beverley wasn't doing much better, as Kate's mum was systematically picking all the toppings off every single slice of pizza, before eating the mangled remains with an if-I-must expression on her face.

'That lamb would have tasted so much better than this rubbish,' Helen said, carefully trying to lift a slice out of the box with a knife and fork, instead of grabbing it with her fingers like a normal person. 'It would have been better for the children, too, I don't believe in feeding them junk food.'

'You could always have trimmed off the bit the dog ate,' Kate said, sarcastically.

'Certainly not!' Helen retorted with a theatrical shudder. 'That's disgusting.'

Portia sniggered and Sam gave his sister a nudge.

'I was joking,' Kate pointed out. 'We don't

have junk food that often.'

'I've seen the contents of your freezer,' Helen said. 'There are enough frozen chips in there to feed the whole street, as well as chicken nuggets and sausages.'

'Nana is the junk food police,' Sam said, stuffing a large slice of meat fest in his mouth with one hand, and vigorously scratching his armpit with another.

'Don't do that at the table,' Helen said. 'You're behaving worse than a chimp.'

Kate could have told her it was the wrong thing to say to an eleven-year-old boy, if her mother-in-law had taken the trouble to ask her beforehand. But Helen never asked, she only lectured, so the words were no sooner out of her mouth, than Sam was bouncing up and down on his chair, doing a monkey impersonation complete with sound.

'Does he have to make so much noise?' Beverley implored. 'It's bad for my nerves.'

'He's a child, Mum, of course he makes noise,' Kate said, then turned to her son. 'Just not at the table, eh?'

Sam carried on scratching, although the silly noises and the bouncing stopped.

'Anyone would think he's got fleas,' Helen pointed out.

'Pepe hasn't got fleas,' Beverley said indignantly. 'I have him wormed and treated for fleas three times a year, I'll have you know. And he goes to the parlour every two weeks; he's cleaner than you are.'

'I sincerely doubt it,' Helen retorted.

It was Sam's turn to snigger. 'Just think, if people had fleas, like dogs do,' he began, but his paternal grandmother cut him short.

'That's not a suitable conversation for the dinner table,' she said, loftily, then went off on a completely different tangent. 'I could have dished up the roast potatoes and vegetables.'

'Pardon?' Even Brett was flummoxed by this comment.

'With the pizza,' Helen explained. 'It would have saved them going to waste. I hate throwing food out.'

'Ew, cabbage with ham and pineapple on stuffed crust? No thanks, Nana.' Portia wrinkled her pierced nose.

'If you ate more vegetables you mightn't look so peaky,' Helen retorted.

'Mum, what does peaky mean,' Sam wanted to know.

'Pale and slightly ill-looking,' Kate replied.

'That's funny, Nana.' Sam was chortling. 'Portia is peaky, Portia is peaky,' he chanted, then he changed it to, 'Peaky Portia, Peaky Portia,' until his sister threw a slice of garlic bread at him.

'Sam, that's enough,' Kate said. 'Portia, stop throwing food.'

'He started it,' Portia whined. 'Anyway, I'm not pale, It's my makeup.'

Helen snorted. 'I thought make-up was supposed to make you look prettier. Yours just makes you look ill.'

Portia's eyes filled with tears. 'I'm a Goth. I don't expect you to understand. You're too old.' And with that, she pushed her chair away from the table, got to her feet and flounced out of the door, but not before she'd grabbed another slice of mushroom, pepper, and sweetcorn thin and crispy on her way.

Kate took a deep steadying breath as her mother-in-law tucked into a generous portion of garlic bread.

'I thought you said you had a dairy and gluten intolerance,' Kate said to her. 'You do realise garlic bread has both in it?'

'I never said such a thing,' Helen replied, chewing carefully.

'You did! I bought you some gluten-free bread especially.' Kate was holding onto her patience with both hands.

'Nonsense. I've never been intolerant of anything in my life!'

Kate bit back the obvious retort.

Before she could say anything less antagonistic, Ellis put in an appearance in the form of barging in through the front door, yelling, 'I'm just going to get my charger,' and darting up the stairs.

Oh, shit... Kate began to count, one, two, three.

'Mum!' Ellis's shriek could probably be heard on the moon. 'What's this blow-up bed doing in my room?'

Kate winced as her eldest child thundered back down the stairs.

'What?' That came from Portia, who hadn't ventured into her sister's room to steal anything so far this evening and therefore hadn't seen the new sleeping arrangements. More thundering.

Ellis burst into the living room first, Portia hot on her heels. 'There's an inflatable mattress in my room and I want to know what it's doing there,' Ellis ranted, her hands on her hips and her eyes flashing.

'It's obvious, stupid,' Portia said. 'They expect me to sleep in your room. Huh! I don't think so.'

'Don't call your sister stupid,' Brett said, and Kate practically snarled at him.

Trust him to focus on the least important thing. The girls called each other far worse things than "stupid", and name-calling was the least of her worries right now.

'Why don't you make Portia sleep on the living room floor?' Ellis suggested, pulling a face at Portia. 'She can sleep there just as easily as she can bunk down on the floor in my room, and it would mean I don't have to put up with her all night. Do I have to think of everything around here?'

'Ellis, I'm not having your sister loll about in the middle of the living room until lunchtime. It's not fair on everyone else,' Kate said.

'You're just being selfish, making me have her in my room. Why don't you have her in yours, if you're so worried about where she's going to sleep?'

'I know,' Portia said to her sister, 'why don't *you* sleep on the living room floor?'

'I'm the oldest. I should have certain privileges. It's not fair.' Ellis stamped her foot.

Kate stared at her daughters in dismay. Brett kept his eyes down and his mouth occupied by cramming it full of meat feast with added spicy chicken, so he didn't have to speak to anyone, least of all have to deal with the situation. Kate sent him a furious look.

'Ellis, Portia, you'll do as you're bloody well told,' she hissed. 'I don't care if you don't like it. Portia, you'll sleep on the air bed in Ellis's room, and Ellis, you'll just have to suck it up. Mum, you can have Portia's room. As soon as we've finished eating, I'll put some fresh sheets on the bed.'

There, that told 'em, she thought. But of course, it hadn't. She should have known better.

'I don't want to put the girls out,' Beverley said, giving Helen a sly glance out of the corner of her eye. 'It's not fair to oust Portia from her bedroom. I slept really well in your bed, Kate.'

I bet you did, Kate thought uncharitably. Their nice, huge comfortable bed, with its en suite and its dormer window with the fantastic views. Who wouldn't sleep well in a bedroom like that?

'Your mattress is better for my arthritis than the one in Portia's room,' Beverley added.

'How do you know, Mum; you've never slept in Portia's bed.'

'No, but I've sat on it, and it's awful hard on old bones. If I have a flare-up, I won't be able to travel.' Beverley's smile was radiant.

Kate heard the sub-text, and so did Helen by the sudden look of horror on her face. If Beverley didn't get to stay in Kate and Brett's room, she was threatening to stay until the New Year.

Dear lord, take me now, Kate pleaded silently. She wasn't sure how much more of this she could deal with.

Ellis and Portia, sensing victory, fist-bumped each other in a rare show of sisterly solidarity, before going their separate ways, leaving Kate open-mouthed and close to tears in their respective wakes.

Helen silently fumed, knowing it was useless to object; Beverley tucked into what was left of her decimated pizza with a serenely smug smile; Sam stared at all of the adults in turn, a chocolate-chip cookie halfway to his mouth, his eyes wide; Brett gave a resigned sigh and reached for a spicy chicken wing and a couple of potato wedges.

Kate sat there, feeling blindsided. Dear God, what on earth had just happened? One minute she'd been reading her girls the riot act, the next she'd had the rug pulled from underneath her and was now very much on the back foot.

She knew she wasn't making much sense, but the situation itself didn't make much sense. Her whole bloody family didn't make much sense. Her life didn't—

'Ow! Damn and blast!' Kate felt a set of sharp canine teeth sinking into her ankle as Pepe took his revenge for Kate taking the leg of lamb off him, by giving her a quick nip when her guard was down.

It was at that point she took herself off to the bathroom for a bit of a cry.

CHAPTER 19

It wasn't like Brett to bunk off work, but he'd seriously had enough, and he wasn't just referring to work, either. Sleeping on the sodding air bed again hadn't helped his mood or his back. Since when did it become a thing for the lower spine to play up? His hips hurt too, and he briefly wondered if he would need a hip replacement in the future. If he did, he'd lay the blame on having spent two nights on the floor. OK, he'd actually slept on the sofa the night before, but it hadn't been that comfortable, either.

He'd also cut himself shaving and had left

the house with a piece of toilet paper dabbed on the nick. He hadn't bothered with breakfast because the ache in his back made him feel a little nauseous. Besides, there was no coffee left in the jar, so he hadn't been able to make himself a hot drink, then the car had needed de-icing, and he'd discovered that one headlight was out.

'Bugger it,' he muttered, reached for his phone, and called in sick.

Then he had no idea what to do with the rest of his day. He could hardly go into Worcester, because someone might spot him. Pershore was out of the question for the same reason, and besides, Kate knew most of the people who shopped there, and someone would be bound to shop *him*.

He sat there for a moment, his breath steaming up the inside of the windows, while outside they began to refreeze. He'd go to the garden centre, that's what he'd do. He'd buy a newspaper and sit in their little café and read it. All day, if he couldn't think of anything else to do.

It was far too early for it to be open, though,

so he decided to drive to the nearest retail park where there was a greasy spoon café, and treat himself to a fry up. A big plate of bacon, sausage, and eggs should see him right, then he'd have a coffee and a cake at the garden centre, and read the adverts pages where jobs were listed.

He didn't expect there'd be much he could reasonably go for, not if he wanted to maintain the family's current standard of living (and he did want to do that), and especially not at this time of year, but at least he'd feel as though he was taking a step in the right direction.

His New Year's resolution would be to find another job, one without The Abyss in it, breathing down his neck with her unrealistic demands.

Decision made, he headed towards the city, then skirted around the ring road until he came to a truckers' café. The tea would be so strong and dark you could stand a spoon up in it, the eggs would be swimming in grease, and tomato ketchup would be served with everything, but Brett didn't care. He felt like a ton weight had been lifted from his shoulders. Admittedly, it hadn't been lifted far, and he could sense it still hovering, waiting for him to return to work, when it would thump back down like a coffin lid; but for now, he felt lighter than he'd done in ages.

He needed this little break, a chance to regroup and rethink. He considered confiding in Kate, but she was so exhausted all the time, so stressed with the kids, that he didn't want to add to her worries. Besides, he did feel like he was the last on the list when it came to his wife's priorities. She always put the kids first, was a bit of a martyr to them, if he was honest.

Brett, waiting for his greasy, salty, fat-laden, mouth-wateringly delicious fried breakfast had to admit that he sometimes felt left out, ignored, overlooked. He was sick of her running around after the kids when they were mostly old enough to sort themselves out. Sam needed a bit of help now and again, but he was nearly twelve, almost a teenager. It was about time the three of them learned to stand on their own feet a little more, especially the girls, take a bit more responsibility, and stop expecting their mother to fetch, carry, and pick up after them.

Then there was the problem of his sex life. He didn't exactly have much of one. He and Kate couldn't seem to coordinate their sex drives – if one of them was up for it, the other couldn't be bothered. To be honest, he was the one who was usually up for it, and Kate was the one who couldn't be bothered. His wife seemed to say yes to everything and everyone, except him.

And now that her mother was here, he was last in line after the blasted dog, who by the way, also seemed to have more of Kate's attention than he did. Even a sharp telling off (like she'd given the dog last night after it had tried to take a chunk out of her ankle) was better than being ignored.

He knew she was tired and doing too much, but some of it was her own fault. The kids were perfectly capable of tidying up their own things, finding their own lost phones, doing their own homework without supervision. He supposed he could help a bit more, but he worked such long hours and the job was so stressful and demanding, and took so much out of him, that all he wanted to do when he got home was to collapse in front of the TV and let his brain wallow in a couple of hours of mindless drivel until bedtime.

CHAPTER 20

Doris felt better, so her text to Kate said that she'd be in work today as normal – which was a good thing, considering Kate wasn't. Kate was sitting in the coffee shop opposite, eating a fried breakfast and wondering how much she had in her bank account and how far it would take her.

She was so tired and fed up, she could cry – and it was only Wednesday!

As she shovelled bacon and egg into her mouth, she hated to admit it, but most of the events over the past few days (and the previous few years, if she was being totally honest) was all her own fault. It was a hard thing to accept, but it was true. She'd let her family get away with murder (not literally, of course), and now she was harvesting the results.

The kids, the girls especially, were nightmares – spoilt, entitled, selfish brats. They expected, no *demanded*, that she drop everything to see to their immediate needs; and while this had been essential when they were babies, she'd carried on the practice for far too long and was still doing it now, as last night sleeping on the air bed showed. Although all three of them were well-behaved, polite, accommodating children outside the family home (thank God for that; even Portia, the more challenging of the three, was often called "delightful" and "a sweetheart" by teachers and other parents alike) they slipped into their alter-ego of stroppy, opinionated (none of them had enough life experiences to be so opinionated in Kate's eyes), dramatic, stubborn (the list could go on...) horrors once they were at home.

Her husband took her for granted and

regarded her as part of the fixtures and fittings – he probably wouldn't even notice if she wasn't there, except to wonder why there were no clean shirts in his wardrobe and why the fridge was empty.

Her mother…? Hmmm, that particular relationship was rather more difficult to quantify. Mothers and daughters didn't always hit it off (she should know – her own daughters had turned into unrecognisable strangers), and she wondered if Beverley felt the same way about her. Guilt-tripping was what her mother was especially good at – she could go on Mastermind, with her specialist subject being "How to make daughters feel guilty". Her mother would more than likely win that damned contest, too.

Kate mopped up some egg yolk with a piece of toast and chewed thoughtfully, and slightly guiltily, too. It wasn't like her to pull a sickie. She was hardly ever ill, and on the rare occasions she did feel under the weather, she'd always make an effort to go into work. After all, she reasoned, if she was well enough to deal with three children, then she must be well enough to go into work.

She didn't only feel guilty about taking an unwarranted sick day, she also felt guilty she wasn't using it to remain at home and keep the peace between the various factions. At least they hadn't coalesced into two warring groups – in Kate's house it seemed it was every man for himself, and every other family member was viewed as the enemy. No one got on. Her kids hated the sight of each other, her mother and his mother played a subtle game of one-upmanship and putting each other down. They also tried to play Kate and Brett off each other, but the children had been doing that for years, so it was a bit like water off a duck's back. The children didn't particularly enjoy having either of their grandmothers to stay; Kate didn't see eye to eye with Helen, and Brett barely tolerated Beverley.

As for her and Brett themselves, the least said about that the better, she decided.

Peace, that's what she craved. *Solitude.* The

word almost made her feel faint with wanting. Imagine not having to answer to anyone, having nothing to do all day but please herself?

The thought was so decadent, it was practically obscene.

Kate wondered if it was normal to feel like this – if her family was normal. Despite many of the school's mums posting Facebook images of familial bliss she wondered if, underneath the surface of those seemingly happy, perfect lives, all those other families were equally as disjointed and miserable. Because if her situation wasn't typical and wasn't being reflected in families all across the country, then she had an awful feeling she wanted to opt-out of Christmas altogether.

Which was why she was speculating on how much she had in her bank account. She hadn't checked it recently, having used it to purchase most of the Christmas presents for the children, and a few things for Brett, too, of course.

If she left it up to her husband to ensure there were presents under the tree, the kids would be lucky if they got a bag of nuts each, and an orange to share – and those would only be given because there were several bags of assorted nuts and raisins in the cupboard and the fruit bowl was full.

Kate logged onto internet banking and winced. She didn't have enough to fly to the Caribbean for a fortnight, but she might be able to manage a few days in a guest house somewhere and the odd meal out.

She put her knife and fork neatly on her plate, pushed it to the side, and picked up her coffee. Taking a sip, she leant back and narrowed her eyes, staring unseeingly into the distance.

It would be so lovely to have some peace and quiet; no screaming, yelling, shouting; no stamping upstairs, no slamming of doors, no music turned up loud enough to burst eardrums. No arguments, no drama. No crises over mislaid phones, keys, earbuds, homework. No accusations of stolen hairbrushes, borrowed favourite eyeliner, or the top left off someone's mascara so that the contents had gone all gloopy. Then there would also be the wonderful relief at not finding empty orange juice cartons placed back in the fridge; of not discovering that the last loo roll had only a few sheets left on it, and no one thought to mention it to her. She'd particularly enjoy not falling over shoes abandoned in the middle of a room, discovering plates with unidentifiable messes on them left in bedrooms, not having to drive three children to three separate places at three different times when, with a little bit of cooperation and consideration from her offspring, she might have only had to make the one journey.

As for Brett, while she was on a roll he might as well get it with both barrels, too. It would make a nice change not to have to wrestle the duvet from him in the middle of the night because he'd wrapped himself up in it like a snoring burrito. It would be strangely liberating not to have to wonder whether he was too tired for sex and would therefore rebuff her advances (not that she made many herself these days, because she was always so dammed knackered), or would be hoping for a quick fumble and would sulk if she didn't make the first move. It would also be wonderfully nice to be free of the low-grade resentment she felt towards him because he hadn't given her enough help or support. She wasn't sure whether she believed in "absence makes the heart grow fonder" but right now she was more than willing to give it a go.

Daydreaming about escaping was wonderful and had provided her with a tiny respite, but her conscience (the annoying little nag) kept prodding at her, telling her to go back home immediately and make sure no one had hit anyone else with a shovel and was burying the body in the garden.

In her present frame of mind, the prospect of a corpse under the patio didn't bother her unduly – it was just one less person she'd have to deal with; although she did pray that if anyone was going to be planted six feet under, it would be Helen.

Cheered slightly by the thought, Kate

gathered her hat, coat, and scarf and sidled out of the café door with as much nonchalance as she could muster and scuttled around the corner praying Doris hadn't spotted her through the shop window.

It might be mid-morning, but everyone had their Christmas lights on, probably more out of necessity than festive cheer because the day was a dank, dreary one, with an overcast sky and a grim chill in the air.

The café had had Christmas songs playing just that smidgeon too loud, and an under-decorated tree in front of the customer loo, partially obscuring it from view. Still, they were trying, which was more than could be said for Kate. She asked herself if she truly hadn't had time to pop to the garden centre to buy a tree, or if she'd had an attack of the "bah humbugs". She suspected the latter.

Convinced that this year (like previous years, but worse) would be a total wash-out, she'd not made the slightest effort on the Christmas front, apart from buying and wrapping presents and sending the odd card. Of course, she'd ordered the turkey and had stocked the fridge, freezer, and cupboards with the usual Yuletide treats, but what had she actually *done*?

When Beverley and Helen had arrived there wasn't a sprig of holly or a berry-scented candle in the house. Which was probably why Helen had taken it upon herself to go out and buy that hideous tree.

Determined to rectify the situation (although she didn't intend to take Helen's tree down and put another in its place), she decided to dig the strands of twinkling lights out of the garage and drape them artfully over the small fir tree at the side of the drive, as she'd done in other years. She could always weave more lights up the bannister, and yet more along the shelves in the kitchen. There was a wreath still to buy and crackers to purchase, and she should think about buying a little something for Pepe to open on Christmas morning so he didn't feel left out.

Keeping her hat pulled down over her ears and her scarf wrapped around the lower half of her face, Kate slinked into the little general shop and spent a good few minutes weighing up the pros and cons of the assorted boxes of crackers on display, before choosing ones with jokey "gifts" inside. No doubt Helen would turn her nose up at the crassness of it, but the kids would have a few minutes (seconds?) of amusement, and Brett might even crack a smile. Her mother would complain about crackers being a waste of money, but then, she complained about most things, so it wouldn't matter which ones Kate bought.

After that, she popped into the little florist for a wreath, and followed it up with a visit to the pet shop. Not knowing what Pepe liked apart from stolen lamb and ankles, she bought him his own doggy stocking with a selection of canine treats inside.

She then darted into a lovely little shop which sold home-made soaps, shampoo bars, silky moisturisers, and the most gloriously scented candles and fragrant oils. Kate chose a diffuser, inhaling the aromas of cinnamon, clove, frankincense, and orange with delight. With the scents of the festive season in her nose, she finally began to feel more in the Christmas mood. Splashing out a little, she bought another diffuser for the hall and several candles which she intended to dot along the mantelpiece; they'd look lovely when they were lit, the large mirror behind reflecting the flickering light back into the room. If she had to cut the plug off the TV so everyone would be forced to enjoy the candle and twinkly light atmosphere, then she bloody well would. It wouldn't hurt her family to take a moment to reflect in peace without the TV blaring. Maybe she'd try to find some Christmas carols on her phone and play those at the same time. They could all enjoy a glass of something alcoholic, even the kids (just a small one and definitely not to be repeated) and stand around the tree in harmony.

At last! She was finally beginning to feel the spirit of Christmas flowing through her, and her feelings of angst and irritation flowing out.

Her family was no different from anyone

else's. They had their ups and their downs, their squabbles and their good times. It was inevitable that with three generations in the house, and seven lots of opinions, likes, and dislikes, there were going to be clashes. The only thing that mattered was that they were all together, celebrating the most magical time of the year. Kate was surrounded by the people who meant the most to her (she struggled manfully to include Brett's mother in that); she was loved and cherished, and she loved and cherished them in return.

Not quite ready to leave the giddy sights and sounds of Pershore behind, Kate decided to consolidate her rediscovered love of Christmas by doing something she'd not done for years – she paid a visit to Pershore Abbey.

It was a magnificent building, not far from the High Street, but set in extensive gardens and open lawns with tall, old trees dotted around. Square-towered, built of buttery yellow stone, the abbey had been constructed in Anglo-Saxon times and was over a thousand years old. Now a parish church, it hadn't lost any of its grandeur by being relegated. The high vaulted ceiling and huge arched windows behind the altar were truly breath-taking, and at this time of year, the abbey was alive with light and song, and the smell of... coffee?

'Hello, and welcome to our Yuletide coffee morning,' a lady said with a smile, gesturing towards a row of trestle tables groaning with cakes, cups, and a large silver urn. Individual tables were laid out with chairs, most of them occupied, and behind those, a group of children were singing carols in sweet, high voices.

Oh, how lovely! This was just what she needed to bolster her before she returned home. She was under no illusion that her Christmas spirit would be sorely tested in the days to come, but if she could remember this feeling, then she stood a chance of hanging onto that Christmas spirit without resorting to several large glasses of grapefruit gin.

Grabbing a hot chocolate and a slice of rich fruit cake topped with marzipan and gleaming white royal icing, she took a seat and let the singing flow over her. It reminded her so much of when the children were younger and took part in the school's carol service; although as Kate went down the ranks from Ellis, through Portia, and finally to Sam, so the carol service became less about carols and the Christmas story, and more about popular Disney songs and whatever happened to be in the charts at the time.

Ooh, this cake is delicious, she thought, taking a large bite and letting the explosion of flavours flood her mouth. Soft, rich fruit, combined with the slightly harder bits of chopped nuts, had been given added warmth by being soaked in a liberal amount of alcohol – brandy, if she wasn't mistaken.

This was what Christmas was all about – a visit to a church, beautiful singing, and mouth-watering food, with a wonderful family at home waiting for her return.

Buoyed up by her illicit morning, and feeling calmer and less stressed than she had for days (although she still felt awfully guilty about letting

Doris down, but she realised she'd desperately needed the little break) Kate set off for home with a lightness in her step and good-cheer-to-all-men in her heart.

CHAPTER 21

Brett had to wait outside the garden centre for a few minutes until it opened, and he spent the time in his car listening to Radio 2. It felt awfully strange to just sit there, with nothing to do; no emails to open, no meetings to attend, no phone calls to make.

Of course, he did have all those things to do – he just wasn't in work to do them. He felt an odd mixture of naughty relief and guilt, and an uplifting sense of freedom, and he wished every day could be like this, with nothing much to do, except potter about. He was realistic enough to realise that if he didn't work, the opportunity for "pottering" would be considerably less because he wouldn't have the money to do much pottering with, and certainly not any spare cash to spend on expensive slices of cake in garden centre cafes. It was ironic, he mused – if one had the time, one didn't necessarily have the money, but if one had the money then one didn't have the time, because one spent all their sodding time trying to earn the sodding money in the first place. There must be a happy medium, and he didn't mean when he retired, either. He didn't want to have to wait another fifteen years or so; he might be able to afford to retire before then if he accessed his private pension early, but the state said his official retirement date was over a decade and a half in the future, when he might be too old and decrepit to enjoy it. He wanted to enjoy it now, while he was young enough to appreciate it.

Dear God, there must be more to life than this.

Sod it, now he'd gone and depressed himself,

just when he was enjoying his stolen day, too.

Desultorily, he clambered out of his car, shutting the door with a soft thunk, and dawdled over to the entrance, clutching his newspaper. He deliberately left his phone in the car. Work shouldn't be bothering him anyway, not when he was ill, and if Kate called him, she'd assume he was in a meeting or something. His mother, if she wanted him, would have to wait. There was no life or death situation he could think of that would require his input. She could decide for herself whether she cooked anything for dinner – she didn't need his approval. Although, when she'd suggested cooking the lamb (dear lord, that lamb… it had been almost farcical), she'd been lining her ducks in a row, so if Kate had made a fuss, his mother could have legitimately claimed that Brett had agreed for her to cook it. His mother could be a wily old girl at times.

After ordering a hot chocolate (it was Christmas, after all) and a mince pie with a dollop of cream, Brett selected a table and shook open his newspaper, immersing himself in the goings-on in the world. He usually read it from cover to cover when he got home from work, as a kind of escapism, while Kate watched a soap on TV, and it was strange to sit in a café and read it. He felt a little out of sorts, but in a good way. Christmas songs were playing softly in the background and twinkly lights had been strung everywhere. With the enticing smell of coffee, and the alluring scent of spices from the stand of candles and oils just by the café entrance, he was starting to feel a teensy-weensy bit Christmassy. The festive season had failed to touch him at all so far this year, but taking the time to relax and soak in the atmosphere today was doing wonders when it came to ridding himself of the bah humbug frame of mind he'd been in. It was a bit cheesy that he had to sit in a garden centre café to experience it, but he'd grab it anyway he could.

'Would Father Christmas please come to Santa's Grotto,' a nasally voice said over the tannoy.

Oh, he used to love taking the kids to see

Santa. Yes, it might be overpriced and rather tatty, but his children hadn't thought so at the time. He vividly remembered Ellis's little face one year. She couldn't have been more than four – old enough to understand that Christmas meant magic, unbearable excitement, and presents, but not too old for doubt and disbelief to have started to creep in. She'd been fully immersed in the experience, telling Santa what she wanted in her high-pitched lisp (which she'd grown out of), her face alight with wonder and joy.

However, by the time Sam was four, Ellis had been ten, going on twenty, and Kate had been forced to bribe her not to tell Sam the truth about Father Christmas.

The magic didn't last long, and that made him feel incredibly sad.

'Would Father Christmas *please* come to Santa's Grotto!' The voice over the tannoy was beginning to sound a little desperate.

Brett checked the time. It was nearly midday, to his surprise. He'd been sitting in the café for almost two hours, enjoying his quiet, uninterrupted perusal of the paper and soaking in Christmas spirit, like osmosis, almost against his will.

He'd better fetch himself another drink, if he didn't want to be kicked out. It was lucky the café wasn't busy yet, the lunchtime crowd of pensioners only just beginning to trickle in.

He didn't want or need anything else to eat or drink, but if he wanted to remain here, he'd better had; because there wasn't anywhere else he could think of to go. If it was summer, he could have driven out to one of the villages by the river and taken a stroll, but a dismal December day didn't lend itself to gentle strolling, especially along muddy river banks while wearing a pair of brogues.

As he queued for a coffee, he glanced over the low partition, dividing the café area from the Christmas tree and lights area. The whole thing had been quite artfully done, the garden centre using the display of trees, figures, and lights which were for sale, to make a magical forest path leading towards Santa's Grotto. Already there were a number of small children squirming impatiently, accompanied by their equally impatient parents, as they waited for the big man himself to put in an appearance.

Make the most of it, he wanted to tell those harassed mums and dads (although the few grandparents who were in the queue appeared to be rather more serene) – this magical stage of belief and trust wouldn't last long. In far too short a time, those same children would be refusing to be seen in the company of their parents, and questioning the commercialism of the whole thing, while happily accepting every present they were given as long as it was something they'd asked for.

Brett, for all the hard work those early years with his children had meant, wished with all his heart he could turn back the clock to a time when Christmas was filled with happy, shiny faces, and squeals of unadulterated joy.

'Please, Father Christmas, you are needed at the Grotto.' The voice sounded desperate, and Brett grimaced.

Poor little kids. Poor parents too, if Santa didn't show up.

He paused. Without thinking too hard about it, he darted out of the queue and headed for the customer service desk.

'What's happened to Santa?' he asked when he got there.

'There's been a slight delay, sir, but if you return to the Grotto, I'm sure it won't be much longer. Tell your little one, that one of the reindeer is poorly, or something. We'll get Santa to his Grotto as quickly as we can.'

'You don't have a Santa at the moment, do you?'

'As I said, sir, I'm sure it won't be much longer.'

'I'll be Santa, until the real one shows up,' Brett offered, in a rush, then realised he sounded a bit deranged. 'I mean, until the man who is supposed to be Santa arrives. I don't honestly think Santa is real.'

The young man behind the counter eyed him dubiously. 'I'm not sure that would be allowed—

' he began.

'Go and check,' Brett said.

The two of them locked eyes, and Brett saw suspicion in the other man's, and abruptly understood why. Oh dear...

'Never mind,' Brett said. 'I can see how this looks, and I'm sorry. It's just that I remember when I took my kids to see Father Christmas and how their little faces lit up. I just didn't want those children,' he waved an arm in the general direction of Santa's Grotto, 'to miss out. But I can understand your caution – you can't just let any old Tom, Dick, or Harry waltz in and play Santa.'

Shoulders slumped, as much from disappointment as embarrassment, Brett turned away.

'Wait a sec,' the young man called after him. 'I'll have a quick word with my manager.'

Brett wasn't sure he wanted to play Father Christmas, after all. He clearly hadn't thought his impulsive offer through, not imagining how it might look to have a total stranger rock up and offer to haul small children onto his knee. These days, one couldn't be too careful. He just hoped the sales assistant wasn't on the phone to the police right now, reporting him for—

'That's a very kind offer,' a woman wearing a sweatshirt with the garden centre's logo on it said, bustling up to him with a sheaf of papers in her hand. 'Fortunately, Santa has just arrived – his car wouldn't start, or should I say, sleigh?' She laughed. 'If you'd like to be considered for next year, you can fill in an application form.' She held out the sheaf of papers. 'Of course, any offer would be subject to the necessary pre-employment checks, and for this role you'd need a valid DBS certificate, too.'

'DBS?'

'Disclosure and Barring Service. It's a criminal records check, as you'd be working with young children.'

'Oh, I see. Thanks.' Brett took the form automatically. He wasn't exactly going to apply for the job (however much he thought he might enjoy it, being Father Christmas was a tad on the seasonal side), but he didn't want to appear rude. However, it did give him food for thought, and he hurried back to his table and to the newspaper he'd left lying there.

These days not many jobs were advertised in it because most vacancies were placed online, but he *had* seen one thing that had caught his interest...

CHAPTER 22

Good-cheer-to-all-men didn't extend to her children, her mother, her mother-in-law, or the bloody dog, Kate discovered when she stepped through the front door an hour or so later, the peace and contentment of her illicit day fading faster than a layer of cheap fake tan in a swimming pool.

It was the noise that hit her first, somewhat surprisingly considering it was still the morning side of noon and she hadn't expected any of her offspring to have surfaced yet. Two different songs blared down the stairs, competing with the sound of Sam's Xbox which sounded as though it was being played at full volume, and two sets of teenage female lungs screeched and bellowed, and they weren't singing along to the records, either.

In among the caterwauling, Kate heard Helen trying to soothe the savages, but from her pitch, tone, and volume (almost as loud as her granddaughters) Helen wasn't getting anywhere.

Accompanying the cacophony was a small dog's frantic, high-pitched yapping.

'What are you doing home so early?' Beverley yelled in Kate's ear, and Kate let out a resounding shriek.

'God, you scared me,' she cried. 'What the hell is going on?'

'From what I can gather, Ellis got up early – well, early for her – to meet some boy called Riley, only to discover that Portia had "borrowed",' Beverley made quotation marks in the air with her fingers, 'Ellis's new Christmas top and had managed to get something all down it.

Ellis is accusing her of ruining her top, her day, and her life. Portia is telling her sister that the top looked awful on Ellis anyway and she was doing her a favour. I think the throwing of hairbrushes and other blunt objects was involved at some point. So, now they're not talking to each other, and to reinforce the point that they're not speaking they've turned their music on and are playing it at full blast, while still screaming at each other.' Her mother toddled back into the living room, saying, 'Oh, and Sam was upset because they woke him up, Pepe seems to like singing along to one of the records, and Helen is sticking her pointy nose in, as usual. There, I think that covers it.' She sank into a chair and picked up her knitting.

'Right, er, thanks for the update,' Kate said faintly.

The noise grew louder as Ellis opened her door (Kate recognised The Wombats blaring out of her eldest daughter's bedroom) only for her to quickly slam it shut again so hard it made Kate's teeth rattle.

She sighed, and debated turning on her heel and going into work after all. Anything was better than being roped into this drama.

Shit, too late. Helen had spotted her from the top of the stairs.

'Oh, Kate dear, thank God you're here, I'm worried one of them will kill the other,' Helen cried, dramatically.

Kate had the vague, unmotherly thought that it would certainly be one solution... 'Shall we take bets?' she replied flippantly. This was nothing compared to some of the humdingers she'd witnessed over the years.

'I don't know how you can take this so lightly,' her mother-in-law said, raising a wilting hand to her brow and making her eyes roll as if she was about to faint.

'Easily,' she said. 'It'll calm down in a minute.'

'I do hope so, because it's not doing my head or my nerves any good. I think I might have to lie down.'

Good luck with that, Kate thought – the spare

room was sandwiched between Portia's (The Chemical Brothers at ear-splitting volume) and Sam's (the sound of Fortnite's gunfire was of epic proportions) bedrooms.

'Your mother isn't helping,' Helen stated when Kate didn't respond. 'All she does is sit in that chair and knit. I don't even know what she's supposed to be making; it looks a shapeless mess.'

'Oi! I heard that, and for your information it's a jumper,' Beverley yelled above the noise.

'Not a very good one,' Helen shouted back.

'At least I can knit, and I don't spend my time poking my nose in and interfering,' Beverley retorted.

'At least I'm trying to do something.'

'You wanna try a bit harder, then, because from where I'm sitting you don't appear to be doing a very good job.'

'All this is making me ill,' Helen announced.

'Never mind what it's doing to *you*, look what it's doing to poor Pepe.'

"Poor Pepe" was bouncing around the hall on

stiff little legs, yapping excitedly and seeming to be enjoying every second of it.

'He'll not settle for ages after this, my poor baby,' Beverley cried.

'Your poor baby has just shredded all the toilet roll in the family bathroom. That's what I was coming downstairs to tell you. Please clean the mess up – I don't see why I should have to do it,' Helen said, all indication that she might faint having now been replaced with indignation and outrage.

'Mum!' Kate glared at Beverley. 'Please can you make sure he stays in the kitchen. If he's not having little accidents everywhere, he's being destructive.'

'He's bored,' Beverley said.

'Why don't you get up off your backside and take him for a walk?' Helen suggested. 'It might wear the little blighter out.'

'Why don't you mind your own business?' Beverley retorted.

'My son's house *is* my business. I can't believe you let Brett spend the last couple of nights on the floor when he's got work the next day. How you can be so inconsiderate astounds me.'

'You're just cheesed off because I'm sleeping in Kate and Brett's room. I don't see you giving up your bed.'

'Why should I?' Helen was starting to lose her composure, her voice rising an octave or two. 'I was here first.'

Kate put a hand to her head and massaged her temple. She didn't think she could take another four days of this. Maybe she'd be better off in work after all. It was peaceful there; the only music would be the soft playing of Christmas carols, and no one shouted unless it was from out the back asking if anyone wanted a cuppa.

Yes, that's what she'd do – she'd go into work and let this lot bloody well get on with it. She might be abdicating responsibility and she did feel rather guilty about it, but she honestly didn't think she could take any more argy-bargy.

'You're only here first because you were told

I was coming to my daughter's for Christmas,' Beverley was saying. 'You made sure you turned up early just to get the spare room. Ha! Backfired on you, didn't it?'

Kate looked at her mother's smug expression, then looked at Helen's furious one.

Then she looked longingly at the front door and uttered another deep sigh. She supposed she'd better begin sorting everyone out and she'd start with the easiest – the loo roll situation.

'You're nothing but a selfish old woman,' she heard Helen cry as she marched up the stairs and into the bathroom.

She stopped. Dear God, there were tiny shreds of tissue paper everywhere. The poodle hadn't just pulled all the paper off the roll, he'd annihilated every sheet. The bathroom looked like there'd been an explosion in a confetti factory.

She needed the vacuum cleaner for this, but before she had a chance to fetch it from the cupboard under the stairs, the wall of noise from

Ellis's room ceased and her daughter flung the door open.

'Mum! Tell her,' her eldest yelled, pointing a rigid finger at Portia's bedroom. 'I only bought that top last week, and she's gone and ruined it. I can't wait until I'm eighteen and can leave home!'

'Where were you thinking of living?' Kate asked, probably not the best response under the circumstances, but she was curious.

'Anywhere! I don't care!'

'You've given this a lot of thought then?'

'You're no help, you always take her side. She's always been your favourite.'

'Ellis, I don't have a favourite child. Now, let me have a look at that top and see what I can do.'

'Don't bother – it's ruined – and I wouldn't wear it now anyway because it stinks of that awful perfume she wears. She smells like bubble gum. It's hideous.'

'I can pop it in the washing machine—'

'I'm wearing this now,' Ellis interrupted. 'I

haven't got time to mess about, I'm meeting Riley in town.' She pulled at the jumper she was wearing. 'He's seen this before – he's going to think I've got nothing else to wear.'

'Don't be silly, he's not going to think anything of the sort. He's a boy. Boys don't notice stuff like that.'

'Riley does!' Ellis wailed. 'He's different from other boys, he's so sensitive and observant and lovely. If he breaks up with me because of this, I'm going to kill her.'

Okaaay, that was a bit extreme. 'I'm sure he isn't going to break up with you because you're wearing a jumper he's already seen you wearing,' Kate began.

'What do you know? You and Dad have been together since the dawn of time. It's different these days. Boys care about personal grooming and stuff. Not like Dad.' Ellis's glance swept over her, and she heard her daughter's unspoken, "not like you, either."

Yeah, you wait until you've got three kids, a house and a job to sort out. You won't care how many bloody times your husband has seen you in the same outfit, Kate thought. Some days she was lucky if she managed to drag a brush through her hair and find a matching pair of shoes.

Ellis sent her mother a narrow-eyed glare. 'I bet you won't even tell her off. It's so not fair.'

With that Ellis charged across the landing and took the stairs two at a time. Kate heard the front door slam a second or so later. She pitied any family who purchased this house at some future date, when she and Brett decided to move into something smaller – they'd need to replace all the doors and possibly do some serious replastering; and that was just for starters.

Portia, undoubtedly having waited until her sister had stormed off downstairs, yanked her bedroom door open, and yelled, 'She's so mean, she never lets me borrow anything, and she's got way nicer clothes than I have and lots more than me, and it's not fair because she has more pocket money than I do, and if I had the same amount that she does I wouldn't need to wear her stuff, and if she wasn't so selfish—'

Portia paused to take a breath and Kate jumped in. 'Wait there, young lady. She's older than you so it's only right she has more of an allowance. When you get to her age, you'll have the same as she does now.'

'Inflation,' Portia said. 'You've got to take that into account.'

Kate blinked. Fair play, her daughter had a point and kudos to Portia for her negotiation skills.

'We'll deal with that when the time comes,' Kate said. 'That doesn't excuse you for taking Ellis's top without permission. You know better than to help yourself to other people's things. It's up to you – you can either have your phone taken off you for the next three days, or you're grounded. Your choice.'

Kate knew that both of the options would hurt.

Portia had an excellent line in pouting. She crossed her arms, dipped her head to stare belligerently out from lowered brows, and thrust out her chin. 'You never tell anyone else off, it's always me! You hate me! Well, that's OK because I hate you too!'

Kate stared in open-mouthed shock as her middle child whirled on her heel, dashed back into her bedroom and slammed the door. Of course, she slammed it. Hell would freeze over before any of her children ever shut a door quietly.

She made a vow that once Portia had a home of her own, she would visit her for the sole purpose of repeatedly slamming every door in the house. If her daughter objected, she'd blame it on the menopause, or encroaching old age.

Let's see how she'll like that, Kate thought, turning her attention back to the confetti-filled bathroom. What was she doing? Oh, yes, she'd been about to fetch the vacuum cleaner—

Her trouser pocket buzzed. It was a text from Ellis.

If you don't tell Portia off, I'll never forgive you.

Another buzz, another text, this time from

Portia. **I hate you your ruining my life.**

Phone or grounded? She replied to Portia, not even faintly amused that she was holding a conversation via text with someone who was only about ten feet away.

Ground me. I dont care was her daughter's reply.

This was followed by Portia's furious screech, 'I didn't want to go to that stupid party anyway, because I'VE GOT NOTHING TO WEAR!'

The music was turned up even louder, and she feared for her daughter's eardrums. 'I swear to God, I'm going to cut the plug on every single electronic device in this house,' she muttered. 'Except for the kettle.'

Kate tried not to stomp as she went downstairs to fetch the vacuum cleaner, but it was hard not to resort to her daughters' methods of showing displeasure. She not only felt like stomping, she felt like slamming doors and yelling, too.

'Oh, shut up,' she griped to Pepe, who continued to yap that annoying high-pitched bark of his.

The nans were still hard at it, arguing in the living room, and Kate tried to ignore them as she wrestled with the Dyson which had got caught up in some scarves and a coat that had been flung into the little cubby-hole under the stairs, instead of being hung on a hook.

'Whose fault is that? He never should have married her,' Helen shouted, and Kate paused.

Married who? Surely Helen wasn't talking about *her*?

Kate stopped her rummaging and took a step towards the living room to peer through the door. The two nans were in a face-off, barely three feet apart and scowling at each other. Beverley was standing up for the occasion and Helen had her hands on her hips.

She debated whether to butt in now and calm things down, or let the pair of them have their say once and for all. This row had been building for years. They may as well get it over with; it might even clear the air.

'You've never worked in your life, so you

don't know what you're talking about,' Beverley was saying.

'I have!'

'You did three months in a travel agency before you fell pregnant with your precious Brett. I hardly call that working. After that, Derrick kept you. You don't know what it's like to work and run a home.'

'Better that, than try and do it all and end up being a bad mother.'

'Are you calling me a bad mother?' Beverley sounded furious.

Kate winced as her mother waved a long and very pointy knitting needle in the air. That's it, she had to step in before things got out of hand.

'If the cap fits,' Helen retorted as Kate moved into the room. 'And your Kate is going the same way. As I said, Brett never should have married her.'

Helen had her back to Kate, but she realised something was wrong when Beverley's eyes widened. Slowly turning to face her daughter-in-law, Helen's face was ashen. She opened her mouth and closed it, then shook her head.

Kate felt the blood drain from her own face, and nausea roiled in her stomach.

Without a word, she whirled around and fled into the kitchen, Helen's call of, 'Kate, Kate, wait, I didn't mean...' following her.

The last thing she heard before she darted through the door, the still-yapping Pepe hot on her heels, was her mother saying, 'Now you've gone and done it, you nasty old bat.'

She didn't slam the door, and neither did she slam the one on the garage. Her movements were deliberate and measured, as she took one of the small suitcases off a shelf and let herself back into the house.

Her mother and mother-in-law were still going at it, but this time Kate hoped her mother *would* stick Helen with the knitting needle.

Quietly, and with the minimum of fuss, she slipped up two flights of stairs and into her bedroom, and threw an assortment of clothes and toiletries into the case, paying little attention to what she packed, except for her charger. She must have her charger; how else would anyone reach her—

Kate hesitated and took it back out again.

She needed her phone just in case of an emergency, like breaking down on the M5, or if she got lost, but once she arrived at her destination, she'd switch it off. And if she didn't have much battery, then she wouldn't be tempted to keep checking her phone.

Brixham, that's where she'd go, she decided. Someone had recently told her it was nice there. A bit of sea air and some time to breathe was what she needed. Peace, quiet, and no drama was what she craved. She didn't want Christmas either, and although she knew she couldn't avoid it, she suspected that it might be a bit less obvious at the seaside, with the sounds of the waves and the calling of gulls drowning out carols and cheerful Christmas tunes. There wouldn't be any squabbling children telling her they hated her, no mother-in-law saying Brett should never have married her, no husband ignoring her.

Let them get on with it and see how they liked it without her holding everything together. Either they'd realise just how much she did for the family, or they'd manage perfectly well without her. And right now, Kate, with tears pouring down her face and despair in her heart, didn't particularly care which one of the options they'd take.

But there was something else that niggled her as she threw the suitcase into the boot of her car and slid into the driver's seat – she had an awful feeling they'd only miss her when they came sniffing around the kitchen on Christmas morning and discovered there was no turkey in the oven.

CHAPTER 23

The only reason Kate pulled into the services was because she was desperate for the loo. She was thirsty, too. She hadn't had a drink since the cup of coffee in the abbey, and she'd shed so many tears on the drive to Exeter that she thought she might be slightly dehydrated.

As she sat in Costa Coffee, sipping her drink, she took out her phone and switched it on.

It was mid-afternoon, two and a half hours since she'd done a runner, and it seemed no one had missed her yet, although she did have several texts.

Beverley – U let Pepe out hes been outside for ages I think hes got a chill

Ellis – Can you wash that top, I'll wear it tonight

Beverley – If U R passing that nice sweet shop can U get me lickorish humbugs

Sam – Wots for dinner

Portia – I want a lift to the stables. Where are you?

Portia – Don't bother Annies mum will pick me up.

Portia – I'll need a lift back tho

Portia – Mum

Portia – Mum???

Portia – Answer me!!!!!

Portia – Ignore me then, I dont care

Helen – I'm going back to my own house. I'm clearly not wanted here.

Beverley – And some toffees plz btw shes packing as soon as shes gone ill move into the spare room n u can have yours back

Kate had to read this last one a couple of times before her mother's meaning was clear and, despite herself, she gave a tiny smile. Her mother could write beautiful letters, but when it came to texting…

Portia – **Forget it. I'll walk back and probably die of hypothermia or something**

Doris – **Hope you're feeling better, my lovely. Don't come into work until you are xxx**

It was amazing to think that the only person who had bothered to put a kiss on the end of their text was her manager – the woman who was having the wool pulled over her eyes by a definitely not-ill Kate.

Abruptly, she felt even worse than she'd done a few hours ago. How could she be so mean and deceitful to the only person in the world who appeared to care about her?

Sniffing, she dabbed her eyes with a soggy, crumpled tissue and checked Google maps. It was roughly one hour to Brixham, and it was already nearly dark. Examining the route carefully, she saw it was a more or less straight run into Paignton and then a short dab from there to Brixham itself.

She took another good, long look at the online map, made sure she knew where she was going, then she switched her phone off again, vowing to only turn it back on if she got lost. Although, she would send Brett a quick message to let him know she was safe and well as soon as she checked into a hotel.

That was a point, and one she hadn't considered when she jumped into her car – would there be any vacancies over the Christmas period? She guessed that some of the smaller places might not be accepting guests at this time of year.

Oh, well, she'd deal with that issue if it arose. For now, she was intent on reaching her destination without falling apart.

Feeling very fragile and extremely unloved, Kate got back into her car for the final stage of her journey.

It was late afternoon by the time she arrived in the little fishing village, which wasn't as little as she'd anticipated. The shops were still open, and light spilt from their windows and doors. The streets were strung with fairy lights, and individual homes glittered and sparkled with festive cheer. Kate had never felt less like Christmas in her life. It might all look very pretty, but it left her feeling a little sad and rather deflated.

At least there were plenty of small hotels and guest houses to choose from, she saw as she drove along the one-way system before finding a car park and pulling into it. She got out and stretched, easing the kinks out of her back, took the little suitcase out of the boot, and headed towards the nearest hotel, The Pirate Inn. There was a restaurant next to it called The Pirate's Parrot, and a gift shop on the other side named The Pirate's Gold. All three businesses appeared to be open, so she pulled her case towards them, hoping the inn would have a room free.

'Arr, we do, as it happens,' the man behind the small reception desk said when she asked if he had a room for tonight. Bizarrely, he was wearing a patch on his right eye which he kept lifting up to see what he was doing, and had an extremely realistic-looking stuffed parrot on his left shoulder.

'Pirate,' Kate said, bemused.

'Arr, that I am. Call me Dave, Cap'n Dave.'

Kate smiled weakly, thinking the joke a bit overdone, and wondering if perhaps she should try somewhere else.

'How long be you wantin' the room for?' he asked.

'Um...' She honestly didn't know. It was Wednesday today, Christmas Day was on Saturday. Did she really intend to stay here over Christmas?

Her mind flitted back to earlier, when her daughters had told her they hated her, and her mother-in-law had said Brett should never have married her. She thought that maybe she *would* stay that long. Christmas was hardly going to be celebrated in her house, not when every single family member, including the dog, seemed to be at war with everyone else. It was just another day – but one where people were forced to spend time together watching crap TV and eating too much. No wonder they argued and fought. It was like sticking a bunch of rats in a too-small cage and expecting them to live in peace and harmony.

Peace my backside, Kate thought. The only peace she was going to get was in Brixham, where no one knew her, no one made any demands on her, and she wasn't being yelled at or hated.

'Four days, possibly five,' she replied. 'If you're open to guests over Christmas, that is.'

'Aye, that we be,' the man said, lifting his eye patch up again, and peering at the screen on the desk in front of him. Kate watched as he laboriously entered her details on the computer. Every now and again, she glanced at the grey parrot on his shoulder. Its fake beady eyes watched her closely, and she could have sworn it moved.

Ugh, creepy. How he could stand having that thing (it was stuffed and not a plastic fake one) on his shoulder was beyond her. She thought it was quite gruesome.

He got her to sign in, took her card details, then lifted a key off a hook behind him. 'Follow me, and I'll show you to your grotto.'

Kate blinked. 'Excuse me?'

'Your grotto? Your room?'

'Oh, I see.'

'You're not into the pirate thing, I take it?' he asked, leading the way down a narrow corridor and up a steep flight of stairs.

The building looked to be at least a couple of centuries old, and the low ceilings and small, quaint windows reflected its age. Thankfully, there were no more stuffed parrots, that Kate could see, though there was the odd lobster pot dotted around, and lots of lengths of coiled rope with buoys on them.

'Not really,' she replied. 'I'm not sure I like pirates.'

He looked hurt. 'Here I am, dressed in my best pirate costume, with Polly on my shoulder and you're telling me you don't like pirates?'

'No, sorry.'

'You've not heard of the smugglers which

used to be rife around these parts?' He'd lost his pirate accent by now and was speaking to her in a normal voice. 'The Pirate Festival is a big attraction,' he added.

'Oh, is it on now?' That would explain a lot.

'No, it's held in May, but this is called The Pirate Inn, so...'

'Ah, I see.' It was a bit over-the-top, but if the pirate thing appealed to people and helped keep customers happy, who was she to complain?

'Here's your room,' he said, halting outside a sturdy wooden door and inserting an old-fashioned key into the lock.

The door swung open and he stood to the side to let her in.

As Kate sidled past him, she could have sworn that damned parrot was staring at her. Who in their right mind liked having dead creatures around them? It was downright morbid.

Oh, but the room was, in fact, lovely. It was decorated in pirate style (naturally) and the owners had done their best to make it look as though it was in a ship, with wooden panelling, a tapestry on the bed, and an old dressing table with a gorgeous enamel jug and bowl sitting on it. There was also an en suite, the door to it hidden among the panelling, and was surprisingly modern, apart from a wonderful, free-standing, roll-top bath with gold, fish-shaped taps.

'There's a TV in here,' he said, opening yet another panel to reveal a large, flat-screen telly, 'and this here, is your wardrobe. There are tea and coffee making facilities in this cupboard and a fridge. Breakfast is between seven-thirty and nine-thirty, and if you need anything, just shout—' He paused dramatically, and Kate glanced around at him, wondering why.

'Pieces of eight!' yelled the parrot, with a flap of its wings, and Kate let out a little shriek.

'That's... great,' she said, once she had regained her composure. 'Very clever.' Not.

'Polly is a clever girl. Most parrots are,' he said. 'She's an African Grey, and is about thirty years old. Say hello to our guest, Polly.'

'Hello, hello,' the parrot squawked.

Kate leaned against the dressing table, her heart thudding. 'I assumed it was stuffed,' she said. 'No wonder I kept thinking its eyes were following me.'

'She loves surprising people. It's her thing. I just let her get on with it. Right, is there anything else, or shall I leave you to settle in?'

'I'm good thanks,' Kate replied, her heart rate slowly returning to normal.

Dear God, what with silly poodles and parrots who liked to scare people, Kate's nerves were starting to unravel. And she simply didn't want to think about mothers, mothers-in-law, children, or husbands.

She did, however, need to tell Brett she was safe. It wouldn't be at all fair of her to let him worry, so she turned on her phone again and braced herself.

Ellis – **Don't bother with washing the top. Portia can have it. I've bought a nicer one.**

Portia – **You didnt clean up the mess in the**

bathroom and I cant find any loo roll. This house is a pigsty.

Beverley – **she chickened out the witch is staying**

Helen – **I'm not going anywhere until we can sit down like adults and discuss this properly.**

Sam – **Im itching. I think im allergic to Nannys dog**

Abruptly, Kate felt considerably better about absconding. No one had missed her, no one had even noticed she'd gone – apart from the inconvenience of no loo roll (there was plenty of toilet paper in the cupboard, but obviously no one had bothered to look) and shredded tissue paper all over the bathroom. That's all she was to them – a skivvy. Someone to sort out their problems, clean up their messes, make their lives easy and comfortable; and none of them, not even her own mother, had any consideration for Kate at all. And Brett hadn't been in touch all day, either.

She sent her husband a message, **Gone away for a few days. Need some space. I'm OK, I'll be** back after Xmas.

Kate hesitated, wondering if she should put a kiss at the end of the text, then decided against it. Lately, Brett's texts had a severe lack of kisses, or anything at all affectionate, so she pressed "send" before she could change her mind.

Then, in a right old funk, she answered the rest of her family.

To Portia – **Clean the bathroom yourself – you're perfectly capable. The toilet roll is kept where it's always kept. Open your eyes.**

To her mother – **Take Pepe for a much-needed walk and buy your own humbugs. The fresh air will do you both good.**

To her mother-in-law – **I really don't want to talk to you. Ever.** That text was a bit on the childish side, but it was the way she was feeling and after hearing what her mother-in-law believed, she honestly didn't want to talk to Helen for a good long time. Maybe never.

To Sam – **Ask your father to give you an antihistamine.**

There, that made her feel a little better.

And with that, she threw herself down on the bed and had a good, long cry.

CHAPTER 24

Brett was feeling much better about life when he stepped through the front door of his house. Unfortunately, the much-better feeling only lasted three seconds.

'Your wife has gone off in a huff,' his mother said, before he'd even managed to take his coat off. '*And,*' Helen paused dramatically, 'she told me she wanted me to leave.'

'She actually said that?'

'No, she didn't say—'

'There you go, then. I'm sure you've just caught hold of the wrong end of the stick.'

'She said she didn't want to talk to me ever again. I've got it in writing, so there's no denying it.' Helen's voice was triumphant, and she waved her phone at his face, inches from his nose.

Brett batted it gently away. 'Why would she say something like that?' he asked, scratching his head. Maybe he was allergic to Pepe, too; not that he thought his mother was allergic to the dog. Or maybe it did have fleas. Sam was certainly scratching a lot.

'I don't know, I'm sure,' Helen sniffed.

'Yes, you do, you liar,' Beverley shouted from the living room. 'I can hear you, you know.'

'Take no notice of her,' his mother hissed. 'She likes causing trouble. Oh, hello Beverley.'

Beverley had stepped through the living room door, one foot in the hall, and one foot still in the living room. 'You're the one who's causing trouble, going around telling people that other people should never have married them.'

'Eh?' Brett looked questioningly at Beverley.

His mother-in-law stared balefully back at him. 'She wanted me to fetch my own humbugs.

Said I should take Pepe for a walk.'

'Has he been out?' Brett asked, fearful of the dog's propensity to cock his leg and sprinkle anything that took his fancy.

'No, I was hoping Kate could do that. It's too dark for me, and I don't like the cold neither. It plays havoc with my rheumatism.'

'I thought you had arthritis,' Brett said.

'It's the same thing,' Beverley retorted.

Brett was fairly sure it wasn't, but he let it go. 'Where's Kate?' he asked again.

'I told you – she went off in a huff,' Helen said, pursing her lips together in disapproval. 'I don't know what she's planned for dinner, but I hope it's not fast food again.'

'You mean, she's not here?' Brett asked, looking around the hall as if he expected his wife to be hiding under the stairs ready to jump out at him.

'That's what I've been trying to tell you,' Helen grumbled. 'It's been pandemonium here this afternoon and Kate stormed off, leaving me to deal with it all.'

'What kind of pandemonium?' Brett asked.

'The kind where your mother tells your wife that you should never have married her,' Beverley said with a get-out-of-that-one look on her face.

'Mum...?'

'I never said that,' Helen said.

'You did. I heard you with my own two ears, and so did Kate. You need to apologise.' Beverley folded her arms and nodded, as if that was the final say on the subject.

'I don't have anything to apologise for,' Helen retorted. 'It's true, Brett never should have married her.'

'Mum...' Brett's voice was low and a bit growly. He really, really hoped Beverley was exaggerating and his mother hadn't said anything so nasty.

'Well, it is,' Helen said. 'You were going out with that nice little girl from over Droitwich way – she's a barrister now you know – and then you met Kate, and you didn't have eyes for anyone else.'

'What nice little girl from Droitwich?' Brett wanted to know.

'Her mother worked in the post office for years. Dark hair. Lovely skin.'

'Her mother?'

Helen sighed. 'No, the girl. I think her name was Darlene?'

'Oh, her?' Brett barked out a laugh. 'She wasn't my girlfriend.'

'What was she, then?' Helen's brows had shot up to her hairline.

'Just a friend who happened to be a girl.'

'But…but…you said you were going out with her. You even brought her home once.' His mother's eyebrows rose even further.

Brett shook his head. 'Have you been thinking that I dumped Darlene Wilberforce for Kate, all this time?'

His mother's expression turned sheepish. 'She's done extremely well for herself,' Helen said. 'Her mother's always telling me how well she's doing.'

'She had an affair with a solicitor,' Brett said,

273

'and the last I heard, her husband left her because of it.'

'Well, I never!' Helen's indignation verged on the comical. 'Her mother never told me that!'

'She wouldn't, would she?' Beverley piped up. 'That's not the sort of thing you brag about. At least my Kate has never been unfaithful.'

'That we know about,' Helen muttered.

'Mum. Stop it. If this is the way you behaved, no wonder Kate doesn't want to speak to you. If you don't apologise to her, I'll send you home.'

Helen's eyes filled with tears.

'Don't bother turning on the waterworks because no one's interested,' Beverley said. 'No one likes a cry baby.'

Helen's tears dried up quicker than a raindrop in a desert. 'No one likes a miserable cow, either. You've done nothing but moan about how you hate Christmas ever since you got here.'

'You're a fine one to talk! All you've done is carp and snipe. Nothing is ever good enough for you, is it? You've got to stick your beak in.'

'At least I try to help. All you do, is sit on your

274

backside all day and watch TV.'

'STOP IT!!!' Brett yelled.

The two women fell silent and stared at Brett, their mouths open, their eyes wide.

'Right, now that I've got your attention, can someone please tell me where my wife is?'

The front door slammed open, ricocheting on its hinges. 'Yeah, that's what I'd like to know, too,' Portia exclaimed. 'She said she'd pick me up from the stables. I had to cadge a lift off someone.'

'At what time?' Brett asked, glancing into the living room and taking a quick look at the clock on the wall.

'I dunno, she didn't say.' Portia shrugged, pushing past her father to get to the stairs.

'You didn't ask her?'

'I told her I needed a lift back.'

'But you didn't arrange a time?'

Portia shrugged again, and Brett took that as a "no". Phew, she'd had him worried for a minute. He thought Kate might have had an accident or something…

He slapped a hand to his head. She'd probably tried to call or message him, but he'd turned his phone onto silent and hadn't looked at it since.

Checking it for messages, he saw there were twenty-three, twenty-two of them from work. The other one was from Kate. **Gone away for a few days. Need some space. I'm OK, I'll be back after Xmas.**

He read it, then he read it again.

'She's gone,' he said in a quiet voice.

'Who's gone?' Helen wanted to know.

'Kate.'

'Yes, I know. I told you she's gone out. She left me to deal with the mess in the bathroom.'

'What mess?' Brett asked absently, still staring at his phone.

'The mess Beverley's dog made.'

'It wasn't Pepe's fault. He was just playing,' Beverley retorted hotly. 'Dogs will be dogs.'

'Gone?' Brett repeated. 'Gone where?'

'That's what I'd like to know. These children need a proper meal, and I'll be damned if I'm cooking it, not after last night.' Helen glared at Beverley. 'Your blasted dog ruined that, too.'

'It wasn't his fault. Someone moved a chair and he jumped up on it.'

'It's never your fault, is it? It's—'

'She's gone!' Brett shouted, although not as loud as a few minutes ago, and once again the nans ceased their bickering for a moment.

'Yes, Brett, you keep saying,' his mother sniffed, 'but I'm sure she won't have gone far.'

Brett marched into the kitchen for a bit of privacy and called his wife's number.

It went straight to answerphone, so he left a voice message. 'What do you mean, you've gone away for a few days? Stop being silly and come back home. My mother said you stormed off in a huff.'

He still didn't believe it. Not really. Kate was winding him up, making them worry a bit as a punishment. Wandering back into the hall where the two nans were still hovering, he opened his mouth to say he'd left Kate a message when a bloodcurdling scream made everyone jump.

It came from upstairs.

The hairs on the back of his neck stood on end, and a shiver of absolute dread travelled down his spine.

'Mum! Mum!' Portia cried, her voice breaking on a sob.

Dear God!

Brett raced up the stairs, taking them two at a time, and burst into Portia's room expecting to see...

He wasn't sure what he'd been expecting to see, but the awful thought that it might involve blood or a body stayed with him for a moment, until he'd calmed enough to focus on what Portia was holding in her trembling hands and staring at, with a horrified expression on her face.

One solitary Doc Marten boot.

The pink, red, and grey skull pattern which adorned the side of the boot wasn't quite as pristine and sharp as Brett remembered it being when Portia had proudly shown them off to him a couple of weeks ago. He remembered thinking at the time, that they were rather attractive in a morbid kind of way. He could also remember thinking that Portia had only waved them under his nose to get a reaction from him, and not because she expected him to approve her fashion sense. Wisely, he'd refrained from saying much at all, not wanting to be dragged into an argument over whether such boots were suitable attire for a fourteen-year-old girl to wear to school, which they weren't, obviously, as Portia had found out when she'd received a detention.

Now, though, they were looking decidedly chewed.

'Look what that effing dog has done to my Doc Martens,' Portia screamed, taking a step forward and waving the solitary boot in Brett's face.

Brett took a step back and bumped into his mother, who had raced up the stairs behind him and was now panting in his ear.

'Brett, are you going to let her get away with that kind of language?' Helen demanded.

'Butt out, Nana, this is nothing to do with you,' Portia snarled.

Brett peered behind his mother, looking for Beverley, but she was nowhere to be seen. Hopefully, she was rounding up that poodle of hers and putting it someplace where it couldn't do any more damage.

'OK,' Brett said, as an opening gambit, trying to think. Should he tackle his daughter's foul mouth first, then take her to task over the way she'd spoken to Helen, or should he let it slide for the moment, and concentrate on what had caused her outburst in the first place.

Damn her, but Kate should be dealing with this. She was so much better at handling the drama than he was – she was always able to smooth things over and calm everyone down.

He tried her number again, hissing, 'Kate, answer your phone,' when it went to voicemail yet again.

Christ, he hadn't even managed to change out of his work clothes yet, and the house was already in an uproar.

'We'll get you another pair,' Brett tried to say but was interrupted by a furious Portia who yelled, 'You can get me another pair in the next half hour, can you?'

'Why in the next half hour?' he wanted to know.

'Because I'm supposed to be going to Taylor's party. Duh!' Portia sneered.

Brett didn't help the situation by saying, 'Didn't your mother say you were grounded?'

Portia's scream of fury set Brett's teeth on edge. 'I hate you. All of you. I wish I was old enough to move out! I wish I was dead!' she shrieked, then threw herself on her bed and sobbed loudly.

Brett thought it best to retreat and regroup. His daughter might be more amenable to reason when she'd calmed down a bit.

He turned around and pushed Helen away from the door, closing it softly behind him, and winced when a loud thud indicated that Portia might well have thrown her ruined boot at the door.

'Well I never,' his mother said with a huff. 'I've never seen such a display of temper, bad manners, and sheer rudeness from a child.'

Brett was tempted to tell her to hang around for a while – this was nothing compared to some of the meltdowns his kids were capable of, but before he'd opened his mouth a little voice floated up the stairs.

It was Beverley. 'See, I told you Christmas was shite. Now, do you believe me?'

Brett honestly thought the evening couldn't get any worse. And it mightn't have, if Pepe hadn't chosen that very moment to sidle across the landing and decide to cock his leg and water Brett's trousers. The fact that they were turn-ups made the whole thing just that tiny bit worse...

CHAPTER 25

Hunger drove Kate from her room an hour or so later. She'd eaten nothing since the piece of cake at the abbey and now she was starving, and there was no better thing to have at the seaside than fish and chips, no matter what time of year it was.

She splashed some water on her face, noting with dismay her blotchy skin and the bags under her eyes. Thinking of bags made her remember her suitcase, sitting where she'd left it by the door, and she went back into the bedroom and lifted it onto the bed. She supposed she'd better unpack, considering she intended to stay for a few days, but when she opened the lid she was bewildered to discover exactly what it was she'd brought with her: three T-shirts, a summer skirt, pyjama bottoms (no top), her toothbrush but no toothpaste, two pairs of knickers, a bright red bra, a pair of slippers, one Wellington boot, and the hairdryer.

Dear God, what had she been thinking? Clearly, she hadn't been thinking at all, too busy being shocked and hurt by Helen's words.

She glanced at the clock on the bedside table. It was too late to go shopping now, so she'd have to go out this evening in what she was already wearing, but tomorrow she'd see what the local stores had to offer in the way of fashion. At least she could wear the pyjama bottoms and one of the T-shirts to bed, and her slippers might come in handy. The bra was festive, even if no one would see it and she was suffering from a serious lack of the Christmas spirit.

At least she had enough underwear for a couple of days, even if she had to rinse a pair of knickers out in the sink.

Wrapping up warmly in her coat, hat, and scarf, she left her phone on the bed, grabbed her handbag and the hotel key and went in search of supper.

Brixham was more of a small town than the little fishing village she'd been expecting. As she wandered towards the harbour, she saw loads of shops (selling mostly tourist stuff), but there were a couple of places where she should be able to find a pair of jeans and some socks. She was in dire need of socks, only having brought with her the pair which were currently on her feet.

There were plenty of restaurants too, but the image of golden, battered fish and salty, vinegary chips drove her on until she reached the harbour itself. It was difficult to tell in the dark, but it looked pretty enough. Many of the boats had Christmas lights strung on them and together with the official decorations on the lamp posts and draped overhead, the whole harbour twinkled, the water reflecting the lights like stars shining in its depths. The little streets were thronging with people off out for some liquid festive cheer, and the aromas of cooking competed with the smell of the sea. She'd never been to the seaside at Christmas time before and she felt slightly disorientated.

'Isn't it odd—' she started to say, before she realised Brett wasn't by her side, and intense loneliness swept over her.

What was the point of being in this cute little village if she had no one to share it with, and for a moment she was tempted to jump in the car and high-tail it back up the motorway.

"He never should have married her."

Helen's words slipped, unbidden, into her mind, stopping Kate in her tracks. What if her mother-in-law was right? What if she was totally wrong for Brett? It might explain why, for the past few years, her husband seemed to view her as little more than part of the fixtures and fittings.

Of course, she didn't expect harps and flowers. She didn't expect her heart to leap out of her chest whenever he phoned. She didn't expect to go weak at the knees at the sight of him. They'd been married for over twenty years, for goodness sake! She knew that the first flush of love couldn't possibly last and that the can't-keep-their-hands-off-each-other stage had to wear off. But she had thought their love had matured and developed into something less transient and more mature.

Maybe she was wrong. Maybe Brett didn't feel the same way and was only staying because of the children.

Surely not. She'd have noticed it. OK, they didn't make love as often as they used to (who did?), because life got in the way. Both of them were exhausted by bedtime, and the one time they'd tried slipping off to their bedroom on a Sunday afternoon when all three kids were out, they'd been continually interrupted by first her phone ringing, then Brett's, then the house phone as Ellis had wanted a lift back from town because she'd fallen out with her friend and she wasn't prepared to wait another second longer to go home.

They'd tried again, the following week, but this time it had been Sam who'd had the emergency in the form of forgotten football boots. It hadn't been Sam who had called, it had been the coach. Four times.

After that, they'd given up on afternoon loving, and kept their romantic encounters to when the kids had gone to bed. It worked for a while, but as Ellis had become older, so her bedtime had grown later, until neither Kate nor Brett could keep their eyes open. Unless, Ellis was out, that was, because Kate was unable to fall asleep until she knew their daughter was safely back in the nest. Unfortunately, it also meant she was too strung out to concentrate on lovemaking, because she was either listening for Ellis's key in the lock, or she was bracing herself for a phone call.

God help it when Ellis passed her driving test and bought her first car – Kate didn't think she'd ever sleep again.

Food, that's what she needed to lift her mood, and the tantalising aroma of a fish and chip shop drew her in.

Ooh, lovely, it was one of those places where you could eat inside, and she opted to do exactly that. She would have preferred to have eaten them directly from their paper wrapping rather than off a plate, but it was freezing outside and wonderfully warm inside, so she slid into a booth and waited for her meal.

This was distinctly surreal, she thought, as she tucked into her steaming plate of crisply battered fish and scrummy chips because, for the first time in as long as she could remember, she didn't have a timetable. She could take as long as she wanted over her meal and the thought of eating it in silence (apart from the staff, the other customers, and the obligatory Christmas songs, which she could ignore) without anyone nagging her was rather weird.

If she was honest, she felt a little lost. As she looked around the chip shop or out of the window, everyone seemed to have someone else, or were hurrying on their way to somewhere else. She was like a single, motionless snowflake in the middle of a swirling blizzard. It was the strangest feeling, and she didn't know what to do with herself.

Maybe she'd buy a book or two; she couldn't remember when she'd last read a decent novel. Or any novel, come to that. There were still a couple of half-read paperbacks lying around the house, a left-over from the last time she'd tried to find some time and space for herself in her busy life. But each time she'd picked up one of them, she'd either been interrupted or had been so tired she'd fallen asleep with it in her hands.

She'd look for a bookshop tomorrow, she vowed. If it had been the summer, she could have spent the day on the beach, but the most she could hope for in the depths of winter was a brisk walk followed by a hot chocolate and a mince pie. So, she'd either be sitting on her own in a café or a restaurant and staring at other people's happiness, or she'd be curled up in the armchair in her room wondering whether she should turn her phone on and deal with the fall-out.

A book was by far the better option.

She ordered a cup of tea to wash down her meal (wishing it was a large glass of red wine), and watched the world go by for the next twenty minutes. She found it difficult to shake the feeling that she should be picking one of the kids up, or arranging the insurance on Brett's car, or writing a to-do list of outstanding Christmassy things. She was always busy, never had a minute to herself, but now that she had at least three whole days full of lovely minutes ahead of her, she had no idea what to do with them.

Guilt threatened to overwhelm her, and she forced it away by getting to her feet and going for a quick walk to the nearest pub.

A drink or three would take the edge off it, and if that didn't work, she'd have a few more.

CHAPTER 26

Kate hadn't walked into a pub on her own in maybe... never? Or if she had, she'd known there'd be a bunch of friends already there, or she was meeting Brett (in their early days). Tonight, she was totally and utterly on her own, which was another odd feeling. Not unpleasant, just odd, as though she was watching someone else stroll casually into The Mason's Arms and order a pink gin and grapefruit juice. That other person took her drink and found a corner table where she could people watch, yet not be too visible herself.

Kate thought she might be having some kind of out-of-body experience, while still being very much awake and compos mentis.

She was alone, but she didn't feel lonely – OK, maybe she did, just a little bit, because the only other person who appeared to be on his own was a very elderly gentleman in a flat cap who was nodding by the log burner. Everyone else had someone to talk to or ignore. A couple seated at a table nearer the bar were very definitely ignoring each other and were making a pretty good job of it. But at least they weren't sitting on their own.

She took a long swallow of her drink, grimacing slightly at the unaccustomed but not unpleasant bitterness. It was an acquired taste, she decided, finishing it off and enjoying the little buzzing tingle the alcohol gave her. She'd have one more, then go back to the hotel – where she'd be even more alone in her gorgeous room than she was now. At least there were people to watch and listen to here, even though she felt terribly self-conscious. If she was watching herself, she mused, she'd probably think she'd been stood up.

The pub was warm and cosy (except when the door opened and a blast of biting sea air swept in), and if she wasn't in such a funk, she'd have to acknowledge that the atmosphere was lovely and festive. With the crackle of logs burning merrily on the fire, the scent of wood smoke and beer (a surprisingly aromatic combination), the glow from the various lamps dotted around the lounge contrasting with the tiny sparkling fairy lights strung behind the bar and around the little tree, it certainly looked very Christmassy. The barman wore a jumper with a reindeer on it and some wobbly antlers on his head, and his colleague, who also served drinks and collected the glasses, sported an elf outfit, which suited her sweet heart-shaped face and spiky hair.

Feeling slightly more mellow and not quite as emotional, Kate ordered a third drink. She could get quite addicted to this, she thought, trying to remember the last time she and Brett had gone out together just the two of them, and failing. This time of year tended to be Christmas parties (his company always held one, but they hadn't seemed to have done so this year, she realised – or if they had, Brett hadn't mentioned it), or meeting friends for a boozy meal (they hadn't done that this year, either).

Even before Christmas, Kate and Brett hadn't been out together for ages. Having a quick meal in a gastro-pub just outside Birmingham while they waited to pick Ellis up from the NEC where she'd gone to see some band play, didn't count. They'd been hungry and they'd had a couple of hours to kill – which was hardly the same as having a date night.

Date night? Huh! They didn't do such things; and maybe that was part of the problem. They'd stopped seeing each other as lovers a long time ago. Now they were just an old married couple hurtling towards empty nests and tartan slippers. How tragic.

Kate was quite scared to follow those depressing thoughts – when Sam eventually left home, what if she and Brett discovered they had nothing in common, that the only thing holding their marriage together had been the joint task of raising the children? Not that Brett had taken a very active role in that side of things, leaving most of the parenting to her. In fact, he left most of everything to her. OK, he had a responsible job and he earned good money, but that didn't excuse his lack of interest in the kids, or in her.

Oh, bugger, now she was feeling maudlin, and rather cross again. It wasn't a good mixture on top of three large pink gins. Or maybe her mood was *because* of those gins.

Time to head back to the hotel, before she was tempted to have another drink and make a fool of herself by dancing on the table or trying to snog the old gentleman in the corner – Hark the Herald Angels Sing was hardly a tune to bop about to, and the elderly man would probably have a heart attack if she was to dive on him and demand a cuddle.

Cuddles, that's what she missed the most, she decided as she made her slightly wobbly way out of the pub and into the street. There was a time when she was overrun with cuddles, the kids trying to outdo each other for hugs and kisses, each of them wanting as much of her love and attention as she could give. Brett, too, used to cuddle her. It might have only been when they were in bed and too exhausted to do anything except spoon (she was always little spoon), but at least it was human contact with the man she loved.

Kate put out a hand to steady herself, feeling the cold, hard stone of the pub's wall against her palm.

Did she still love him?

The very fact that she asked herself the question, was extremely telling indeed.

Oh dear, had she fallen out of love with him, and if so, when?

She rooted around in her heart, tears stinging at the back of her eyes, as she pondered the question.

No, she decided, trying to imagine her life without him in it; she hadn't fallen out of love with him. She did love him, more than he would ever know. But she wasn't *in love* with him, and there was a big difference between the two. Was it even possible to stay in love with a person you'd been with for twenty years?

There she was, coming full circle to the conversation she'd had with herself earlier, and she still didn't have an answer. Perhaps she never would.

She needed more alcohol. Halfway between being drunk and sober, she was currently neither one thing nor the other, but somewhere in the middle. She would either have an early night or buy a bottle of wine from the off-licence she'd seen earlier on her way to the harbour.

The wine won.

CHAPTER 27

Brett changed out of his soiled trousers and deposited them gingerly in the laundry basket, wrinkling his nose in disgust. He'd have to tackle Beverley about her dog in a minute; it wasn't hygienic having the pooch widdling wherever and whenever it felt like it. Where the bloody hell was Kate? She should be here dealing with this.

He'd tried calling her again, but her phone went straight to voicemail. Again.

Brett could hear Portia still howling, wailing down the phone to one of her friends, her voice loud and strident even with two closed doors between him and her. It wasn't right what Pepe had done, but neither had it been right for Portia to have been so rude. He could understand that she was upset – he would have been too, if it had happened to him – but her reaction had been way over the top.

'Portia?' Brett made his way onto the landing and tapped on her bedroom door. Gone were the days when he used to walk straight in. His daughter was too old for that, but when she failed to answer him, he knocked a little louder.

'What?' she shouted.

The aggression and disrespect in her voice irked him. This little madam was getting too big for her boots, even if they were funky, skull-daubed Doc Martens.

He pushed the door open and walked in.

'Do you mind? I might have been undressing.' Her eyes were narrowed, and her face had that hard, pouty, defiant look he detested. She was such a pretty girl when she wasn't wearing her obnoxious face.

He saw the phone in her hand, the screen

illuminated, and guessed she was still on the phone.

'I'm sorry Pepe chewed your favourite boots,' he began, but his daughter didn't let him finish.

'What are you going to do about it? I want a new pair. Right now.'

'Right now isn't going to happen and you know it. Stop being so childish.'

'You owe me, so I want to go to Taylor's party. It's the least you can do, and I still want a new pair of boots.'

Brett guessed she was playing up to the audience on the other end of the phone, and his ire developed into downright annoyance. How dare she speak to him like that, and in earshot of her friend, too?

'You might want to say goodbye to whoever's on the other end,' he said mildly, nodding his head at the mobile.

'Just say what you're going to say and get out of my room,' Portia retorted.

'OK, you asked for it.' He took a deep breath. 'You're a spoilt brat with an attitude no one likes.

I – *we*, your mother and I – are fed up of it. She's already told you that you are grounded because you can't respect your sister's things; and, by the way, you don't like it when the shoe is on the other foot, do you? Or should I say, boot? Now you know what it feels like to have someone take something of yours and damage it. The dog didn't do it on purpose, although he should have been trained not to chew things, but that's another matter. You, on the other hand, knew it was wrong to borrow Ellis's top without asking her, and when you got it dirty you didn't even apologise. Do you want me to continue with your friend listening, or would you prefer we did this in private?'

Portia, still with a defiant and not-at-all-apologetic expression, hurriedly muttered into the phone that she'd call her friend back. 'I can't believe you just embarrassed me like that—' she began, but Brett jumped in before she could continue.

'I *was* going to replace those boots, he said, 'but I'm not going to now, and yes, before you say it, I know it's not fair. But you need to learn a lesson, my girl. You can't carry on being horrid, rude, and obnoxious, and not have to face any consequences.'

'Why do you care? You've never bothered before.'

She was right, Brett admitted silently; he hadn't. It had been so much easier to bury his head in the paper, the footie, a documentary on TV, than to become embroiled in his daughters' many dramas and tantrums. He had a moment of absolute clarity when he realised that his non-interaction must have been viewed by his children as tacit agreement with them. Hardly ever had he backed Kate up. Maybe once or twice he'd managed a weak and desultory "Don't speak to your mother like that", or something equally as bland, but he'd never shown any solidarity with his wife.

'I'm bothering now,' was his reply, and Portia scowled.

'Why now? You could wait until after Taylor's party,' she snapped. 'I want to go to that.'

'Tough, you're not. And you're not going to the stables or anywhere else, either.'

'That's so not fair.' Portia threw her phone on the bed and got to her feet. 'You can't stop me.'

'I think you'll find I can,' he replied, keeping his tone even.

'I'll report you to the RSPCA.'

'I wouldn't go that far,' Brett said, 'although you do behave like a little beast. Don't you mean Childline?'

He daughter's scorn was palpable. 'I know what I mean. You're making me be cruel to Silver and Stanley. I have to muck them out, and check they've got fresh water, and groom them. You're being cruel.'

Brett bit back a smile, his anger turning into amusement. 'Those horses don't belong to you; they belong to the stables, and Cheryl will no doubt make sure they're well cared for. She did it before you started riding, and she'll continue to do it if you're not there.'

'She's relying on me to muck them out on Christmas Eve and Christmas Day!' Portia cried.

'Just you?'

Portia nodded, a spark of hope in her eyes. 'Just me. No one else volunteered.'

'I bet they didn't,' Brett said. 'Who did you think is going to take you there, hang around while you do what you need to do, then drive you back?'

Portia became wary. 'Mum…?' The word was uttered with a hint of uncertainty.

'She'll have enough to do with preparing Christmas lunch.'

'Can't she do that the night before?' Portia suggested.

Brett was taken aback by his middle child's sheer selfishness. It was also a little disconcerting to see that Portia was prepared to let her mother be run ragged, but she didn't even consider asking him.

That's because you never do any of the taking or picking up, a little voice in his head said. It was right – he didn't. But to be fair, that was usually because he was in work, and so couldn't even if he'd wanted to.

'What about whether your mother wants to spend her Christmas Eve chopping vegetables, and sticking her hand up turkey's bottoms? Have you thought about that?' he asked her.

'Ew. Gross.'

'Here's an idea – how about if *you* helped her? After all, you're the one who wants to go to the stables. Or, I've got another suggestion – you tell Cheryl that she'll have to find someone else to muck out the horses, because your mother might like to have a glass of something stronger than lemonade while she's slaving over a hot stove.'

'Why can't *you* help her instead?' Portia muttered, undeterred. 'You don't do anything, ever. If you gave her a hand, she'd—'

'What? Have more time to run around after you?'

Portia had the grace to look sheepish.

'We're all guilty of being selfish,' Brett said, ignoring Portia's sotto voce comment of "Too right, you are", and ploughing on. 'It's got to change, and it stops right now. Today. You need to apologise to your grandmothers – both of them – and you also need to blow up that air bed and put it back in Ellis's room, because that's where you'll be sleeping until the nans go home.'

'It's not fair! I don't want to sleep in Ellis's room. She's mean, and she's on the phone to her boyfriend half the night. You ought to hear her. It's enough to make you feel sick.'

'You can always sleep in the living room, or we can have the air bed in our room,' Brett suggested.

'And listen to you snore? No thanks.'

'Portia, it's up to you. I don't care which room in the house you sleep in, as long as it's not your own.'

'It's not fair,' his daughter repeated.

Christ, he was sick of hearing that phrase. 'Life isn't.'

'What if I refuse?'

'Do you honestly want to go down that path?' Brett asked. 'You might want to have a think about that before you answer.'

'Mum will back me up. She doesn't want to

upset Nanny. What does Mum have to say about you making Nanny sleep in my room when she likes sleeping in the attic?' Portia wanted to know. She saw his expression. 'Mum doesn't know, does she? She won't be happy.' Portia practically crowed.

'She's not here, so it doesn't matter,' Brett said, a sudden wrench twisting his heart. Where the hell was she, and what was she playing at?

'When will she be back?'

'I don't know.' It had better be soon, the kids needed to be fed. So did the nans, and he, himself, was getting a bit peckish, too.

'Where is she?' Portia demanded.

'I don't know.' He could see his vague panic reflected in his daughter's eyes.

Then Portia seemed to gather herself, her usual belligerence draped around her once more like a favourite scarf. 'She won't have gone far,' she said confidently. 'She never does.'

'Right,' he said. 'I'm going to find the laptop. While I'm doing that, you can have a serious think about your behaviour.'

Brett caught a glimpse of his daughter in her bedroom mirror sticking her tongue out at him but he chose to ignore it.

Instead, he had yet another go at calling his wife, and ended up leaving yet another message. 'Kate, where the bloody hell are you? You do realise the kids haven't had their dinner? Kate, answer your phone. Kate?'

This wasn't funny anymore!

CHAPTER 28

Brett was already exhausted and he'd only been home for a half an hour. Bloody hell – being in work was a darned sight easier than dealing with the two nans and Portia, and he hadn't had to tackle Ellis yet. At least Sam was behaving himself; as far as Brett could tell, because the child hadn't emerged from his room yet.

His stomach rumbled loudly, and he briefly debated whether to venture into the kitchen and see what was in the fridge, but he decided against it. He quite fancied Indian food. A plate of chicken passander would go down a treat.

Without consulting either his mother or Kate's, he sloped off into the kitchen, sidling around Pepe who was sprawled on the tiles with his tongue sticking out of the side of his mouth, and reached for the pile of menus. If Kate wasn't here to cook, then it would have to be a takeaway for dinner.

He ordered their usual, plus an extra dish or two for the nans. He didn't bother asking them what they wanted. Just seeing their faces while they picked at the pizza last night, had been enough. No, he decided, if they were hungry, they could either eat some curry and rice or cook themselves something.

He plodded downstairs, ready to face the next task. Really, Kate should be sorting this out – Beverley was her mother, after all. He had enough to do what with keeping his own mum happy. What he was about to say would probably bring a smile to his mum's face; Beverley, on the other hand, wouldn't be as pleased.

'What's for dinner?' Beverley asked, as soon

as he entered the room.

'I've ordered Indian,' he said and watched the pair of them wrinkle their noses.

'It's hardly healthy, all these takeaways,' his mother said.

Beverley shuddered. 'I don't like that curry stuff. It's too spicy.'

'Just try some,' he suggested.

'It's not the spice that bothers me, it's all the fat and salt,' Helen said. 'It can't be good for growing children. Anyway, I think takeaways are the height of laziness.'

Brett did a double take. He loved his mother dearly, but she could be so hypocritical at times. There speaks the woman who goes out to lunch with her cronies several times a week. But of course, she didn't consider herself to be lazy at all – it was purely so she could enjoy the company. Or so she said. Brett, for one, didn't believe it; his mother couldn't be bothered to cook for just herself, although she always used to cook when he still lived at home. She was pretty good at it, too, but she hadn't particularly enjoyed cooking. He suspected the only reason she'd cooked the unfortunate leg of lamb last night, was to make a point, and to possibly annoy Kate.

As for Beverley, she'd eat the food and enjoy moaning about it. It would give her something to grizzle about for the next few hours.

'Not very festive, is it?' his mother-in-law said.

'That should suit you, then; I didn't think you liked anything festive.' He didn't "think", he "knew" she didn't, because she kept telling him and anyone else who'd listen. It was like having your own personal Scrooge sitting in your living room. No wonder all the joy and magic seemed to have been sucked out of Christmas this year.

Brett cleared his throat. 'Portia is sleeping in Ellis's room tonight,' he announced, 'so you, Beverley, can have her bed.'

There was a stunned silence for a second, then Beverley's mouth pursed up like a cat's bottom, while his mother's mouth turned into a Cheshire Cat's grin. If his mother smiled any wider, Brett thought uncharitably, then her face was in danger of turning itself inside out.

Kate's mother rallied swiftly. 'What about my arthritis?' she asked. 'It'll play up something terrible if I have to sleep in Portia's room.'

'It's either that, or you sleep on the inflatable mattress down here,' Brett said, firmly.

Beverley thought for a moment. 'You and Kate could always have Portia's bed, and I can stay where I am. It's only for a couple more nights.'

'Five, to be exact, unless you're planning on travelling back on Boxing Day,' he pointed out.

Beverley's eyes widened.

'I didn't think so. It's quite unfair to expect Kate and I to squash into a small double bed, when there's a perfectly good super-king-size one in our bedroom. So, for this visit, you can have Portia's room. For subsequent visits, if you both plan on being here at the same time and are going to stay longer than a night or so, you can share a room. After Christmas, I'll buy two single beds, which should fit in the spare room nicely.'

There, he thought, let them put that in their pipes and smoke it. He'd gone past the point of caring.

'I'd like to go home,' his mother announced. 'I don't want to stay where I'm not wanted, but my car won't start.

Beverley snorted. 'How convenient,' she muttered, and earned herself a scathing look from Helen.

Aren't families great, he thought, with a sigh, wondering if this was normal. All of them – him, Kate, the kids and the two grandmothers – hadn't ever been in the same place at the same time, as far as he could remember. If this was how it was going to be going forward... He shuddered.

While he waited for their takeaway to arrive, Brett called Portia from her bedroom, and he dropped into an armchair, hearing his youngest daughter thunder down the stairs.

She sidled in, looking sullen.

Brett raised his eyebrows, and she replaced her expression with a slightly less sullen one.

'When's Mum back?' she asked.

Brett could read her like a book. 'Not soon enough to save you from this,' he said. 'Now, what do you have to say to your grandmothers.'

'Sorry?'

'Are you asking me or telling them?'

'Telling them,' she said.

'Then you could at least sound as though you mean it,' he said.

Both Helen and Beverley were sitting side by side on the sofa. Beverley looked quite miserable, but then she often did, so it was difficult to tell what she was thinking. His mother looked stern and rather forbidding.

'I'm sorry,' Portia said again, but this time she sounded more sincere. 'Dad says I made you feel unwelcome,' she said to Beverley. 'I didn't mean to.'

'And...?' Brett prompted.

Portia looked at Helen. 'I'm sorry I was rude.'

'Apology accepted,' Helen said, although she looked as though she hadn't quite forgiven her granddaughter.

'Can I go now?' Portia asked her father in a small voice.

'You may. Dinner will be here in about twenty minutes.'

His daughter hesitated. 'When *will* Mum be back? You never said.'

Brett flinched. He hoped she'd be back later this evening, despite her text. But what if she wasn't? And at what point did he tell the children?

'I'm not sure,' he said.

'Where is she?'

'She's popped out for a bit.'

'How long is a bit?'

Portia was certainly persistent, Brett thought. 'I'm not sure,' he hedged.

'Is she at a party, or something? She didn't say she was going out? If she's gone out with Patty or Freda, I bet she'll come home tipsy, like she did the last time.' Portia giggled. 'She's funny when she's had too much to drink.' Her expression sobered. 'She *is* going to work tomorrow, though, isn't she? I mean, she won't have too much of a hangover.'

Ah, so that was it – Portia wanted to make sure both her mother and her father were out of the house for the day. No supervision (the nans didn't count as far as Portia was concerned), meant not being grounded – at least, not until he or Kate came home.

'I expect she will,' he replied mildly, his insides churning as he considered the possibility that she mightn't.

Brett saw the gleam of delight in his daughter's expression, and knew his assessment was correct. 'I won't be, though,' he added.

'You what?' Portia blinked.

'I don't have work tomorrow.' He did, but he intended to have another sick day, and another, right up until Christmas. After that, he intended to be working somewhere else entirely.

'Bummer,' she muttered, slinking back upstairs.

'I'll call you when the Indian arrives,' he shouted after her. 'And tell Sam to finish his game because dinner will be here soon.'

Brett didn't expect a reply from his daughter, so he wasn't disappointed. But he did expect a reply of some sort from his wife.

But when he checked, there was nothing from her whatsoever.

This was starting to become irritating. He didn't appreciate having to cope with three kids, two mothers, and a dog, on his own. She was annoyed, he appreciated that, but going off alone to sulk wasn't the answer.

He tried her again and was forced to leave another voice message. 'Why the hell don't you answer your phone?'

He'd phone her again after they'd eaten, but Brett and Portia were the only ones who seemed to have any appetite. Sam – so unlike him – was moving most of his food around his plate. Brett examined him out of the corner of his eye, wondering what could be wrong with the boy.

'You OK, son?'

Sam shrugged.

'It's your favourite, chicken passander.'

Another shrug.

'Don't you feel well?'

Sam stared at the table. 'Mum said for you to give me an antihismatine.'

'A what?'

'Antihismanine?'

'Oh, you mean an antihistamine? Why?'

'I think I'll allergic to Nanny's dog.'

'Do you know what, Sam?' Helen piped up, pushing her food around her plate, and wrinkling her nose. 'I'm allergic to it, too.'

'Does he make you scratch, Nana?'

'Um, not really.'

'I've got spots, too.' Sam announced.

Oh, bless him. He did have a couple on his forehead, Brett noticed. It looked like teenage acne was going to be a thing for Sam. Both the girls had gotten off lightly, with only Portia having the odd break out now and again. He knew, because she was very vocal about it, crying that she looked like a leper (not that Portia could possibly know what a leper looked like), and that she usually tried to refuse to go to school until the tiny spot had gone.

Sam, it seemed, was going to have much more of a problem.

It didn't help that whenever the child wasn't playing footie or rugby, or was in school, he was entrenched in his bedroom staring at a screen and trying to shoot things. He should get out more; play with the other lads on the close— Hang on; *were* there any other boys of Sam's age in their street? Brett had to admit that he didn't know.

'Ask Portia if she's got any spot cream,' he suggested. Then, 'When did Mum say for me to give you an antihistamine?'

'I dunno. Half an hour ago?' Sam shrugged. Brett wished he'd stop doing that.

'Did you speak to her?'

'Text.'

'She texted you?'

'I just said so, didn't I?'

Bloody hell, this boy of his was getting as sullen as the girls. Annoyance shot through him – Kate could text Sam, but she couldn't be bothered to reply to him. At least he knew she had her phone with her; he'd definitely call her after he'd eaten, and give her a piece of his mind.

'Kate used to have spots. Not many, though,' Beverley said. She wasn't exactly tucking into her food, either. None of them were, apart from Portia, who was gobbling down curry and naan bread as though it was about to be taken away from her at any second.

'Don't you like it?' Brett used his fork to point at Beverley's plate.

'It's too spicy for me,' his mother-in-law said. 'It'll upset my tummy.'

He resisted the by-now very common urge to roll his eyes. Chicken korma wasn't in the least bit spicy. Maybe he should have ordered her a vindaloo instead, just to see her eyes water.

Ellis was still out, God knows where, and there was so much food left over that he felt positively guilty, especially when his mother said, 'You've ordered far too much, Brett. It's such a waste.'

As he carried the barely-touched cartons out to the kitchen, he called Kate again, without any luck, so he left yet another message. 'Pick up, Kate, you're starting to worry me.'

It was so unlike her. She'd never done anything like this before. Surely a silly comment from his mother wouldn't make her go haring off in the car? He thought she had thicker skin than that. Besides, she knew what his mother was like, and he was certain Helen didn't mean what she'd said. It had just come out wrong, that's all. His mother was always putting her foot in her mouth, but she never meant it the way it sounded.

Brett wasn't sure whether he should be concerned with, or annoyed at, his wife.

The fact that she'd replied to Sam and not to him, tipped the balance in favour of being cross, and he seethed for a bit while he cleaned up.

As he tackled the dirty dishes, a horrible thought occurred to him, and he rang Kate again. 'Is there someone else, is that it?' he demanded.

Even as the words left his mouth, he knew it was ridiculous for him to think such a thing. For one, when would Kate have time for an affair?

She was always either in work or running around after the kids. For another, he knew their sex life wasn't brilliant, but he didn't think it was bad enough to drive her into another man's arms. Besides, Kate wasn't the type – she was loyal and faithful. She simply didn't have it in her to sneak around behind his back and cheat on him.

A short while later, feeling he should apologise for his last message, he called her again, but when he realised her phone was still turned off, his good intentions vanished.

'Where are you?' he snapped. 'I've left message after message. Now you're being ridiculous and childish. For your information, we've had a takeaway. Again!'

He stared at the remains of the Indian in disgust. His mother was right, living off fast food wasn't healthy, and he didn't feel that the kids should have yet another takeaway tomorrow evening. It wasn't fair on them, or on him. He needed good, wholesome food after a hard day in the office, with vegetables or a salad, freshly prepared and nutritious, not fast food swimming in cream or fat, and laden with salt.

Right, this was the last time he was going to call her tonight. If she didn't answer, so be it…

'Kate!' He gave a loud huffing sigh down the phone, then muttered, 'For God's sake,' under his breath.

Before he went to bed, he couldn't resist sending her one last message. 'We'll talk tomorrow when you've had a chance to come to your senses.'

He didn't want to think about what he'd do if she refused to speak to him in the morning. Surely, she'd have gotten over whatever funk she was in, and she'd come back home where she belonged?

Because, if she didn't, he had absolutely no idea what he would do without her.

CHAPTER 29

Since when did hangovers get to be so bad?

Kate prised one eye open then the other, thankful that even if it was morning, it was still dark outside. The thought of having bright sunlight stabbing her in the head made her feel ill.

Actually, she didn't need another reason to feel ill – she felt positively horrid as it was. Her stomach was doing slow, nauseating rolls, and her tongue was stuck to the roof of her mouth.

Ug!

With great effort and a considerable amount of grunting, she clambered stiffly out of bed, heading for the mini-bar and the bottled water she knew it contained, gulping half of it.

Oh, no! Too much, too fast—

She only just made it to the bathroom and afterwards she stood on wobbly legs staring at her gruesome reflection in dismay.

If Brett could see her now…

Ah, well, it was a good job he can't then, she told herself tartly. Anyway, it was his fault she was in this state to begin with. Him and his sodding mother.

Kate rinsed her mouth out a couple of times, then ran a shaking hand through her shoulder-length hair, catching her fingers in the tangles and wincing. All she wanted to do was to finish that bottle of water, take a couple of aspirin, and go back to bed, but—

Wait, she really could do that, couldn't she? She didn't have to make breakfasts, or packed lunches, or take various children to several different destinations. She was on her own and she could do what she bloody well liked.

So what, if she went back to bed and missed

breakfast. It didn't matter, she had no one to please but herself.

Except...breakfast was part of the cost of the room, and it would be a shame to miss it. Besides, a fry up would do her good, and she was desperate for a glass of orange juice. She was up now, so she might as well just get on with it.

After a shower, a cup of tea, and a couple of painkillers from a stray blister pack she'd found in the bottom of her bag (she'd also found an ancient sachet of Calpol which must have been in there for ages, because she hadn't given any of the kids any of the baby pain relief for years), Kate began to feel more like her normal self. She still felt a little sick and her head still throbbed, but she was functioning, albeit at a lower level than normal. She'd eat her breakfast and then see how she felt. If she continued to feel lethargic and out-of-sorts, she'd go back to bed for a nap.

Breakfast was surprisingly good, served by Dave who'd signed her in yesterday, minus the parrot.

'Where's Polly?' Kate asked, tucking into a

bowl of chopped fruit and honeyed yoghurt.

'She's not at her best in the mornings,' he said, placing a pot of tea on the table. 'I've left her in her cage with her head tucked under her wing. How about you, did you sleep well?'

'Yes, thanks.' If she could call passing out, sleeping.

'Are you here on business or pleasure?' he asked.

It was probably a standard question of his, but Kate gave it a moment's thought as she wondered how to answer. 'Pleasure,' she said, eventually.

'Have you been to Brixham before?'

'Never; a friend recommended it, and I needed somewhere... I mean, I was at a loose end, so I decided to come here.'

'You'll be sightseeing then,' he said. 'There are some brochures on a stand in reception, if you're interested. The harbour is lovely, and we've got a replica of The Golden Hind moored up which is well worth a visit. There are some glorious walks along the coast.' He leaned closer

329

as if what he was about to impart was a secret. 'The weather forecast for today is good – cold but sunny, with very little chance of rain.'

'Great,' Kate said, thinking that the way she was feeling now, she might just manage a trip to a café and back, but that was about it.

Yet, once a hearty English breakfast had done its job and with a large glass of orange juice and several cups of tea under her belt, Kate felt almost back to normal.

A stroll around Brixham might be nice, she thought. Actually, it was essential if she didn't want to wear the same clothes several days in a row or try to rinse them out in the shower. She also needed to pick up a few toiletries and a book or two. Of all the shopping she intended to do, choosing a book excited her the most.

Kate popped back to her room for her coat and bag, and as she did so, her mobile phone glared accusingly at her. Still switched off, it nevertheless managed to make her feel guilty. Should she check it for messages? Make sure everyone was OK at home.

Maybe something had happened when she was out gallivanting and getting drunk last night – something awful – and no one had been able to get hold of her—

In a sudden panic, Kate grabbed the phone and held the on-button down.

'Start, start,' she muttered, a fresh wave of guilt vying with a sudden churning in her stomach, making her feel nauseated again. Please let everyone be alright, please…

It came on, and the text icon appeared in the corner of the screen.

With shaking fingers, she opened up her messages.

Ellis – **This is the top I bought. Don't let Portia anywhere near it**.

Portia – **I need a lift into town tomorrow at 6. Evening, obvs lol**

Sam – **is it normal to have so many spots**

Kate paused. All the messages had been received yesterday evening, and her first instinct was to send reassuring replies back.

A pause gave her time to think.

Ellis, she conceded, did have a point. Portia shouldn't be taking Ellis's things without permission and as a parent, it was Kate's responsibility to make sure her middle child respected boundaries. Portia, she recalled, should have been grounded, but the punishment appeared to have been conveniently forgotten, even to the point where Portia was demanding the mum-taxi. And, yes, Sam was getting to the age where acne was a definite thing.

There was nothing further from her children, but there were a couple from the nans.

Beverley – **she ses her car wont start rubbish thats why shes staying don't believe a word of it**

Helen – **We need to talk. Stop being so childish.**

Followed by another from Helen saying, **How could you do this to him?**

Kate narrowed her eyes – a huge part of her felt as guilty as sin for running away, even if it was only for a couple of days. Another part, a much smaller but more vociferous part, whispered loudly that it was about time her family realised how much she did for each and every one of them, and that it was high time they stopped treating her like a doormat. Admittedly, Christmas wasn't the ideal time to make a stand, but a woman could only take so much, and she was at the end of her tether.

Finally, she gathered enough courage to listen to the voicemails from Brett.

'What do you mean, you've gone away for a few days? Stop being silly and come back home. My mother said you stormed off in a huff.'

'Kate, answer your phone.'

'Kate, where the bloody hell are you? You do realise the kids haven't had their dinner? Kate, answer your phone. Kate?'

'Why the hell don't you answer your phone?'

'Pick up, Kate, you're starting to worry me.'

'Is there someone else, is that it'?

'Kate!!'

'Kate!' Brett gave a loud huffing sigh. *'For God's sake,'* she heard him mutter under his breath.

Kate closed her eyes and gulped back tears. Someone else indeed! Since when did she have the time to have an affair? She barely had time to shower. Even though she and Brett had an en suite, none of the kids felt they could wait for her to come out of it if they wanted to speak to her. Instead, they traipsed up to the attic and parked themselves outside the bathroom door to hold a yelled conversation through it. She couldn't remember the last time she'd washed her hair in peace; or had managed to shave her legs without nicking herself because she'd been concentrating so much on one or another of the kids' problems. Not that she shaved her legs very often, because she was always haring around and chasing her tail.

Brett sounded worried, but he didn't sound upset. Cross and put-out were the things that came to mind when she listened to his final message.

'We'll talk tomorrow when you've had a chance to come to your senses, it said.

So much for missing her. He sounded more

like he was her line-manager and was reprimanding her, than a concerned husband wondering why his wife had suddenly gone off the rails.

That did it – her mind was made up. She'd stay in Brixham until after Christmas. Sod the lot of them. None of them cared, none of them even asked her what was wrong, why she'd done what she'd done. The only thing they cared about was how her absence affected them.

Kate sent one message before she switched her phone off again. It was to Brett.

There is no one else. There's not even you, it seems.

Then she placed it gently on the chest of drawers and burst into tears.

CHAPTER 30

The first thing Brett did when he woke on Thursday morning (apart from noticing that his wife wasn't in her side of the bed and didn't appear to have been, although it was difficult to tell because the duvet was firmly wrapped around his waist) was to check his phone. There was a text from Kate. What did she mean, "there's not even you, it seems"? Of course he was there – where else would he be?

He wished he knew what she was so upset about. His mother might have put her size six feet in her mouth, but Kate was used to Helen and her ways. If his wife had left because of that, then she was overreacting.

He tried calling her again, but this time when it went to voicemail, he didn't bother leaving a message.

He lay there for a while, listening to the silence. The only sound was the occasional slam of a car door from somewhere in the close and the faint hum of the central heating, and he wondered where his wife was and whether she was awake.

It was Christmas Eve tomorrow; surely she'd be home today. Or if not, then definitely tomorrow. He couldn't imagine Christmas Eve without her. Kate was the kingpin of the family, the person who kept everything ticking along, who sorted out problems, who organised everyone else.

She wouldn't have gone far, he decided, not when she had work this morn—

That was it! She'd definitely be in work today. There was no way she'd let Doris down. Surprisingly, charity shops did particularly well in the week leading up to Christmas, with women looking for party dresses that didn't cost the earth, and stocking up on cards and wrapping paper. Kate was bound to be there. She loved her job and she took it very seriously, although Brett honestly couldn't see the appeal of rifling through discarded clothes and assorted household junk. He often teased her about getting a proper job, a full time one and one that paid better, but in fact, he was proud that she worked for a charity – at least one of them was doing some good, because Brett felt that his job was an utter waste of time most days.

Briefly he recalled their squabble the other night when he was blowing up the air bed, and he'd made a comment about earning four times as much as she did. It might be true, but he was a little ashamed that he'd pointed it out. Kate's value to the family wasn't financial.

Keen to talk to his wife and find out what the hell was going on, Brett slipped out of bed and quickly showered and dressed. This particular mountain was off to visit Mohammed, and try to talk some sense into her. Kate could refuse to take his calls or answer his texts, but it would be a whole different ball game when he was standing in front of her and staring her in the eye. He wanted to get this silliness sorted out once and for all, and persuade her to return home before Christmas.

Brett didn't think he'd walked along the high street at this hour of the morning before, and it was quite eerie with the Christmas lights on but none of the shops open, and hardly any people around.

He was intentionally early, wanting to catch Kate before she started work. He wanted her full attention, and not have to vie for it with a pensioner who was looking for a pair of winter boots.

Argh! Talking of boots, Brett tripped over a pair of clunky men's ones which were sticking out from underneath a pile of blankets and some flattened cardboard boxes.

'Are you alright, mate?' a gruff voice asked from somewhere beneath the pile.

'Sorry, I didn't see you there. And I think it should be me asking that question considering I nearly trod on you. Are you OK?' Brett asked.

'Yeah, ta. I'm grand.'

He didn't believe the man for one second. Who could possibly feel "grand" while lying in a shop doorway in late December? The bloke had clearly spent the night there.

'Can I...um...?' Brett looked around. The café across the street was about to open. Staff were bustling about inside. 'Get you a coffee? Once they open?'

'Thanks, mate, but they won't be serving for a bit yet, and you've probably got somewhere you need to be.'

'Uh, no, I haven't. I'm waiting for someone.'

'Then, yeah, a coffee would be great, if you're sure. Two sugars, please.'

'Right,' Brett stuffed his hands into his trouser pockets and rocked back on his heels. 'A coffee it is, then.'

The two men were silent for a moment, then Brett said, 'Is this your normal spot?' He felt a little awkward standing there, without speaking. It seemed a trifle rude.

'I suppose so. The doorway is nice and deep, stops most of the rain if it's not too heavy.'

'It must get dreadfully cold at night,' Brett said. He was already starting to feel the chill and he'd only been standing there for a couple of minutes.

'Yeah, it does,' the man said. 'But I have a wicked sleeping bag. One of the women who works in the shop gave it to me.'

'Doris?' Brett asked.

'No, the other one. Kate. She's lovely, always shares her lunch or fetches me something from the café. She even lets me inside for a warm, when she can.'

Brett's heart did a double thump at the mention of his wife's name. Aww, that was so sweet of her. 'Kate's my wife,' he said, feeling proud of her generosity. 'Always thinking of other people,' he added, realising it was true.

'Nice to meet you,' the man said. 'My name is Ron, and you must be Brett.'

'I am.' Brett didn't know what to make of the fact that this guy knew his name. He wondered what else Ron knew about him. 'She's not mentioned you to me.'

'Why should she?' Ron asked. 'I'm just a homeless bloke she's kind to, now and again.'

Brett shifted his gaze to the café, in the desperate hope it would open its doors soon, because he was wondering what the hell was wrong with him. He'd felt a flash of jealousy there for a moment, which was so unreasonable and so unlike him, that he almost didn't recognise himself. And the guy was right – why should Kate mention that she'd been kind to someone?

'Are you waiting for her?' Ron wanted to know.

'Sort of.' There was no way Brett was going to discuss the situation with this man.

'Is she feeling better?'

'Excuse me?'

'Kate. Is she better?'

Brett shook his head. 'I don't understand.'

Ron's grubby-faced gaze was full of curiosity. 'She wasn't very well yesterday.'

'How do you know?'

'Doris told me that Kate wasn't in work because she wasn't well.'

Brett needed to sit down. Kate hadn't been in work yesterday? Where had she been, and why hadn't she said anything to him about not being well? Was that why she'd taken herself off, because she was ill? But what kind of ill would warrant her disappearing?

Oh. My. God. Brett leant against the shop window, his heart sliding into his boots with fear. Maybe she had something seriously wrong with her and she didn't want to spoil Christmas for the rest of the family. That would be just like her.

No it wouldn't, Brett reasoned. It would be more like her to carry on as normal and not say anything to anyone.

What the hell was she playing at?

'I saw her,' Ron said.

'Kate?'

'Yeah. She was in there.' Ron pointed at the

café which was finally open for business.

'When?'

'After Doris had made me some toast and told me Kate wasn't coming into work because she must have caught what she'd had. A twenty-four-hour virus thing, Doris said.'

'Let me get this straight – you saw Kate in the café *after* she'd phoned in sick? What was she doing?'

'Eating a full English.'

Brett's eyebrows rose. 'Was she with anyone?'

'Not that I could see.'

Had she been planning on disappearing before she overheard his mother saying he should never have married her? If so, that put a whole different slant on things.

'She went to church after that,' Ron added.

'She did?' Brett was even more astounded. He didn't think Kate had stepped foot inside a church since one of the kid's schools had held a carol concert in one.

'The abbey,' Ron said. 'She had coffee and

cake.'

Brett shot him a look. Had this man been stalking his wife? How did he know so much about her movements yesterday, when he, himself, knew absolutely nothing?

Ron smiled as if he knew what Brett was thinking. 'I always pay a visit to the abbey on Wednesdays because that's when they hold their coffee morning. A sit in the warm, with a hot chocolate and a slice of Yule log is very welcome, I can tell you.'

'Do you know where she went after that?' Brett was clutching at straws here, but by now he wasn't ruling anything out.

'Sorry. But she looked much happier on the way out of church than when she'd come in.' Ron got to his feet, and Brett could have sworn he could hear the man's joints creaking.

'Let me get us a coffee,' he said. 'Fancy a bacon sarnie to go with it?'

Ron's eyes lit up and when Brett returned with breakfast, the man tucked in with gusto, making Brett wonder when the bloke had last eaten a hot meal.

'Here,' he said, taking his wallet out of his pocket and handing him a ten-pound note.

'Are you sure?' Ron asked. 'It's a lot of money.'

Which only served to make him feel even worse than he already did. He pushed the money at Ron who took it from him gently and tucked it away inside his many items of clothing.

'She isn't happy, you know,' he said to Brett.

Brett paused, his lips around a bacon roll. He bit a mouthful off, chewed for a while, then said, 'I'm not sure if that's any of your business.'

'It probably isn't,' Ron agreed. 'But I'm not the one who didn't know my wife had bunked off work yesterday. I'm also not the one who's waiting for her to start work today. It makes me think there's something wrong.'

Ron had got that right – there certainly was something wrong.

'What's she said?' Brett asked.

'She told me about the two mothers coming to stay for Christmas and the dog stealing the joint of meat. The way she told the story made me laugh.'

'But?'

'She wasn't laughing, not deep down, I could tell.'

'There's more isn't there?'

Ron heaved a sigh. 'I don't like breaking confidences, but she was talking about going away.'

Brett gulped, his coffee going down the wrong way, and for a few moments he coughed and spluttered. Ron patted him on the back, until he'd regained control of his throat.

'Where?' he squeaked.

Ron said, 'No idea, mate.'

'Why?' It came out as a wail.

'I'm taking a bit of a guess here and I might be wrong, but I think she feels undervalued.'

'But I worship her!' he protested.

Ron gave him a wry smile. 'Have you told her recently?'

He bit his bottom lip. He often told her he loved her. Didn't he? Come to think of it, he couldn't remember the last time he'd said those three little words to her, and he'd certainly never told her he worshipped her.

He assumed she knew how he felt about her.

'There is something,' Ron said, as Brett tried to gather his thoughts and make sense of what he'd just heard. 'When I asked her where she'd go if she ran away, she said the south coast. I told her Brixham was nice. She might have gone there.'

Brett stared at him. He had no idea where his wife might have gone, but Brixham sounded as good a place to start looking as any.

'She's gone away, hasn't she?' Ron said, rolling his sleeping bag up and wrapping it in a piece of plastic.

Brett nodded, miserably. 'I'll hang around here for a bit and see if she shows up for work. If I give you my number, could you phone me if you happen to see her?'

Ron shook his head sadly. 'No mobile, mate. And there's no phone boxes around here, neither.'

'Well if you do see her, will you tell her I love her very much?'

'Not on your nelly. You've got to tell her that yourself. Good luck, mate, and thanks for breakfast.' With that, Ron was off down the street, carrying his every possession with him.

Brett watched him go, feeling humble. He knew nothing of Ron's story, but just speaking with him had made him feel immensely grateful for his family and his home.

He just wished Kate was by his side now, so he could tell her exactly how much she meant to him.

CHAPTER 31

With a selection of shopping bags piled at her feet, Kate sat in a little tea shop which was hidden in a small side street, a pot of tea in front of her and her fingers curled around the handle of a fine, bone-china cup, and stared into space.

She'd had a strange morning, she mused, unable to remember when she'd last spent a couple of hours alone browsing in shops. The last time she'd gone clothes shopping, it had been for school uniforms – hardly a delight – and had involved several arguments about shoes and a stroppy Portia complaining that the regulation school skirts were too long.

Ellis was easier to shop with in some ways, because there wasn't a uniform code in college, but the fuss she made over what she bought was epic. To be honest, the only reason Kate had been allowed to accompany her daughter at all, was to pay for and carry the purchases – she'd had felt like a packhorse with a credit card.

She hadn't gone clothes shopping for herself in ages, possibly years. She tended to buy practical clothes that lasted, and wore them on a rotational basis, with a few outfits which were for "best", but which hadn't seen the light of day in aeons, because she'd not gone anywhere to wear them.

Today had been a revelation. Brixham was hardly the fashion capitol of Devon, but it did have a couple of lovely little boutiques, where she was left alone to browse and try on to her heart's content. She'd even taken some things into the changing room which she wouldn't normally have given a second glance at; there was a good reason for that, she discovered, as she tried the more daring items on and concluded that they weren't for her, but at least she'd given them a go.

She'd treated herself to a couple of skirts, some thick winter tights, a pair of gorgeous leather boots, and some pretty tops. A pair of black slim-fit jeans (her old ones weren't black anymore, but a washed-out shade of grey) completed the bulk of her purchases. She'd added a pack of knickers and some toiletries, and had bought two books. Two! She sincerely hoped she'd manage to read them both.

In fact, she was contemplating starting one of them now, (anything was better than staring out of the steamed-up window and trying not to think of the chaos at home) when a quavering little voice asked, 'Do you mind if I join you? It's just that there aren't any tables free.'

Kate looked up to see a tiny woman of possibly ninety years old wobbling precariously as she tried to manoeuvre herself between a chair and the table, while clutching a shopping bag in one hand and a walking stick in the other.

'Here, let me,' Kate said, jumping up to move the chair so the elderly lady could sit down. 'Have you ordered?' she asked her.

'They know what I want,' the woman said. 'I 'as the same thing every day, excepts when I don't,' and she cracked a crinkle-faced smile. 'This is my second home.'

'It is nice in here,' Kate agreed. 'Cosy, and the cake looks lovely.' She hadn't wanted any herself, still full of the huge breakfast she'd devoured, but the scones, cakes, and pastries looked delicious.

'I'm Mrs Trent, but you can call me Essie,' the old lady said. 'What's your name?'

'Kate.'

'Got a second one?'

'Peters.'

'I've not seen you in here before.'

That's because I've never been in here before,' Kate said.

'Eh?'

'I said, that's because—'

'I heard what you said. There's no need to

shout; I'm not deaf yet, and I've got all my marbles, too.'

'I'm sure you have,' Kate said with a smile. She loved old people. The charity shop had its regular elderly contingent and they were always a hoot. Although, there were currently two elderly ladies in Kate's life who she *wasn't* all that keen on right now...

'Why haven't you been in here before?' Essie wanted to know.

'Because I only arrived in Brixham yesterday.'

'On holiday, are you?'

'You could say that.'

'I *am* saying that,' Essie countered, glancing around and tutting. 'They're slow today. I could die of old age before I get my cuppa.'

Kate smiled again, trying not to let her amusement show in case she offended the old lady.

'Where's your husband?' Essie wanted to know, focusing on Kate once more.

Kate raised her eyebrows in surprise.

'Your rings,' Essie said. 'I'm not blind either, although I do need my specs for reading.'

'In work, I expect,' Kate replied.

'Don't you know?'

'Not really.'

'You gotta keep an eye on fellas. If you don't, they have a habit of straying. About time,' she said, as a waitress arrived with an espresso and a biscotti. 'Ta, love.'

The waitress gave the old lady a fond pat on the shoulder and winked at Kate. 'When this one says jump, we all ask how high. You wouldn't believe she's ninety-seven, would you?'

'Oi! It's rude telling people a lady's age.'

'Get on with you,' the waitress said. 'You love everyone knowing how fantastic you are for your age.'

Essie simpered, picking up her tiny cup with gnarled fingers. 'I even have some of my own teeth,' she announced, to Kate's amusement. 'And I do all my own washing and ironing. I have a woman in to clean, but she's not that good. No one wants to do cleaning anymore – it's too much like hard work. Leaves a ring around the bath, she does. A wipe and a spit, and she calls it done.' Essie peered at Kate over the rim of her cup. 'Don't want a job, do you?'

'No thanks, I've got one.'

'Doing what?'

'I work in a charity shop.'

'Which one?'

'Wyvern Hospice.'

'Never heard of it. Where is it?'

'They're based in The Midlands.'

'Like it, do you, working in a shop?'

'Yes, I do.'

'I used to work in a shop. I've worked in an office or two, a bank, an estate agent, and on a fishing boat during the war.'

'Wow, you've certainly worked in a lot of places.'

'That's not the half of it,' Essie said, dunking her biscotti in her coffee then popping the soggy end in her mouth and chomping enthusiastically. 'It'd make your hair curl if you'd worked in some of the places I have. Mind you, when I got married, my Frank insisted I got a proper job, so I worked in the doctors as a receptionist for years. Used to come in handy when I had trouble with me water works. Didn't have to wait for an appointment, see. The doctors were on tap, so to speak.' She laughed so hard, Kate worried that the old woman was going to fall off her chair, and she guessed Essie had made that particular joke more than once.

'Right, back to your husband,' Essie said, stuffing the rest of her biscuit into her mouth. 'I take it he's not staying with you in Brixham?'

Crikey, but this lady was nosey, Kate thought. 'No, he's not,' she replied, mildly.

'Got any kids?'

'Three.'

'What sort?'

'Teenagers, more or less.'

'I meant, boys or girls.'

'Oh, two girls and a boy.'

'Are they here with you?'

'Er…no.'

'Why not?'

'It's complicated.'

'Life often is, girly; that's what makes it so interesting.'

Kate shook her head. Essie was a character, all right, and a nosey one at that.

'Do you love 'em?' the old lady demanded.

'Of course I do!'

'There's no "of course" about it. You get to choose your husband, but you don't get to choose your parents or your kids. You gets what you're given, like it or lump it. I have the feeling you're lumping your lot right now.'

'You have?'

'You've got a face like a wet weekend in August. Take my advice – not that you'll listen to an old biddy like me – whatever has got you looking like you've lost a shilling and found a sixpence it's got to be better than not having a family at all. I lost my Frank when I was seventy-three. Been without him nearly twenty-five years, I have. We never had any kiddies and both our parents went years and years ago. Well, they didn't last long in them days; not like now, when sixty is the new forty and everyone expects to live to a hundred. Well, let me tell you, old age is a bitch. So is being lonely and on your own.'

Essie stood up and reached for her walking stick before Kate had a chance to hand it to her.

'Let me see you to the door,' Kate offered.

'Nonsense, I can see my own self to the door, ta very much. Now, mind you heed my words. No matter how bad they are, they're still family. Unless they're really, really bad, like murderers or the likes, and then you might have to wash your hands of them.'

Kate watched as Essie toddled towards the door, giving the young man who opened it for her a beaming smile, and Kate shook her head. She had a feeling if she'd opened the door for Essie, she'd have got a scowl instead of a smile. Mind you, the man who'd opened it for Essie was quite a hunk. No wonder Essie had smiled.

'Is she all right going home alone?' Kate asked the waitress who came to collect the cups.

'She's not going home,' the woman said. 'If I know Essie, she's off to the betting shop. Then she'll pop into the pub for a port and lemon afterwards.'

'She seems a handful, but lovely with it,' Kate said, with a laugh.

'Oh, she's a handful all right. Leads her husband a merry dance, she does.'

'She told me her Frank had died twenty-odd years ago.'

The woman rolled her eyes. 'He did. This is her second marriage, and this one is alive and kicking and is a good fifteen years younger than she is.' The waitress lowered her voice. 'Essie says she only married him for sex.'

Kate barked out a laugh. 'Dear God, the woman is incorrigible.'

'She certainly is. She's like one of the family though, and everyone looks out for her, especially since she hasn't got any children.'

Meeting Essie had brightened Kate's morning, lifting her mood from her sombre musings.

The old lady was right, Kate realised. Family *was* everything, but the longer she stayed in

Brixham, the longer she understood just how dysfunctional hers was, especially considering no one had anything to be dysfunctional about. It wasn't as though she and Brett had split up and gone on to have other relationships and other children as a result. There were no step-parents or step-siblings, and the nuclear family was a single unit, with all of its members living under the same roof. So why was everyone so darned miserable all the time?

Kate wanted to return home, she really did. But not just yet. This trip had gone from running away before she'd totally lost it, to teaching them all a lesson – herself included. Now that she had some space (both physically and in her head) she could see things a little clearer. Maybe she wouldn't wait until Boxing Day before she went home. It would be nice to be there when the children opened their presents. She'd never missed that, and she was positive she didn't want to miss it now.

That was it – she'd stay here until tomorrow and drive back in the morning.

She only hoped someone had thought to pick up the turkey from the butcher, otherwise they'd be eating whatever was in the freezer for Christmas lunch.

CHAPTER 32

Home might be where the heart is, but Brett wasn't feeling it when he walked into his hall after his worrying chat with Ron, to be met with a bouncing, hyperactive Pepe, three demanding children, and two equally demanding elderly ladies.

'Will someone please put this dog outside?' he yelled, as the daft animal mounted his leg the second he opened the front door. He hadn't even managed to take his coat off before the silly creature had gripped his calf with its front paws, while wearing an expression of intense concentration.

Trying not to hurt Pepe, Brett gently shook his leg, hoping to dislodge him. When that failed, he prised the dog's front paws from around his leg and stepped away, only for the poodle to launch itself at him again.

'Beverley, will you see to your dog!' he yelled, hoping his mother-in-law was in shouting distance.

'She's in the bath,' his mother said. 'That ghastly beast has been humping everything in sight since I got up. Beverley needs to get it seen to by the vet. Nasty thing.'

Brett, finally free of the over-excited dog, bent down to pick it up.

Pepe growled. Brett flinched back.

The little sod – he was good enough to hump, but when it came to picking Pepe up the dog didn't want anything to do with him.

'Pass me one of the tea towels from the kitchen,' he said to his mother, as Pepe continued to growl and show his teeth. Brett was quite impressed that such a little thing had the balls to stand up to him. Ah yes, talking of balls, Brett agreed that it was Pepe's bits which were causing the problem – he might be a much calmer and more obedient dog without them.

Helen threw him a tea towel; Brett caught it and threw it over the dog. Pepe, as Brett expected, didn't appreciate the manoeuvre, erupting into a frenzy of squirming and growling. Gingerly, careful to keep his fingers away from the bitey end, he wrapped the dog's head as firmly as he could without being savaged through the cloth, picked the poodle up and made a dash for the back door. He opened it quickly and thrust Pepe outside, still with the cloth over the poodle's head.

Brett peered through the glass to check that Pepe had worked himself free of the tea towel, satisfied that the mutt was in no immediate danger of throttling himself as he shook the offending fabric off and launched his irate little self at the door in a flurry of high-pitched barks and frantic scrabbling of claws. Brett winced, hoping the door could withstand the onslaught.

The dog might be small, but he had a darned big attitude. When he turned back to face the kitchen, his mother was wearing an expression of dissatisfaction. 'She's not come back, yet,' she said, her lips a thin line.

'No.'

'Out gallivanting, I expect.'

What the hell was gallivanting, Brett wanted to know, but he couldn't be bothered to ask.

'I'm not surprised,' his mother continued, following him into the lounge as he hunted for the laptop.

'Dad?' His eldest was already in there.

'Hello, Ellis. Have you seen the laptop?'

'I can't get hold of Mum. I want her to drop into Boots in Worcester and pick me up some foundation – I've run out.'

'Why can't you get it yourself? You're not exactly doing anything.'

'I am, I'm meeting Riley. I don't have time to go into Worcester.'

'And you think your mother has?'

Ellis gave him a belligerent stare. 'What are

you doing home?' she asked. Then a calculating look spread across her elfin features.

'No,' Brett said. 'Before you ask, I'm not going to fetch it for you. I've got other things to do.'

'Like what?' she demanded, as if he couldn't possibly be doing anything more important than running errands for her.

'He's got a day off,' Portia said. 'Can you drop me off at the stables?'

'No,' he replied, the laptop still eluding him. He lifted one of the cushions on the sofa, as if he expected it to be hiding underneath.

'Don't be so mean,' Portia said.

'He won't go to Boots and get me my foundation, either,' Ellis added. 'He's just being selfish.' She turned to him, her hands on her hips. 'I expect you're going to play golf, are you?' she demanded.

'No.' He hesitated. It was about time he let the kids know what was happening. 'I'm going to find your mother.'

Ellis rolled her eyes. 'She's in work,' she said,

scornfully. 'And she hasn't bothered to wash that top. I wanted to wear it tonight.'

'Wash it yourself,' Brett said.

Ellis snorted, as if the concept of doing her own laundry was totally alien to her.

'I've got to muck out this morning,' Portia said. 'It's my turn.'

Brett got down on the floor and peered under the sofa. No laptop. 'For one thing, if it is your turn and both your mother and I were in work, like we normally are, how did you plan on getting there? And for another, you're still grounded.'

Portia stamped her sock-clad foot and folded her arms. 'Mum didn't mean the stables,' she said. 'She meant parties and stuff.'

'Your mother's not here, and I am,' he retorted. 'I say grounding includes the stables.'

'I'm going to tell Mum,' she said, furiously.

'*If* you can get hold of her,' Helen said from the doorway. 'She didn't come home last night.'

'Mum!' Brett snapped. 'Leave it.'

Portia's arms dropped to her side. 'Dad?' She sounded a little uncertain. 'What's Nana talking about?'

'Nothing you need to concern yourself with,' he said.

'You'd better tell them, Brett. They're going to find out sooner or later,' Helen said.

'Find out what?' This was from Ellis.

'Brett?' Helen glared pointedly at him.

He glared back, and mouthed, 'Thanks a bunch.' He had every intention of telling the children, but not like this; he wanted to do it in his own time. He'd been hoping to speak to Kate first, before he broke it to the kids that their mother had gone away for a few days.

'Dad?' Both his daughters looked worried.

'Your mum has taken a short break,' he said.

'Hmph!' Helen snorted.

'What do you mean, a short break?' Ellis asked. Portia took a step closer to her sister.

'She's gone away for a few days,' he said.

'Where?' That was from Ellis.

'Your father has no idea,' Helen said.

'Mum! Butt out; you're not helping.'

'Well, I never! Don't you speak to me like

that, Brett Peters. I'm your mother, and I deserve some respect.'

'You don't know where Mum is?' Portia slipped her hand into Ellis's.

'Not at this precise moment,' he admitted.

'Why?'

'She didn't tell him,' Helen said. 'She just marched out without saying anything to anyone. Irresponsible, that's what I call it.'

'I meant, why did she go, not why doesn't Dad know where she is,' Ellis said.

'It's obvious, isn't it?' Helen said. 'It's because of you kid—'

'That's it!' Brett was furious. 'Mum, I want you to go, right now.'

'Excuse me?'

'You heard. You've caused enough trouble; I don't want you causing any more.'

'All I said was—'

'I know exactly what you said, and it wasn't nice.'

'What did she say, Dad?' Portia's voice was small, her face, usually so defiant, creased in worry.

'Just go,' he said to his mother. 'You've done enough damage.'

Helen, her hand over her mouth, let out a sob and made her way unsteadily out of the room.

'Dad, please, tell us what's going on,' Ellis pleaded.

'I want Mum.' Portia sounded like the child she so recently was, and his heart went out to her.

'It's not your fault, it's mine,' he said, leading them to the sofa and sitting them down. He squashed in between them and put an arm around each girls' thin shoulder. 'I've not been pulling my weight around the house, and I think your mum got a bit fed up.'

Ellis pulled away. 'Are you having an affair?'

'Good lord, no! Whatever gave you that idea?'

'Mum wouldn't just go for no reason.'

'It's like I said, I've not been doing enough to help her.'

'You're in work all day,' Ellis pointed out.

'Your mother works long hours, too,' Brett replied.

'She only does nine-thirty to four,' Ellis said.

'That's the day job. Think about all the other things she does as well.' He paused for a moment to give them a chance to ponder it. 'She runs around after all of us, all the time. She does all the cooking, cleaning, shopping, laundry, and all the other things that keep the house and us ticking over. Plus, I think having the two nans here, as well as the dog, became a bit too much for her.'

'Will she come back?'

'Of course, she will. She just needs a bit of time out, that's all.'

Ellis nodded, but Portia looked sceptical. He waited for her to speak, wondering what was going through that pretty little head of hers, hoping that some of what he'd said had struck home, hoping she understood that, although the blame lay with him, the children's selfishness hadn't helped.

Eventually she spoke. 'Am I still grounded?'

CHAPTER 33

With a resigned sigh, Brett let the girls go. 'Don't say anything to Sam,' he warned, 'I'll be up in a minute to tell him myself.'

He wanted a few seconds alone, to think about Ellis's and Portia's reactions. He wasn't sure whether either teenager had completely understood what he'd said, or their part in Kate's disappearance. To be fair, he didn't blame them. It was his fault and Kate's that the children were as inconsiderate and selfish as they were. Kate had given in to their demands because it was easier than battling with them day in, day out;

and he'd done nothing to help. Brett guessed from what he'd seen of his friends' kids, that children, teenagers especially, tended to live in their own little worlds without any thought or consideration for anyone else. It was a parent's job to teach them those things, along with empathy and compassion. And he'd failed. Kate had done her best, but she'd been so busy with the nitty-gritty of running the home, that she'd let some things slide.

When she came back, Brett intended to suggest a family sit-down to discuss everything, and together they should be able to come up with some new rules and new ways of doing things. Responsibility and resilience, that's what was needed in his children, and in himself, too.

He heaved a deep sigh. 'Come home, Kate,' he muttered under his breath, wanting nothing more than to hold her in his arms and tell her exactly how much she meant to him.

Wincing at the thought of what was to come, Brett made his way upstairs to talk to Sam and reassure him that his mum would be home soon, then he needed to find the laptop and start looking for Kate.

A quick visit to the bathroom was in order first, and when he saw the family bathroom was occupied, probably by Beverley taking her bath, he headed up to the en suite in his room.

Deep in thought, Brett pushed open the door of the en suite and—

'Arghh!'

He wasn't sure who screamed the loudest, him or his mother-in-law.

Beverley was sitting bolt upright in the bath, her hands covering her chest, a look of horror on her face.

Brett staggered back, almost losing his footing on the glossy tiles as he hastily zipped himself back up. 'What the hell?' he yelled.

'Get out!' she cried.

He turned his back swiftly and headed for the door. Once safely outside and out of sight of the disturbing vision of his naked mother-in-law, he called, 'Why are you in my bathroom? There's a perfectly good one downstairs.'

'Ellis was in it.' Beverley sloshed around, and Brett hoped she was getting out of the tub and making herself decent.

'Dad?' Brett turned around to see Sam standing behind him. The boy tugged on his sleeve.

'Give me a minute, Sam. Your nan is in my bath.'

'I'm out now,' Beverley said through the door. 'I'm getting dressed.'

'Couldn't you have waited until Ellis had finished, rather than use mine?'

'I'm sure Kate wouldn't have minded.'

'Dad.' Sam was tugging on his sleeve again.

'What?'

'Spots,' Sam said.

'I'm sure one of your sisters can lend you some acne cream, although can you wait a minute because I want to speak to you first.'

'Has Kate come home?' Beverley shouted, and Brett had a feeling of déjà vu. Not again, he prayed.

'Can we talk about this later?' he said.

The door opened, revealing a dressing-gown clad Beverley with a shower cap perched on her head. 'Do the kids know? Have you told them yet?' she asked.

Brett glared at her. 'Later,' he insisted. 'I'm just about to speak with Sam.'

'You can't keep it from them,' she said. 'They'll have to be told that their mum won't be back until after Christmas.'

'What's Nanny talking about, Dad?'

Brett narrowed his eyes meaningfully at Beverley. 'Hang on a sec, Sam.'

'But Dad, I've got spots, real spots. See?' And with that, Sam lifted up his T-shirt to reveal his chest and stomach.

'I'm off,' Helen announced from the landing, and Brett turned to look at her. 'I know when I'm not wanted,' she added.

'You're going?' A huge smile lit up Beverley's face. 'That means I can have the spare room.'

'Dad, what are they?' Sam cried, hopping up and down. 'They itch really bad.'

Brett's eyes widened as he caught sight of his

son's torso, which was covered in a nasty red rash. The child's face didn't look much better, either.

'That looks like chickenpox to me,' Beverley announced.

Helen took a few steps closer and peered at her grandson. 'It certainly does.

'Has he been feeling a bit under the weather these past couple of days?' Beverley asked, and Brett blushed. He had no idea whether Sam had or hadn't.

'Itchy,' Sam said.

'Anything else?' Beverley wanted to know.

Sam nodded. 'Tired, headachy, hot. My legs ache.'

'Typical chickenpox symptoms,' Helen said.

'I'm really itchy.' Sam clung to his father like a three-year-old. 'I want Mummy.'

'Mummy's not here, Sammykins. You'll have to make do with me,' Brett said, bending to plant a kiss on the top of his son's damp head – the only place where the poor child appeared to be spot free.

When was the last time Brett had heard Sam say "mummy"? Not for ages, and Brett hadn't called him Sammykins for a long time without causing his youngest child a great deal of embarrassment.

'Have you got any calamine lotion?' Beverley asked.

Brett wasn't sure he knew what it was, let alone whether there was any such thing in the house. He looked at his mother-in-law helplessly.

'Never mind,' Helen said. 'I'll pop to the chemist and get some.'

'In the meantime, Sam can have a cold shower. It'll take some of the heat out of his skin.' Beverley said. 'Give him some Calpol. You're bound to have some in the house.'

Ah, yes, they did. He knew where it was kept, so he went to fetch it, pouring out the recommended dose onto one of those funny plastic measuring spoons. Sam took it without a murmur, then Brett made him have a cool shower.

'Where's Mum?' he asked, afterwards, and Brett could tell he was beginning to feel a little better. 'Is she in work?'

'Um... no, she's... um... gone away for a couple of days.'

'Where?'

'I'm not sure...'

Sam looked at him doubtfully. 'When will she be back?'

'Soon.' Brett mentally crossed his fingers again.

'Today?'

'Erm, possibly not.'

'By Christmas?'

'She'll be back by then. Stop scratching, you'll make it worse.'

'I can't help it.'

'I know you can't, but try, eh? You'll be as right as rain in a few days,' he added, praying it was the truth.

Sam didn't look convinced. 'If it was a school day tomorrow,' his son asked, 'would you be making me go?'

'I doubt it.'

Sam looked even glummer. 'That's what I thought. Bummer.'

'Yeah, bummer,' Brett agreed. 'Nana will be here with the calamine lotion in a while, and you'll soon feel better.'

'I don't want her to put it on me, I want you to do it.'

'OK, but until she comes back, I've got a few phone calls to make. Is that alright?'

Sam nodded, curling his hands into fists to stop himself from scratching.

'Good lad. I'll be downstairs – once I've found the laptop,' Where the hell was it? He could always use his mobile but reading on a small screen for any length of time made his eyes ache. He should ask Kate to make an appointment at the optician for him.

Ah.

He was doing it again, wasn't he? Expecting Kate to sort things out when he could just as easily make an appointment himself. Easier in fact, because what usually happened was that he would say "any day is fine", only for her to arrange a date, and him to say he couldn't make it. Then Kate would have to ring the optician/dentist/doctor back and rearrange.

'The laptop is in the kitchen on top of the fridge,' Sam said.

'What's it doing there?'

Sam shrugged, and Brett left him in his room taking selfies of his spotty chest and posting them to his mates. From a disaster of epic proportions, Sam, who was now clearly feeling much better, was having great fun showing off his rash, and taking gleeful delight in anticipating which of his friends would come down with the virus next.

Shaking his head (he never would have thought to look up there), Brett went to fetch the laptop and settled down at the kitchen table.

He knew he couldn't possibly phone all the hotels and guest houses in Brixham, but he intended to give it a damn good try.

Starting at the beginning of the alphabet, he dialled the first number he saw.

'Allinson's Guest House, how can I help you?' a cheery female voice sang.

'Er...' he began, and cleared his throat. 'This might sound a little strange, but could you tell me if Kate Peters is staying with you?'

There was silence on the other end for a moment, then a decidedly frostier voice said, 'No, sorry, it's against company policy to give out any information about our guests.'

'Does that mean she *is* staying with you?'

'I'm afraid I can't comment, sorry.'

'But I'm her husband—'

'I don't care who you are, I'm not telling you anything about anyone.' Then she hung up on him and Brett was none the wiser about whether his wife had booked into Allison's Guest House or not. From the way the conversation went, he thought she might have done, but he wasn't totally sure. Also, the fact that this was the very first place he'd tried (and what were the odds of that?) made him think she probably wasn't.

'Dad, what are you doing?' Ellis peered over his shoulder.

'Trying to find your mother.'

'I've already found her. I think.'

'You have? How? Where?'

Ellis gave a long-suffering sigh. 'By using the phone's track and locate.'

'Is there such a thing?'

'Obvs.'

'Eh?'

'Yes.' Another sigh.

'But, I think she's switched her phone off. Every time I call, it goes to answer phone.'

Ellis smirked. 'It'll give you a location history so you can see where she was the last time her phone was on. She was in a place called Brixham.'

'Yes!' Brett punched the air.

'Alright, Dad, keep your hair on. Are we going to get her, or what?'

'I am, you're not.'

'Why not? I'm the one who found her.'

'Yes, about that – do you make a habit of tracking your parents' phones?'

'There's no point. You don't do anything or go

anywhere,' she said.

The front door opened and closed just as Beverley thumped a hand on Brett's shoulder and he yelped in surprise.

'Chill, Daddo, it's only Nanny. I swear you really are going deaf.'

'I'm not,' he protested.

'As soon as Helen has gone, I'll ask Kate to change the sheets on the bed,' Beverley announced, 'and Portia can have her room back.'

'Don't worry, I've no intention of staying where I'm not wanted,' Helen said, having just arrived back. She slapped the bottle of Calamine Lotion on the kitchen counter. 'I'll just have to celebrate Christmas on my own.' She sniffed and dabbed delicately at the corner of her eye.

'It's not that you're not wanted,' Brett began, but she interrupted him.

'You made your position perfectly clear, earlier. To think that my own son has told me never to darken his door again.' Another sniff, this one louder.

'You've been reading too many of those daft

magazines,' Beverley said. 'They've rotted your brain; "Darken his door" indeed. Who speaks like that?'

'First Kate doesn't want to see me ever again, and now my son has cast me out,' Helen cried, ignoring both Beverley's comments and Ellis's incredulous expression.

'I didn't cast you out,' Brett said.

'You did! You told me to go.'

'I wish you'd get on with it,' Beverley interjected.

'This is none of your business,' Helen said to her snootily, her tears momentarily forgotten.

'Yes, it is, because I get to have the spare room. I hope Kate isn't too late back – I'd like her to put fresh sheets on.'

'That does it! I'm calling a family meeting right now!' Brett yelled.

'What's a family meeting?' Ellis asked, not in the least bit fazed by her father's raised voice.

'A meeting of the whole family. Now. Right this minute,' he said.

'Why?'

'Because I said so.'

'Ooh, now you sound like mum,' Ellis replied. 'This should be fun – I'll go and get the others.' She dashed up the stairs, her usual ethereal wafting replaced by thudding and pounding.

'Where's Pepe?' Beverley asked. 'I do hope he's not being naughty.' She gazed around the kitchen hopefully.

'I put him outside about half an hour ago. Maybe more.'

Beverley let out a cry of dismay. 'Oh my God, he'll have frozen to death. He's not used to the cold.' She hurried to the door and yanked it open, calling, 'Pee-pee, darling, come to Mama…Pee-pee,' at the top of her voice.

Brett shuddered, hoping the animal really had gone pee-pee outside and not saved it for a warmer spot indoors.

Pepe slunk inside, giving his mistress a sorrowful wag of his tail and giving Brett an I-hate-you look, but at least the dog didn't growl at him, so that was an improvement.

Brett waited until everyone was present, then

he began. 'Mum is in a place called Brixham—'

'Ooh, it's got a lovely harbour. She'll like it there.'

'Yes, quite. Thank you, Beverley. Can I carry on?'

Beverley subsided, looking sheepish.

'As I said, Mum – Kate – is in Brixham. Now, I don't claim to know exactly what was going through her mind when she left yesterday...' Was it only yesterday? It felt considerably longer. 'But I think it might be because she felt a little overwhelmed.'

Six pairs of eyes stared expressionlessly at him, the dog not wanting to be left out.

'OK, more than a little,' he conceded. 'We're all guilty of taking her for granted, and I believe she's gotten a bit fed up. We're all guilty of being selfish and thinking only about ourselves. I've got to take the lion's share of the blame, because I'm the adult in the house, and I should have helped out more than I have done.'

'Too right,' Portia muttered sullenly. 'You never take me to the stables.'

'See, that's what I mean about being selfish, Portia. Instead of thinking about how this affects you, think about how your mum is feeling right now.'

'You said you hated her, Ellis, and you did too, Portia, I heard you,' Sam said. '*I* don't hate her.' His lip wobbled ever so slightly, reminding Brett just how young his son was, despite his newly acquired high-school bravado.

'And you said Brett should never have married her,' Beverley pointed out to Helen, who gave one of her theatrically loud sniffs. 'No wonder she buggered off.'

'I wish *you'd* bugger off,' Helen muttered under her breath, but loud enough for everyone to hear.

'And that's another thing. I don't know about Kate, but I'm sick to death of all this squabbling and bickering. None of you seem to get on, you all seem to hate the sight of each other, and for that reason, I'm cancelling Christmas this year.'

'*What?*' That was from Ellis.

'You *can't.*' Portia cried.

'Good idea, I hate Christmas.' Beverley's expression was smug.

'We know, you keep reminding us.' Helen said.

'I want my mum.' Sam wailed.

'Christmas should be about families,' Brett said, 'and being together, and being kind to each other, and being grateful for what we have. I don't see any of that in this family.'

'Except for Mum,' said Sam.

'Out of the mouth of babes…' he said.

'I'm not a baby.' Sam scowled furiously, and Brett bit back a smile. He'd always be a baby as far as Brett was concerned, and he felt a sudden rush of love for his youngest child, so strong it made his heart skip a beat.

The solemn, reflective silence around the table was broken by a farting noise from under Beverley's chair, which was followed by a rather disgusting smell.

'What?' Beverley said. 'It wasn't me; it was Pepe.'

'I have been rather awful to her,' Ellis

admitted. 'I didn't mean it when I said I hated her and wanted to move out.' Tears gathered in the corners of her eyes and she dashed them away with the back of her hand.

'Neither did I,' Portia said, quietly. 'I was upset because she grounded me.'

'I know you were, love,' Brett said at the same time as Ellis growled, 'And why was that? Something to do with stealing my top and ruining it?'

'FYI, I didn't steal it, I *borrowed* it; and it's not ruined. You should ask Mum to wash it.'

'I did.'

'Well, then.' Portia leant back in her chair and folded her arms.

'Girls, this isn't helping, and this is exactly the sort of thing I'm referring to. Portia, have you apologised to your sister?'

'No, she hasn't,' Ellis said.

'Then I suggest you do so, and sound as though you mean it. After that, you can wash Ellis's top.'

'But I don't know how!' The aghast

expression on Portia's face was rather comical.

'Then it's about time you learned.'

'What about Pepe chewing my Doc Martens?' she demanded.

'It's not quite the same thing, but I see where you're coming from,' Brett conceded. 'Beverley, if you want to bring the dog when you visit us, then he's got to be better behaved. And he's got to be housetrained. No more peeing on my trousers or pooping on the bedroom carpet. From now on, he stays in the utility room until he's been outside and done his business. And he sleeps in there, too.'

Beverley pursed her lips and folded her arms. 'May never objected.'

'I suspect Aunt May was so desperate for company she wouldn't care. But I'm not, and I do. Pepe is your responsibility and it's up to you to take care of him while you're here. Oh, and another thing; if you mention that you hate Christmas one more time, then I'm putting you on the next train back to Brighton. We don't hate Christmas, and we don't need you making us all feel miserable. If you want to play Scrooge, you can do it by yourself in your own home. You're not spoiling things for the rest of us.'

Helen had a supercilious smirk on her face at Beverley's telling off, but Brett was just about to wipe it off.

'As for you, Mum,' he said, 'I expect you to apologise to Kate unreservedly. How dare you suggest that I should never have married her. She's a wonderful wife, a wonderful mother, and a wonderful person altogether. If you can't accept that, then maybe you *should* go home. I'll continue to visit you, but I'm not going to subject Kate to any more of your snide comments. I've ignored them up until now, trying to give you the benefit of the doubt, because I didn't think you meant what you said. Clearly, I was wrong. Do you think you can apologise and mean it, or do I send you home?'

Helen lifted her chin and stared defiantly at Brett. Then she noticed the unflinching, accusing gazes of the three children.

'Did you really say that, Nanna?' Portia

asked.

'You can talk – you told her you hated her,' Helen retorted.

'I'm a teenager. You're old, you should know better.'

'She's right, Nana. That's our Mum you're talking about,' Ellis said.

Ellis must have wished she hadn't drawn her father's attention, when Brett said, 'And as for you, you keep telling us you're a grown-up and you can't wait to move out. If that's the case, then you need to start acting like an adult, and that means being less selfish and more considerate. I'm prepared to overlook some of Portia's antics because she's three years younger than you, but it's about time you grew up and took more responsibility for yourself and your actions. Sometimes, your attitude stinks, and it's not nice.'

'What about me, Dad? What have I done wrong?' Sam wanted to know.

'You're just being a kid, Sammykins. You've done nothing wrong. But it would be nice if you could get on with your sisters a bit better.'

'They're *girls*,' Sam objected.

'So they are, but they're also your family. Don't forget that.'

'What happens now?' Ellis wanted to know.

'If you decide you want Christmas to go ahead, then the five of you will have to pull together and make it happen. I won't be here, I'm afraid. I'm off to find your mother and bring her back home!'

CHAPTER 34

Kate couldn't believe it was nearly Christmas Eve already. She'd been away from her family for only twenty-four hours, but she felt like she'd been gone for weeks. As she headed to her room to drop her shopping off, she knew in her heart that something good had come out of her headlong flight to the south coast; the first was, as Essie had quite rightly stated, her realisation that family was, indeed, everything; and the second was that Kate felt more in control of her life than she'd done for years.

The children weren't babies. Gone were the

days when they needed her for every little thing. If she wanted her children to grow into resilient, responsible adults, then it was up to her to ensure they did. She took full responsibility for the selfish, spoilt brats they'd become (well, mostly, but Brett had to bear some of that burden) and it was now her job to rectify that. Kate was under no illusion it would be easy – there were going to be some spectacular tantrums as all three children reacted to the changes she was about to enforce, and there might be times when she felt like running away again. If it got that bad, then Brett would have to step up to the mark while she treated herself to a spa weekend, or something.

Of course, she'd do the same for him. Although the lion's share of the home-making and child-rearing would still fall on her shoulders, because, let's face it, Brett worked longer hours than she did, her husband would have to be more supportive. And not only with the children, either. It was high time Kate and Brett, as a couple, stood up to his mother.

If Brett wasn't prepared to do that, or if he agreed with Helen's hurtful comments that Brett should never have married Kate, then the pair of them would have to have a serious discussion regarding the state of their marriage.

'Dave?' Kate caught the hotel owner's attention, as she walked past the reception desk. 'Is it OK if I check out tomorrow?'

'Oh. You're not stopping for Christmas Day?'

'No, sorry. I need to get back.'

'No problem. Thanks for letting me know. Got any plans for the rest of the day?' he asked.

'I'm going to have a nice walk along the coastal path to Shoalstone Pool to try to work some of your delicious breakfast off, then I'm going to come back and read my book before dinner.' It sounded wonderful, so relaxing, but even as her shredded nerves knitted back together, she found she was desperately missing the children, despite how obnoxious they could be. She was also missing Brett, and her heart did a funny little skipped beat when she thought of him.

It was a pity he didn't think of her in the same way.

As she took a stroll past the harbour, then on to the marina and Berry Head (apparently there was a lighthouse at its furthest point, but she didn't intend to walk that far), Kate felt the sting of tears behind her eyes.

Brett had fallen out of love with her, she was convinced of it, although he probably did still love her as the mother of his children and as his long-term companion, but he'd stopped seeing her as *her*. She was just as guilty, she realised. She most definitely loved him, but was she *in love* with him? Her heart did still miss the occasional beat when she thought of him, but somewhere between raising three children and washing his smelly socks, the magic had dissipated, like smoke from a doused fire.

But could not having a fluttery tummy at the mere thought of Brett be enough to turn her back on over twenty years of relatively contented marriage?

She thought not. However, she wasn't so sure

about Brett's thoughts on the matter. She was scared to check her phone (she'd left it switched off in her hotel room for that very reason) in case she saw or heard a message from him telling her they were all getting on just fine without her, thank you very much, and that she could stay where she was and not bother coming back.

A twinge of hurt so sharp it made her gasp, stabbed through her heart. Dear God, what if he didn't want her back? What had she done?

She sank onto a nearby bench and put her face in her hands, ignoring the sea crashing against the rocks and surging into the man-made salt-water pool, and the pretty beach huts, and the odd jogger and dog walker who gave her an occasional curious stare. She'd been so silly, so selfish. Running away, even for a day or two wasn't the answer. In fact, she had the horrible fear that she'd made things worse, that she'd brought everything to a head. And at Christmas, too. The children would never forgive her for ruining their Christmas – hell, she'd never forgive herself. She should have stayed at home and toughed it out. After all, the nans would only be staying until Boxing Day – they were both supposed to go back to their own homes the following morning – and surely she could have gritted her teeth until then. Once they'd left, the family would be back to normal and—

But that was the problem, wasn't it? Normal wasn't good enough. Normal was shouting and griping at each other; squabbling and sulking; ignoring each other one minute and being in someone's face the next. Did she honestly want to continue with that?

She wasn't sure she did...

CHAPTER 35

It hadn't taken Brett as long to drive to Brixham as he'd anticipated, although it had been dark for a good hour or so by the time he found a car park and pulled into it. The Pirate Inn was Kate's last known whereabouts, according to Ellis, so he'd start with that. If she wasn't there, then he was prepared to march into every hotel in the village until he found her.

The guy on the desk was dressed as Jack Sparrow and had a real live parrot on his shoulder. Brett raised his eyebrows. This didn't seem the sort of place Kate would want to stay in. But then, they hadn't been away without the kids for years where every accommodation choice was based on their needs and wants, so he had no real idea anymore what appealed to his wife. Perhaps the parrot had been the selling point for her?

'Kate Peters, please,' he said, in his no-nonsense business tone.

'I'm afraid she's gone out for the afternoon,' the guy behind the desk replied. 'Is she expecting you?'

Brett narrowed his eyes, wondering how to answer. The fact that she'd gone out was a strong indication that she wasn't expecting him, so he'd best not say that.

'She isn't. I wanted to surprise her. I'm her husband.'

'She's booked into the restaurant for dinner, so I'm sure she'll be back before seven, if you'd like to wait in the lounge. I can arrange for coffee or tea, if you want?'

Brett didn't want her first sight of him to be in a hotel lounge. What he wanted to say to her was best done in private. 'If you show me to her room, I'll wait for her there.'

'Sorry, no can do.'

'I've got ID. I'm definitely her husband. Honest.'

'I don't doubt it, but I'm still not letting you into Mrs Peters's room without her permission. And if you stay the night, I'm afraid I'll have to book you in. Don't worry, the room rate is the same.'

Brett didn't give two hoots how much the room cost per night.

All he wanted to do was see his wife. God knows how awful she must be feeling to have jumped into her car and driven all this way. The sooner he told her he loved her and begged her to come back, the better. He didn't think he could stand much more of this.

'I'll have to wait, won't I,' he said, not having any other choice. His shoulders slumped and he let out a sigh.

'She said she was going for a walk to Shoalstone Pool,' the guy with the parrot said. 'If that's any help?'

He wasn't sure it was, but after getting directions, Brett set off. He knew the chances of bumping into Kate were slim, especially in the dark, but anything was better than cooling his heels in the hotel lounge and getting twitchy on too much coffee. A walk would do him good anyway, would blow the cobwebs away and stop his thoughts doing laps in his head.

The same ones kept running through his mind, on a continual loop, and he was fed up of them.

He just wanted to find his wife and get the whole sorry mess sorted.

And he *was* sorry, more than he could ever tell her. To think that she'd felt so trapped was awful. To think that she felt she couldn't talk to him about it was even worse.

Brett didn't see the bright lights spilling out of the shops and restaurants. He didn't see the twinkle and shimmer of the fairy lights strung around the harbour, and he didn't hear the cacophony of festive music filling the air, nor smell the alluring aromas of spiced wine and hot chocolate wafting from the cafes and bars.

His attention was fixed firmly on finding Kate.

She was the only thing that mattered right now.

CHAPTER 36

She'd best be getting back to the hotel, Kate thought. Not that she had anything to go back to, except a hot drink, a warm bath, and her book, although reading had lost its appeal suddenly. How could she concentrate when her mind was filled with images of her husband and family getting on with Christmas without her? Hah! She'd prayed for a typical family Christmas, and now her family's Christmas would be as far from typical as it was possible to get. Especially if Brett decided her absence was something he could begin to get used to, even if he did have to deal with the children all on his own. No doubt his mother was perfectly happy sticking her nose in, and he'd let her, too. He'd probably be grateful for her help because, let's face it, Brett was clueless when it came to the kids.

The sea heaved darkly beyond the rocks, the gleam of white on the crests of the waves only faintly visible. The sound of them breaking was primaeval and relentless, pounding the shore regardless of whether the shore wanted to be pounded or not.

Kate had felt a bit like that. The constant demands of the children were never-ending and persistent; a part of her yearned for it to stop, and another part of her was terrified that when her babies had grown and flown, and the wide-beaked begging for lifts/food/help with homework/money had finally ceased, the silence would overwhelm her. Especially if Brett was no longer in her life, which was looking like a very real possibility.

He'd like it here, she thought. Sitting in the almost-dark of a late December afternoon, the only illumination was from the odd street light on the road behind the pool. The only noise was the loud boom and suck of the waves, and the distant noise of Brixham itself, which she could just see if she craned her neck. The harbour lights were colourful and cheerful; a direct contrast to the way Kate was feeling – she'd never felt less colourful or less cheerful in her entire life.

It was lonely out here, too. The joggers seemed to have jogged back to where they'd come from and the dog-walkers had taken their pooches home.

She shivered. It was time to make a move, but she honestly couldn't be bothered. It seemed too much like hard work to haul herself to her feet and make her way back to the village. She was cold, but not quite cold enough yet. She'd spend another minute or two here, and try to absorb some of the peace and solitude, because once she'd returned home and the subsequent mayhem awaiting her, she might well look back on this little oasis of sorrow-filled peace with nostalgia.

Oh, darn it. There was a walker out to spoil it, and he didn't even have the decency to bring a dog with him. His shoulders were hunched and his hands were stuffed in his pockets, and he was striding along as though he had someplace he urgently needed to be, and she expected him to hurry straight past.

As he grew closer, though, a smidgeon of worry worked itself into Kate's mind. She wasn't sure, but he seemed to be staring at her – she had an uneasy prickle on the back of her neck which made her think he was heading directly towards her and not around the curve of the headland.

Clumsily, stiff from the cold and from sitting too long, Kate got to her feet. He was only about twenty yards away by now, and on a direct course towards her. But there was something about him that reminded her of Brett. He was the same height and build, and she couldn't recall the number of times she'd watched her husband hunch into himself when he was cold, just like this man was doing.

She held her breath, the prickle growing into a full-blown shiver.

It *was* him. It was Brett. She was certain of it.

Then he stopped, took his hands out of his pockets and straightened up. 'Kate? Is that you?'

'Brett?'

'Yeah...'

'What are you doing here?' She knew the question was a daft one as soon as she uttered it. He'd come for her.

Why else would he have driven to Brixham on the eve of Christmas Eve?

'I've come to take you home,' he replied.

He was still about ten feet away and his face was in shadow. But his voice held no hint of recrimination or annoyance. He appeared to simply be stating a fact.

'How did you know where to find me?' she asked.

'Ellis and the track history on your phone.'

'The what?'

'Yeah, that's what I thought. Shouldn't we be

the ones doing the tracking, not our kids tracking us?'

She heard the smile behind the words, and her tense, constricted heart eased a little.

'How are the children?'

His shoulders moved in a kind of shrug. 'Remorseful.'

She nodded. Remorseful was good. It was better than stroppy and argumentative. It probably wouldn't last, though, if she knew her children.

'I'm remorseful, too,' Brett added, 'if that helps you to come back home.'

There was silence for a second or two, then Kate said softly, 'So am I.'

She heard her husband's soft chuckle and it sent an altogether different shiver down her back. 'I don't think you've got anything to be remorseful about,' he said.

'Oh, but I do. I should never have gone away.'

'It's only been twenty-four hours,' Brett pointed out. 'You were hardly gone for weeks.'

'It felt like weeks.' It was true; each minute

without her family had felt like an hour – a blessedly quiet and unpestered hour, but an hour nevertheless. She was so unused to the peace that time had stretched and warped out of all proportion.

'Will you come back home with me, Kate?' he asked, and she heard in his voice the fear that she'd refuse.

'If you want me to.'

'No, *you've* got to want to. I know you've not been happy recently, and I'm sorry. I want nothing more than for you to be happy, and if that means me moving out, then that's what I'll do.'

'You want to move out?' Kate's voice broke. What was he saying?'

'No, I most definitely don't. I love you, Kate, and it would break my heart to be away from you and the kids, but I can't stand to see you like this.' He cleared his throat. 'Actually, I don't just love you – I adore you. I always have, since the first moment I set eyes on you, and that hasn't changed. I'm sorry I don't tell you often enough;

I assumed you knew how I felt. But the most important thing is, how do *you* feel? Do you still love *me*?'

'With all my heart,' she whispered.

It was loud enough.

'Come here,' he said, stepping towards her and opening his arms.

He held her so tightly she thought (hoped) he'd never let her go, but after a few moments of having his nose buried in her hair and feeling the warmth and strength of him, he pulled back slightly.

'I'm bloody freezing,' he said. 'Wanna get a room?'

Kate smiled. 'I believe I already have one...'

Chapter 37

Kate woke with a start and reached across the bed, relaxing when her searching fingers encountered her husband's naked chest. Last night hadn't been a dream, then. The hours they'd spent making love (they'd not done that since before Ellis was born) hadn't been a result of a fevered imagination or wishful thinking. It had been very real and very wonderful.

Crikey, she was starving. She'd forgotten how hungry a good session in bed made her feel, and she glanced at the clock, hoping they hadn't missed breakfast, because they'd most definitely missed dinner last night.

'Come here,' Brett murmured, turning over and slipping his arms around her waist, drawing him into him. 'I haven't finished with you yet.'

Ooh, stuff breakfast, she decided, his lips on her neck, his hands wandering. Didn't somebody once say you could live on love alone?

Afterwards, she decided she couldn't. However nice it had been (nice didn't quite cover it – breath-taking, passionate, wonderful; those were decidedly better words) Kate needed food. A full English with granary toast and lashings of lightly-salted butter should do it, plus a pot of tea and some orange juice.

'I'm hungry,' she announced, slipping out of bed, and she grinned at the matching hungry look in her husband's eyes.

Then she squealed as he launched himself after her, muttering, 'So am I. *Again.* What are you doing to me, woman?'

She darted into the bathroom and shut the door, leaning against it, giggling like a teenager. 'For food,' she clarified. 'We can always come back to bed later. We don't have to check out until eleven.'

'Tease,' he called. 'Food and sex – you certainly know the way to a man's heart.'

'Talking about food, do you think anyone will go to the butcher to fetch the turkey. They'll shut today at twelve.'

'I don't care, but I'll text my mother if you want and tell her to pick it up.'

Kate frowned. Ah, yes, his mother. Her unkind words still rankled. She'd have to have a chat with Helen about it at some point; but not today, because today was Christmas Eve and Kate felt on top of the world, happier than she'd been for a very long time indeed. She vowed to schedule more weekends away with her husband, just the two of them, if this was the result.

'By the way, Sam's got chickenpox,' Brett called, just as she was about to step into the shower, and effectively killing her strangely languid yet energised mood.

She opened the bathroom door. 'He's got what?'

'Chickenpox.'

'And you didn't think to tell me this yesterday? How is he? Is he alright? I mean, how—?'

'He's fine. Spotty and itchy, but otherwise OK. He was plastered in calamine lotion when I left and sending selfies to his mates.'

Kate wrung her hands. 'I should have been there. He needed me.'

'He had *me*,' Brett said, firmly. 'Don't go beating yourself up about it. He's not a baby, although he said he's been feeling unwell for the past couple of days.'

Kate heard the unspoken "when you were there" in Brett's voice. 'Oh, my God, I didn't even notice.' She bit her lip and tried not to cry. 'What kind of mother does that make me?'

'A busy one, with too much on her plate. Now, are you going to get in that shower, or what?'

Kate felt like saying "or what" but she needed a wash, and she needed breakfast. After that, they'd go straight home. Or rather, she would. Brett could stay and have a mooch around Brixham if he wanted, because they both had their own cars to drive. Kate desperately wanted to check that Sam was OK, and she wouldn't be happy until she'd seen him for herself.

Fancy Brett leaving his mother in charge of a sick child! Kate wouldn't leave her in charge of a woodlouse.

The atmosphere was a little cooler over breakfast, Kate noticed, understanding that the deterioration in their previously ecstatic mood was solely because of her, but she couldn't help feeling that she'd let Sam down. Therefore, there was no question of her and Brett retiring to bed for a quick romp before the journey back.

'I'd better let everyone know we'll be back later today,' she said, fretfully.

'It's already done,' Brett replied. 'They can manage without us, without *you*, for another few hours.'

But she turned her phone on anyway and was a little disgruntled to see there weren't any new messages or missed calls since she'd looked at it yesterday. Not even one from poorly Sam.

Maybe Brett was right? Maybe they could get along without her for a while. That's what she'd sort of been aiming for when she'd run off to Brixham in the first place, as well as making them realise just how much she did for them.

It had certainly worked for Brett, she thought, as he drew her to him and gave her a deep, passionate kiss before they checked out of the hotel.

'Later, Mrs Peters,' he promised with the sexy grin she loved so much.

'It's a date,' she agreed. 'Once the kids have gone to bed and—'

'Sod the kids. They should learn that we need alone time, too. And I'm really looking forward to some more alone time. At least twice tonight. And maybe once in the morning...?'

'Oh, yes please!'

Chapter 38

Kate was finally feeling all those Christmassy feels. Every single one of them; from the glow caused by last night's close encounter with her husband (and again this very wonderful Christmas Day morning), to the delight of seeing her children's faces when they opened their presents.

When she and Brett had arrived back home yesterday within minutes of each other, Kate had been astounded to discover that not only had the turkey been fetched, prepared, stuffed, and was in the oven, cooking slowly, but the house was spotless (including the girls' bedrooms – miracle!), and a meal had been cooked by both the nans (*both* of them, together, in the same room where there were knives and other lethal objects. Wow!).

Then there had been the sheepish, but totally heartfelt apologies from her children, her mother, and Helen. Even Pepe had greeted her with a lick instead of a growl, and he'd not widdled on her shoes, either. Or on anything else. Yet.

After that, Brett had dropped the bombshell that he'd applied for a job managing the golf club (not the one he frequented) and had even had a sort of telephone interview. He was quietly hopeful that something would come of it, and so was Kate after he confided in her just how bad things were in his current job. It meant less money, but that didn't matter – the only thing that concerned Kate was Brett's happiness.

All in all, she was delighted to be home, and she felt her family was delighted to have her back, and she was now happily peeling and chopping enough veg and potatoes to feed the whole street, with Helen working companionably alongside her.

'My mother always used to rub the roasties in goose fat,' Helen said.

'I've heard of that. What were they like?'

'Really crispy and the flavour was wonderful. Of course, that's when people were more likely to have goose for Christmas lunch, rather than turkey. You didn't mind me starting to cook it yesterday, did you? It's such a big bird, you'd have had to get up at five this morning, like you usually do, to make sure it was done.'

'No, I'm grateful you thought of it,' Kate replied. The first Christmas after they were married and Helen had come to stay, her mother-in-law had told her to cook it the night before. Kate had ignored her advice, because it hadn't sounded like advice – more like thinly-veiled criticism of Kate's cooking methods. And she'd stuck to getting up before the cock crowed ever since; which hadn't been a problem when the children were much younger because they'd been too excited to sleep past six a.m. anyway.

Now that they were getting older, the last few years Kate had found she'd begun to resent the incredibly early start.

She'd had an early start to this particular Christmas Day too, but it hadn't had anything to do with having to cook a turkey...

Beverley had been trying to keep her recalcitrant pooch out of mischief while the food preparation was taking place, and if that hadn't been an ideal time for Helen to make a sly remark, Kate didn't know what was. But Helen had continued to be remarkably well behaved (unlike Pepe who thought he should be in the kitchen where the turkey was), and her mother-in-law didn't make any comment at all. Kate was tempted to ask who she was, and what had she done with the real Helen. It was like having a totally different woman for a mother-in-law.

Lunch will be ready at two,' she announced, giving everyone fair notice. It was a couple of hours away yet, but Ellis wanted to pop to Riley's house to give him his present, and Brett offered to take her. He'd offered to take Portia to her friend's house yesterday, too, and Kate found it a great help that she didn't have to jump in the car every five minutes to taxi one or the other of her offspring around. He'd been gone rather a long time yesterday, though, so Kate did wonder what else he'd been up to. If he'd left it that late to get her a present, then there would have been very few shops open past midday on Christmas Eve.

He clearly hadn't left it until the last minute to buy her a gift, she saw, when he'd handed her a beautifully wrapped, small box this morning. When she'd opened it, she'd almost cried at the sight of a pair of gorgeous diamond earrings. He'd seemed equally delighted with his new putter, and said he hoped the present was an omen.

'Portia, can you lay the table, please?' Kate called. 'Use the Christmas tablecloth in the dresser.'

She left her daughter to it and returned to the kitchen, but when she popped her head around the dining room door to check on progress, she was curious to see that the table was laid for eight and not seven.

'Portia, there are only seven of us,' she laughed. 'Have you been on your nan's sherry?'

'It's for Father Christmas,' Portia said.

Considering the child had been adamant she didn't want anything to do with Christmas (apart from the presents, of course), Kate decided to let it go. It was quite sweet of her, she thought, looking at Portia's unusually make-up free face, and thinking how pretty she was without all that black around her eyes.

When the front door opened a few minutes later, Ellis burst into the kitchen, her face extremely pale, and Kate hoped she wasn't coming down with chickenpox as well as Sam.

Then a not-unfamiliar smell wafted up her nose.

Surely that wasn't...it couldn't be...

Kate darted into the hall. 'Ron!' she exclaimed, in surprise, a huge grin on her face. 'You came! How did you know where we lived?'

'I brought him in the car,' Brett said following

behind. Her husband also looked a little pale, and Kate understood why. It wasn't easy sitting inside the charity shop with Ron – it must have been so much worse in the close confines of the car, even with, she suspected, all the windows rolled down.

Her husband said, 'Is it OK if Ron joins us for Christmas lunch?'

'Of course it is!' Kate didn't tell Brett that she'd had already invited him, and that she'd been hoping to persuade Ron to have a bit of a clean-up first before she set him loose on the nans, or her foot-in-mouth children.

'I said he could have a shower, and after that I'll kit him out with some of my old clothes,' Brett told her.

'Brilliant idea.'

She returned to the kitchen to deal with the final stages of lunch cooking and by the time it was ready, Ron had finished his ablutions. She left Brett to introduce him to the rest of the family (although Portia and Ellis had been in on the secret) and she marvelled at the distinct lack of complaining from everyone. If she'd have suggested this as little as three days ago, she'd have been shot down in flames.

'OK, everyone, take your seats, lunch is served,' she announced grandly, carrying a mounded plate of carved turkey into the dining room and placing it in the centre of the table.

The two nans followed, carrying an assortment of tureens, closely shadowed by the ever-hopeful Pepe. Kate had made certain not to leave anything on the kitchen table or worktops within jumping up and grabbing distance.

'Pepe,' Beverley warned. 'Sorry, I've been trying to keep him in the utility room while lunch was cooking, but he does cry so, and I feel so sorry for him. Pepe, bed, go to your bed.' When she tried to pick him up, he bared his teeth at her.

'Allow me,' Ron said. He was almost unrecognisable now he was grime-free and had trimmed his beard. Kate realised he was probably much younger than she'd originally thought, and rather good-looking too.

He got to his feet and made a kind of

shushing noise as Pepe stood on his hind legs, nose twitching furiously.

Pepe immediately dropped to the floor, his usual belligerent expression now one of wariness.

'Bed,' Ron said, firmly, and the whole family watched open-mouthed as the poodle, with a look of disgust and disbelief, slunk out of the dining room and into the kitchen, his claws clattering on the tiles.

'What are you, a dog whisperer?' Kate asked him in amazement.

Ron blushed; she could just see a hint of pink on his cheeks above the wiry beard. 'I used to train dogs in another life,' he said.

'Ooh! Can you train mine?' Beverley asked. 'I've been trying but he's got into some bad habits. Brett said you were homeless. Fancy a few weeks in Brighton? I've got a lovely spare room. But I warn you, I don't want to see you begging. I can afford to give you a few pounds-'

Kate caught her husband's gaze and smiled. Her mother wasn't going to change, and she hadn't honestly expected her to. She guessed she'd probably have more than a few run-ins with Helen, too, and would have to deal with the children as they continued to test their boundaries, along with her limits and patience.

But as she gazed around the happy, smiling faces at her table, and the lovely meal they were about to share, she understood that there was no such thing as a typical family Christmas. Each family had their own way of rejoicing, their own way of coming together in love and celebration, their own way of trying to live together with all the inevitable niggles and squabbles. It didn't matter if her family Christmas didn't look like the fake ones on TV.

What mattered was that they loved each other, come what may.

She caught Brett's eye, and saw the love shining from him. 'I love you,' she mouthed at him, and her heart soared when her husband mouthed back, 'And I adore you.'

THE END

ABOUT THE AUTHOR

Liz Davies writes feel-good, light-hearted stories with a hefty dose of romance, a smattering of humour, and a great deal of love.

She's married to her best friend, has one grown-up daughter, and when she isn't scribbling away in the notepad she carries with her everywhere (just in case inspiration strikes), you'll find her searching for that perfect pair of shoes. She loves to cook but isn't very good at it, and loves to eat - she's much better at that! Liz also enjoys walking (preferably on the flat), cycling (also on the flat), and lots of sitting around in the garden on warm, sunny days.

She currently lives with her family in Wales, but would ideally love to buy a camper van and travel the world in it.

Website: https://www.lizdaviesauthor.com

Social Media Links:
Twitter @lizdaviesauthor
Facebook: LizDaviesAuthor1